DEVIN GRAYSON | ALITHA E. MARTINEZ

OMNI

VOLUME ONE | THE DOCTOR IS IN

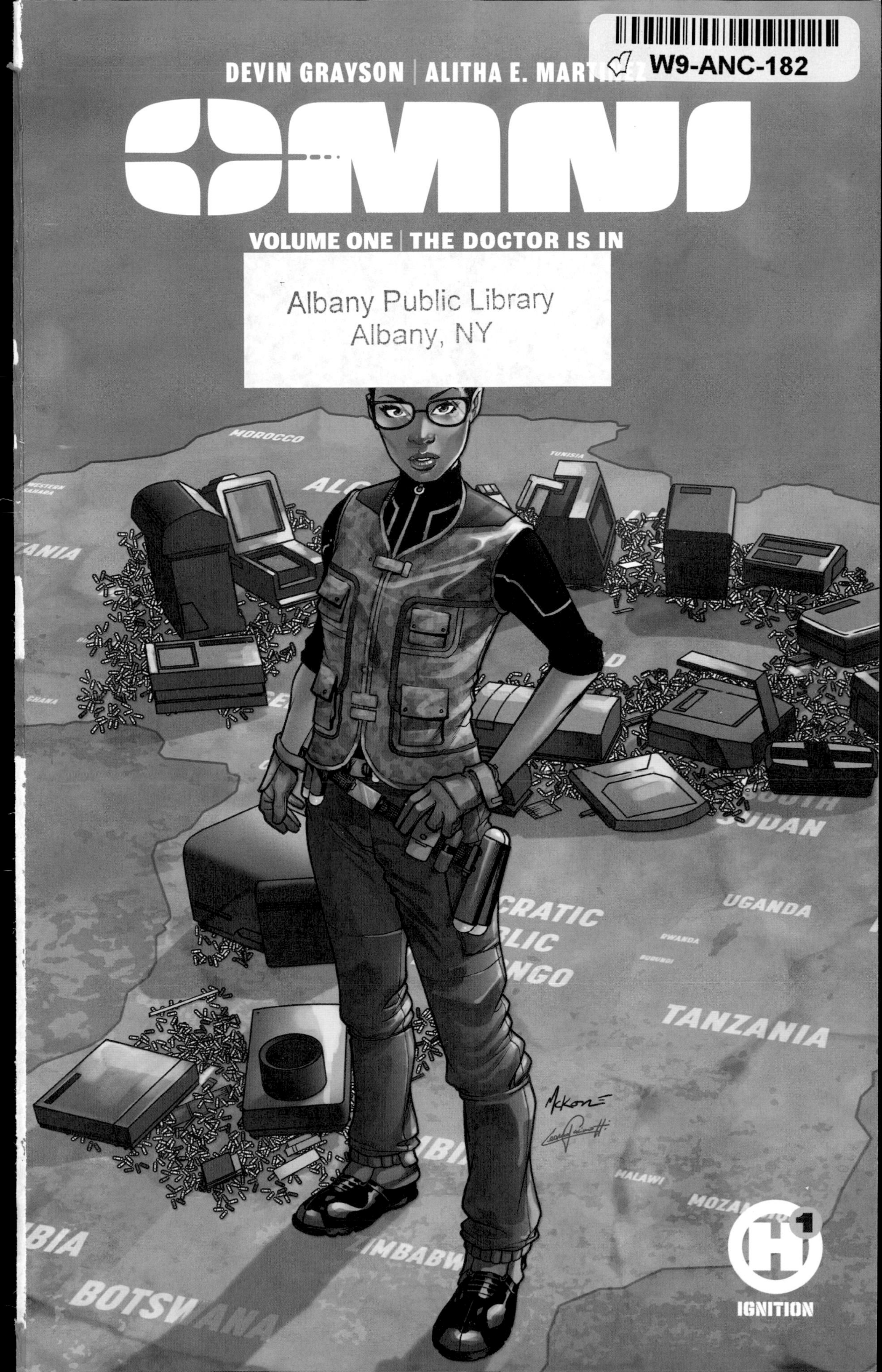
MOROCCO
TUNISIA
UGANDA
TANZANIA
MALAWI

IGNITION

OMNI

WRITER | **DEVIN GRAYSON**
ARTIST | **ALITHA E. MARTINEZ**
WITH **MEREDITH LAXTON** [P. 33-39, 45-46]
COLOR ARTIST | **BRYAN VALENZA**
COVER | **DAVE JOHNSON**

MAE WALTERS MINI-COMICS |
CHRIS ELIOPOULOS [P. 26, 48, 70]
LAYOUTS | **DJIBRIL MORISSETTE-PHAN** [P. 27-46]
AND **GEOFFO** [P. 49-69, 72-92]
TITLE PAGE AND BACK COVER ILLUSTRATION |
MIKE MCKONE
PAGES 2-3 ILLUSTRATION | **AFUA RICHARDSON**
LETTERS | **A LARGER WORLD STUDIOS**

SHARED UNIVERSE BASED ON CONCEPTS CREATED WITH
KWANZA OSAJYEFO, CARLA SPEED MCNEIL, YANICK PAQUETTE

DIRECTOR OF CREATIVE DEVELOPMENT | **MARK WAID**
CHIEF CREATIVE OFFICER | **JOHN CASSADAY**
SENIOR EDITOR | **FABRICE SAPOLSKY**
ASSISTANT EDITOR | **AMANDA LUCIDO**
LOGO DESIGN | **RIAN HUGHES**
SENIOR ART DIRECTOR | **JERRY FRISSEN**

CEO AND PUBLISHER | **FABRICE GIGER**
COO | **ALEX DONOGHUE**
CFO | **GUILLAUME NOUGARET**
SENIOR EDITOR | **ROB LEVIN**
SALES MANAGER | **PEDRO HERNANDEZ**
SALES AND MARKETING ASSISTANT | **ANDREA TORRES**
SALES REPRESENTATIVE | **HARLEY SALBACKA**
PRODUCTION COORDINATOR | **ALISA TRAGER**
DIRECTOR, LICENSING | **EDMOND LEE**
CTO | **BRUNO BARBERI**
RIGHTS AND LICENSING | **LICENSING@HUMANOIDS.COM**
PRESS AND SOCIAL MEDIA | **PR@HUMANOIDS.COM**

OMNI, VOL 1: THE DOCTOR IS IN This title is a publication of Humanoids, Inc. 8033 Sunset Blvd. #628, Los Angeles, CA 90046.
Library of Congress Control Number: 2019910050

This volume collects OMNI issues 1-4.

H1 is an imprint of Humanoids, Inc.

HUMANOIDS

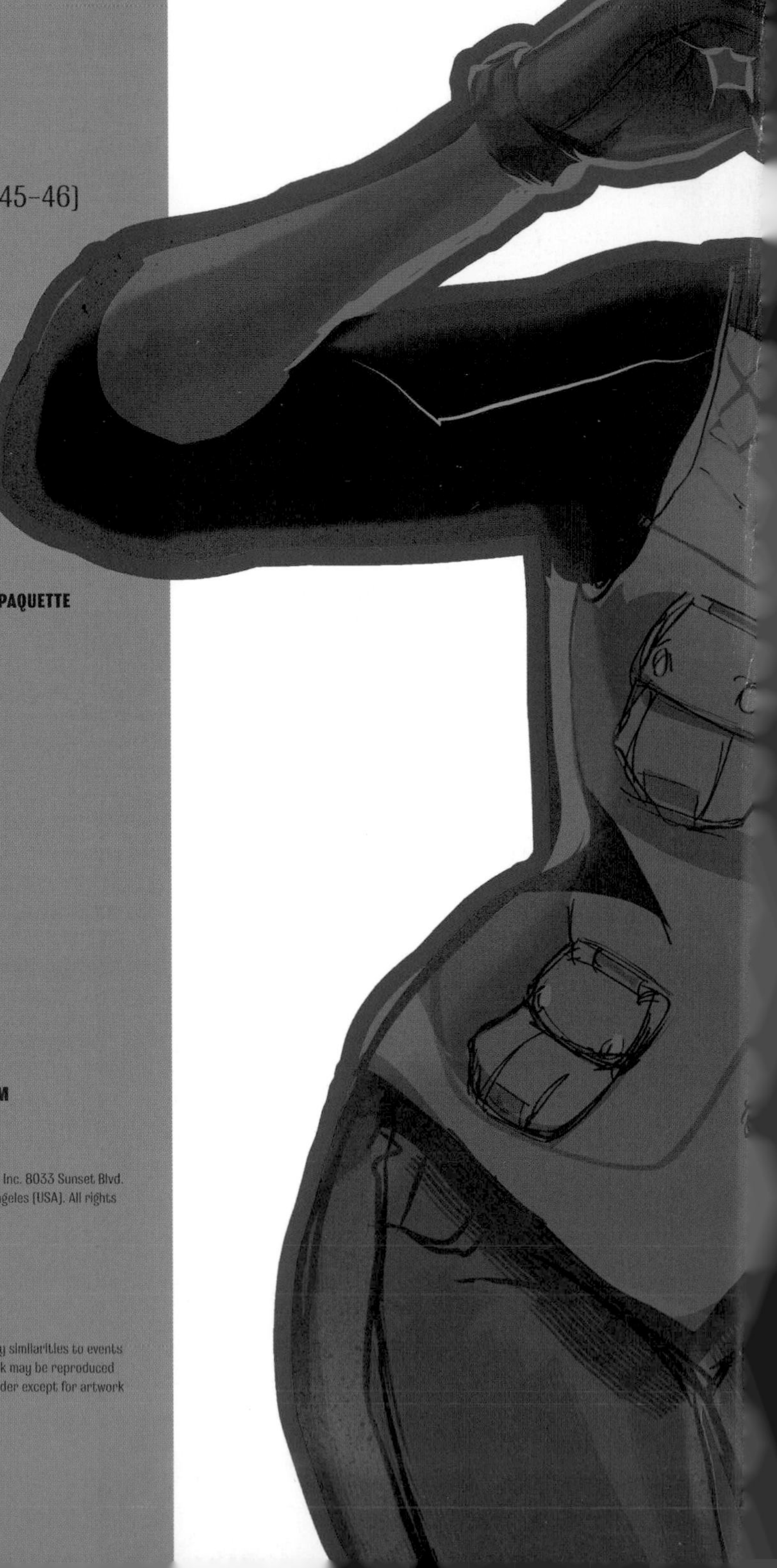

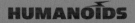

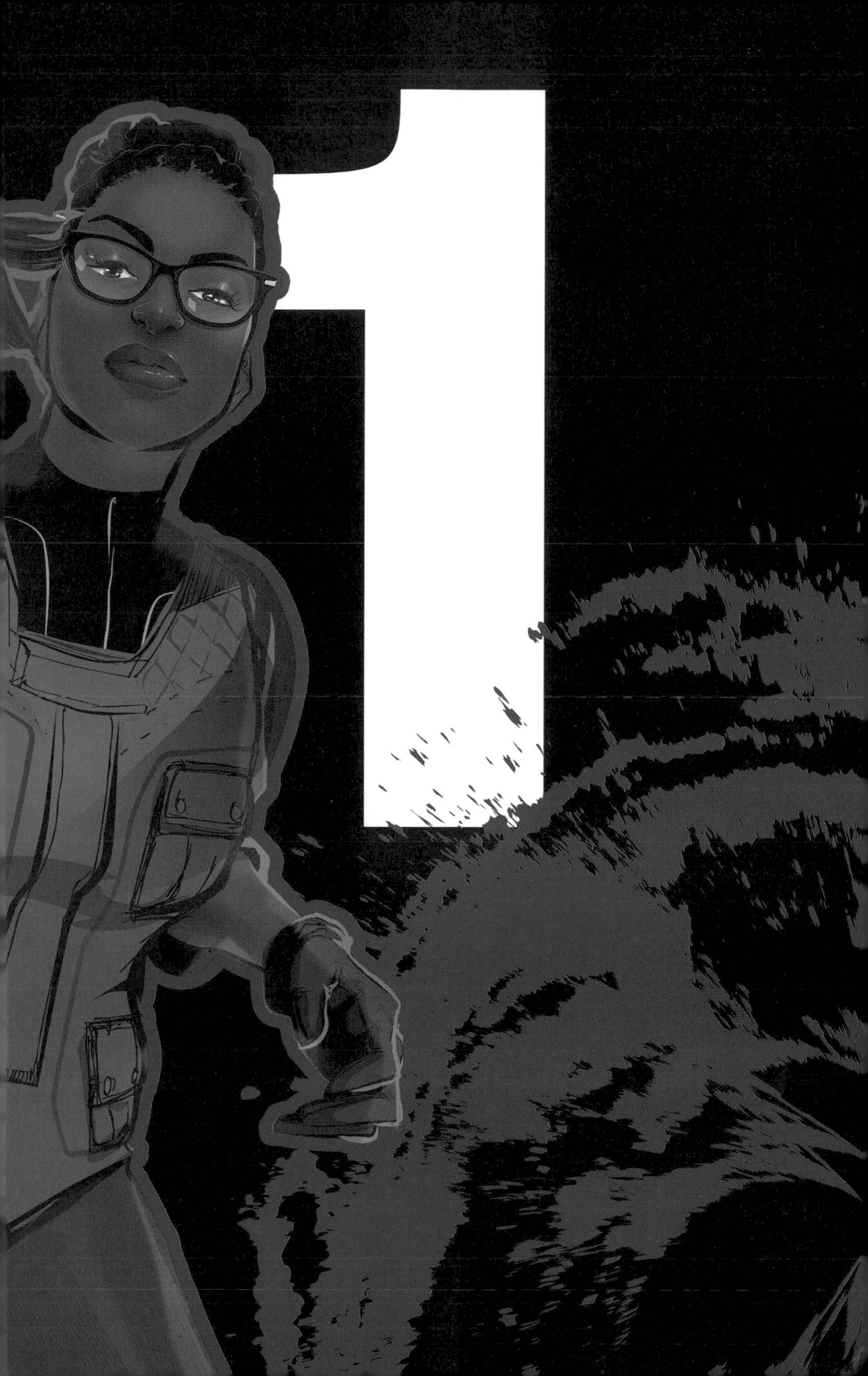
1

OUR WORLD'S DNA IS CHANGING.

UNPRECEDENTED TECTONIC SHIFTS.
SPONTANEOUS, RADICAL CHANGES IN THE ECO SYSTEMS.

IN MOMENTS OF UNIMAGINABLE AGITATION,
THE HUMAN RACE ACTS OUT IN UNIMAGINABLE WAYS.

AND THOSE ARE JUST INDIVIDUAL SPECIES. NOW EARTH ITSELF IS PUSHING BACK.

CERTAIN PEOPLE WORLDWIDE ARE ... CHANGING. ***TRANSFORMING***.

IGNITING WITH ***POWER***.

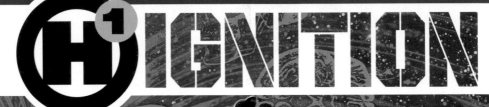

H1 IGNITION

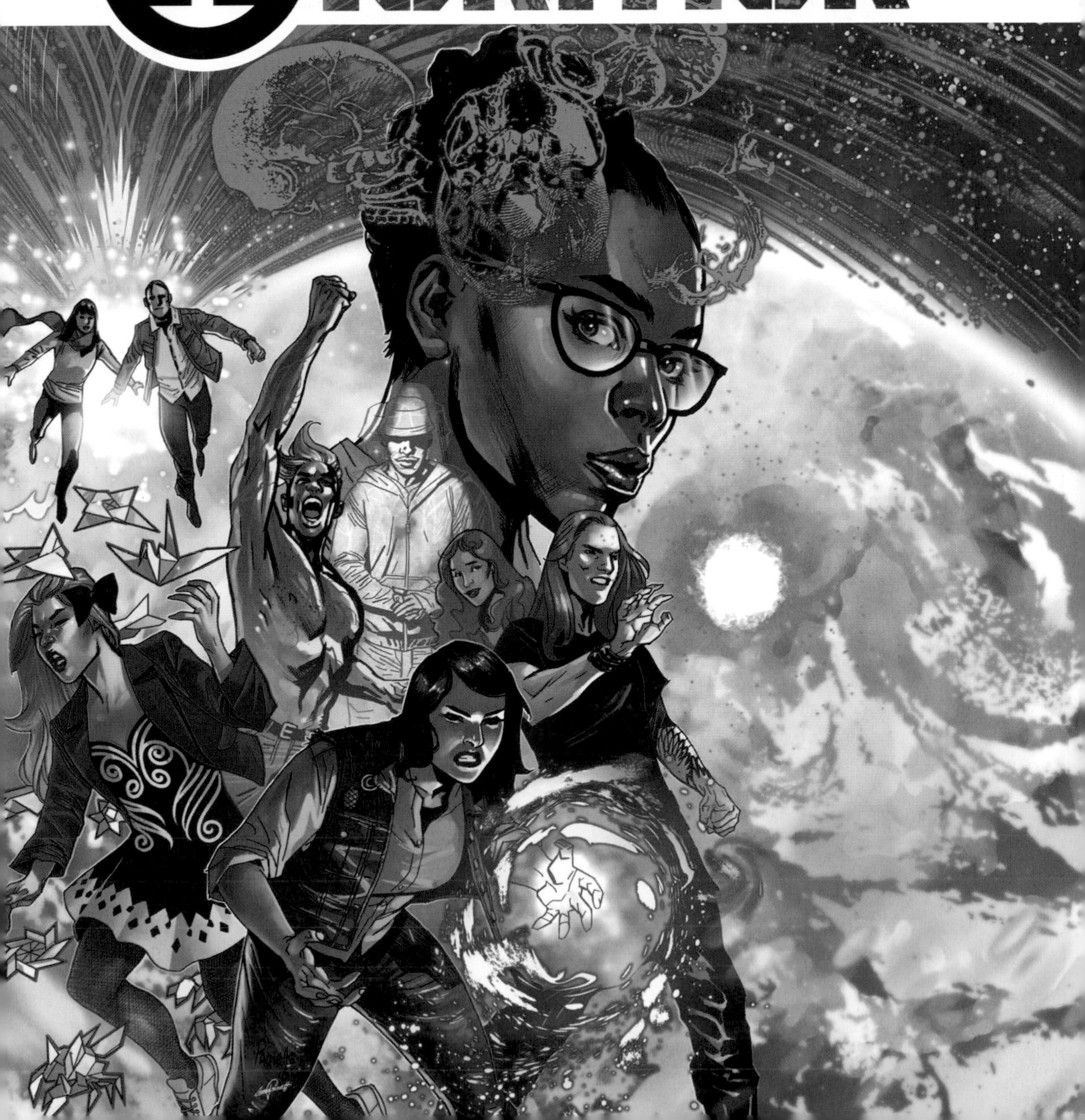

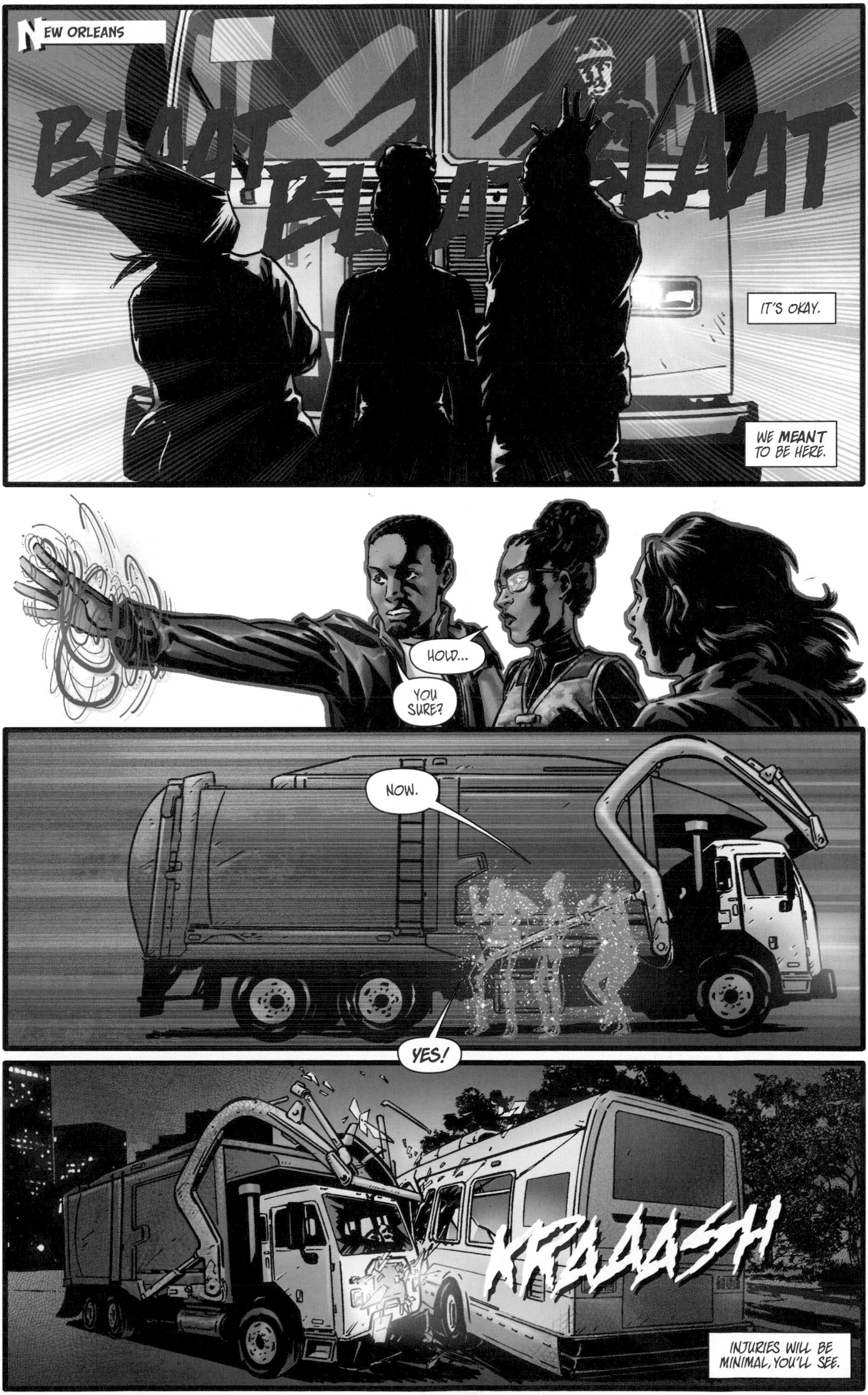
NEW ORLEANS
BLAAT BLAAT BLAAT
IT'S OKAY.
WE MEANT TO BE HERE.
HOLD...
YOU SURE?
NOW.
YES!
KRAAASH
INJURIES WILL BE MINIMAL, YOU'LL SEE.

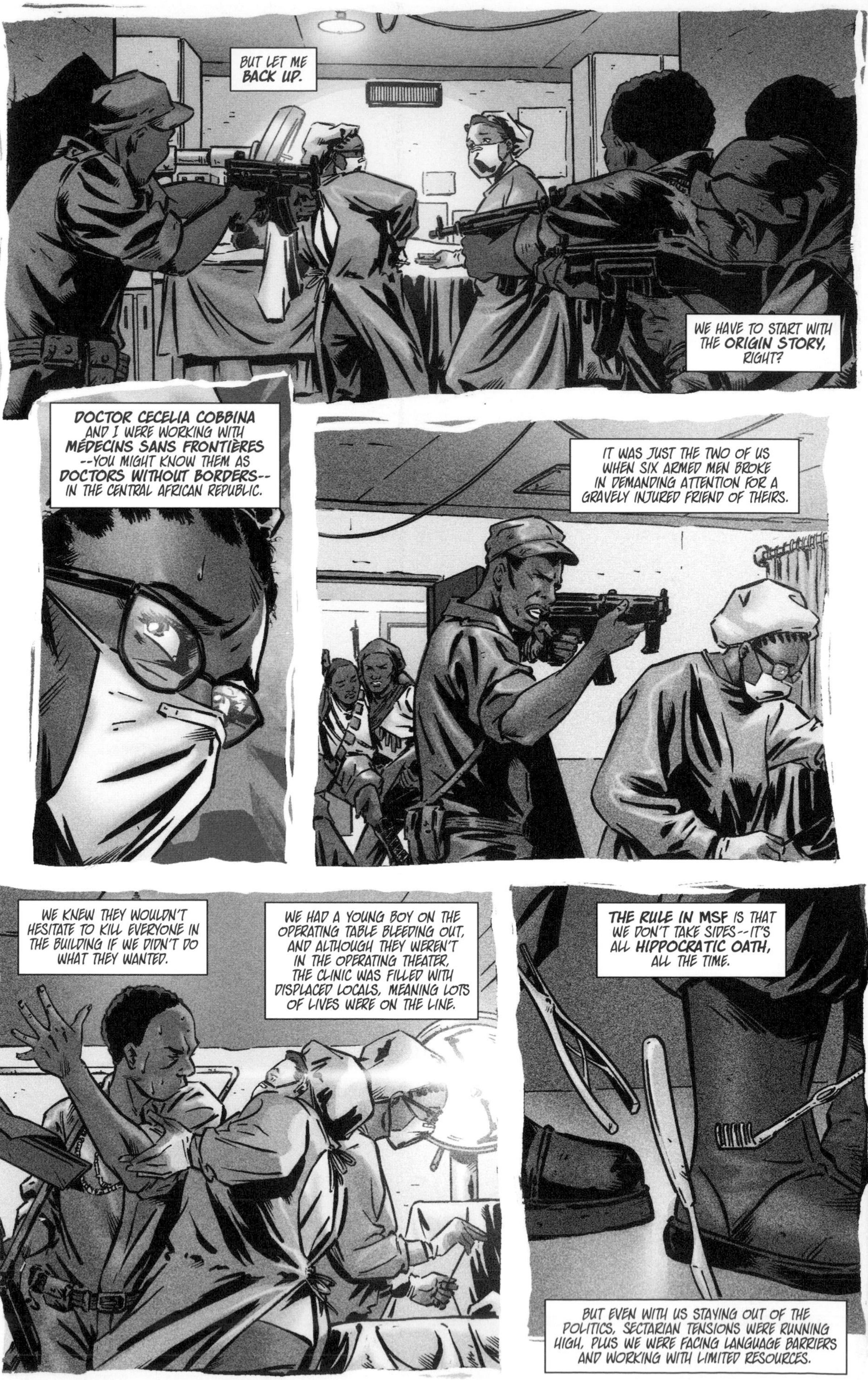
BUT LET ME BACK UP.
WE HAVE TO START WITH THE ORIGIN STORY, RIGHT?
DOCTOR CECELIA COBBINA AND I WERE WORKING WITH MÉDECINS SANS FRONTIÈRES --YOU MIGHT KNOW THEM AS DOCTORS WITHOUT BORDERS-- IN THE CENTRAL AFRICAN REPUBLIC.
IT WAS JUST THE TWO OF US WHEN SIX ARMED MEN BROKE IN DEMANDING ATTENTION FOR A GRAVELY INJURED FRIEND OF THEIRS.
WE KNEW THEY WOULDN'T HESITATE TO KILL EVERYONE IN THE BUILDING IF WE DIDN'T DO WHAT THEY WANTED.
WE HAD A YOUNG BOY ON THE OPERATING TABLE BLEEDING OUT, AND ALTHOUGH THEY WEREN'T IN THE OPERATING THEATER, THE CLINIC WAS FILLED WITH DISPLACED LOCALS, MEANING LOTS OF LIVES WERE ON THE LINE.
THE RULE IN MSF IS THAT WE DON'T TAKE SIDES--IT'S ALL HIPPOCRATIC OATH, ALL THE TIME.
BUT EVEN WITH US STAYING OUT OF THE POLITICS, SECTARIAN TENSIONS WERE RUNNING HIGH, PLUS WE WERE FACING LANGUAGE BARRIERS AND WORKING WITH LIMITED RESOURCES.

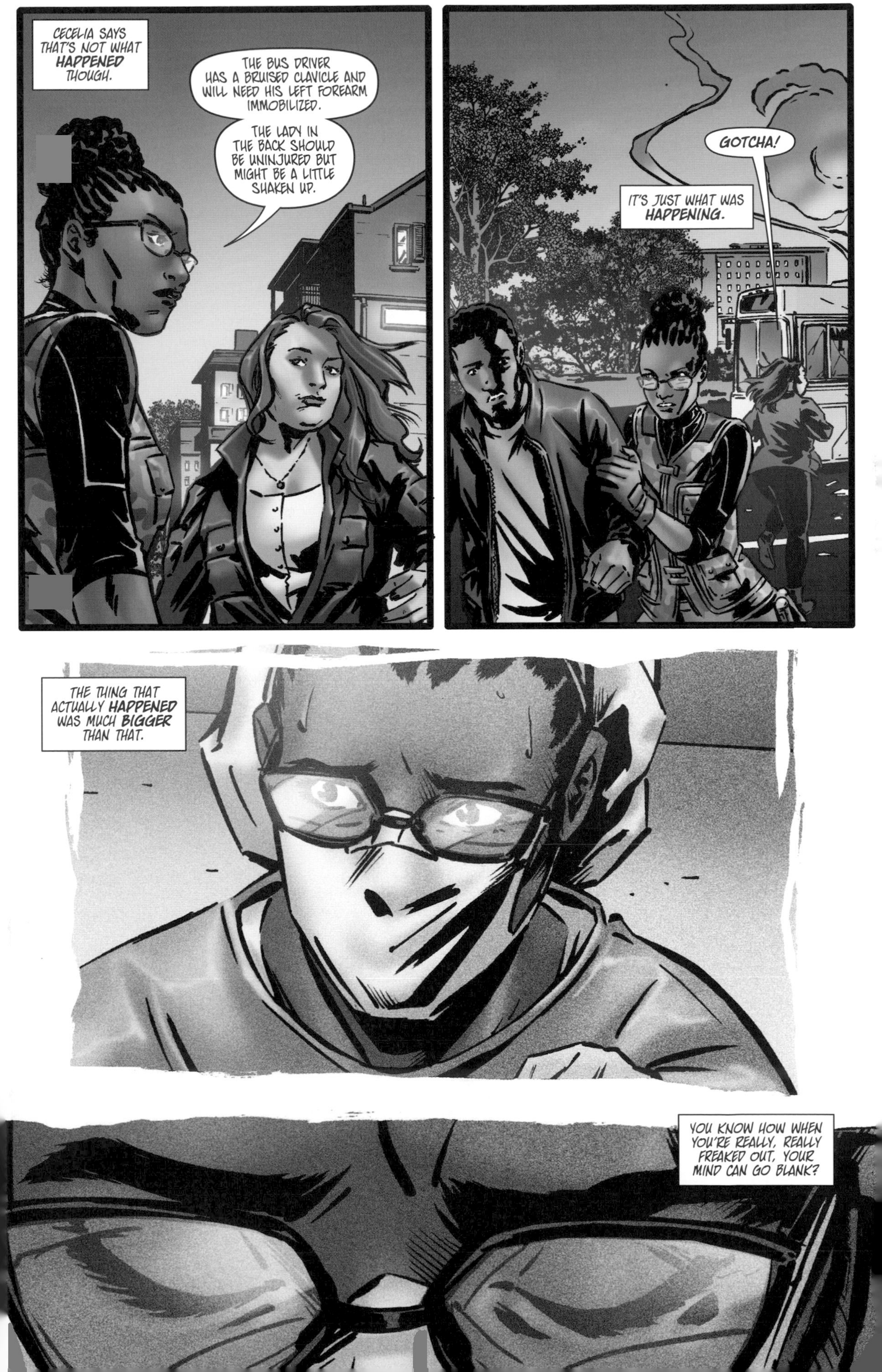
CECELIA SAYS THAT'S NOT WHAT HAPPENED THOUGH.
THE BUS DRIVER HAS A BRUISED CLAVICLE AND WILL NEED HIS LEFT FOREARM IMMOBILIZED.
THE LADY IN THE BACK SHOULD BE UNINJURED BUT MIGHT BE A LITTLE SHAKEN UP.
GOTCHA!
IT'S JUST WHAT WAS HAPPENING.
THE THING THAT ACTUALLY HAPPENED WAS MUCH BIGGER THAN THAT.
YOU KNOW HOW WHEN YOU'RE REALLY, REALLY FREAKED OUT, YOUR MIND CAN GO BLANK?

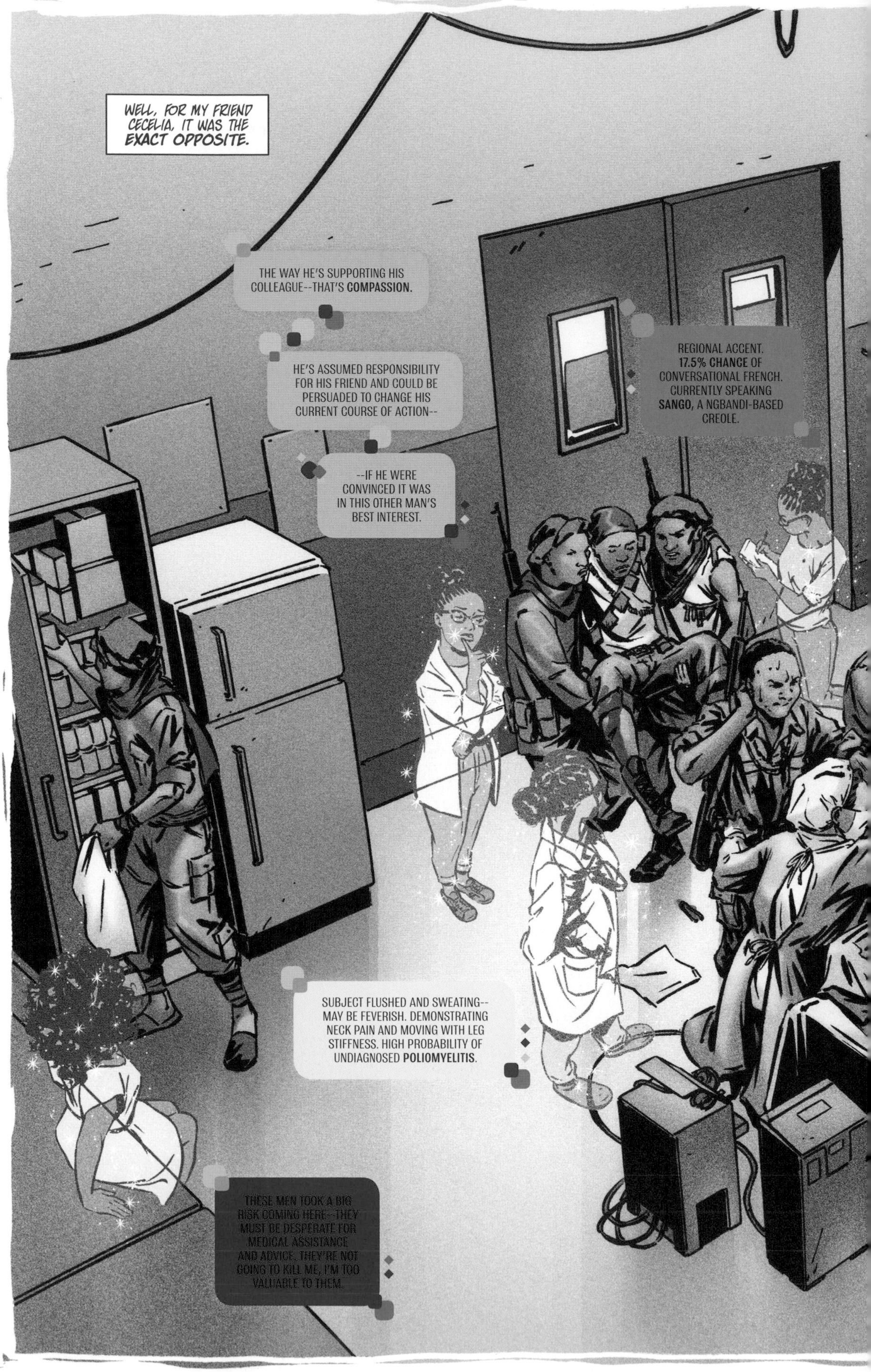
WELL, FOR MY FRIEND CECELIA, IT WAS THE EXACT OPPOSITE.
THE WAY HE'S SUPPORTING HIS COLLEAGUE--THAT'S COMPASSION.
HE'S ASSUMED RESPONSIBILITY FOR HIS FRIEND AND COULD BE PERSUADED TO CHANGE HIS CURRENT COURSE OF ACTION--
--IF HE WERE CONVINCED IT WAS IN THIS OTHER MAN'S BEST INTEREST.
REGIONAL ACCENT. 17.5% CHANCE OF CONVERSATIONAL FRENCH. CURRENTLY SPEAKING SANGO, A NGBANDI-BASED CREOLE.
SUBJECT FLUSHED AND SWEATING--MAY BE FEVERISH. DEMONSTRATING NECK PAIN AND MOVING WITH LEG STIFFNESS. HIGH PROBABILITY OF UNDIAGNOSED POLIOMYELITIS.
THESE MEN TOOK A BIG RISK COMING HERE--THEY MUST BE DESPERATE FOR MEDICAL ASSISTANCE AND ADVICE. THEY'RE NOT GOING TO KILL ME, I'M TOO VALUABLE TO THEM.

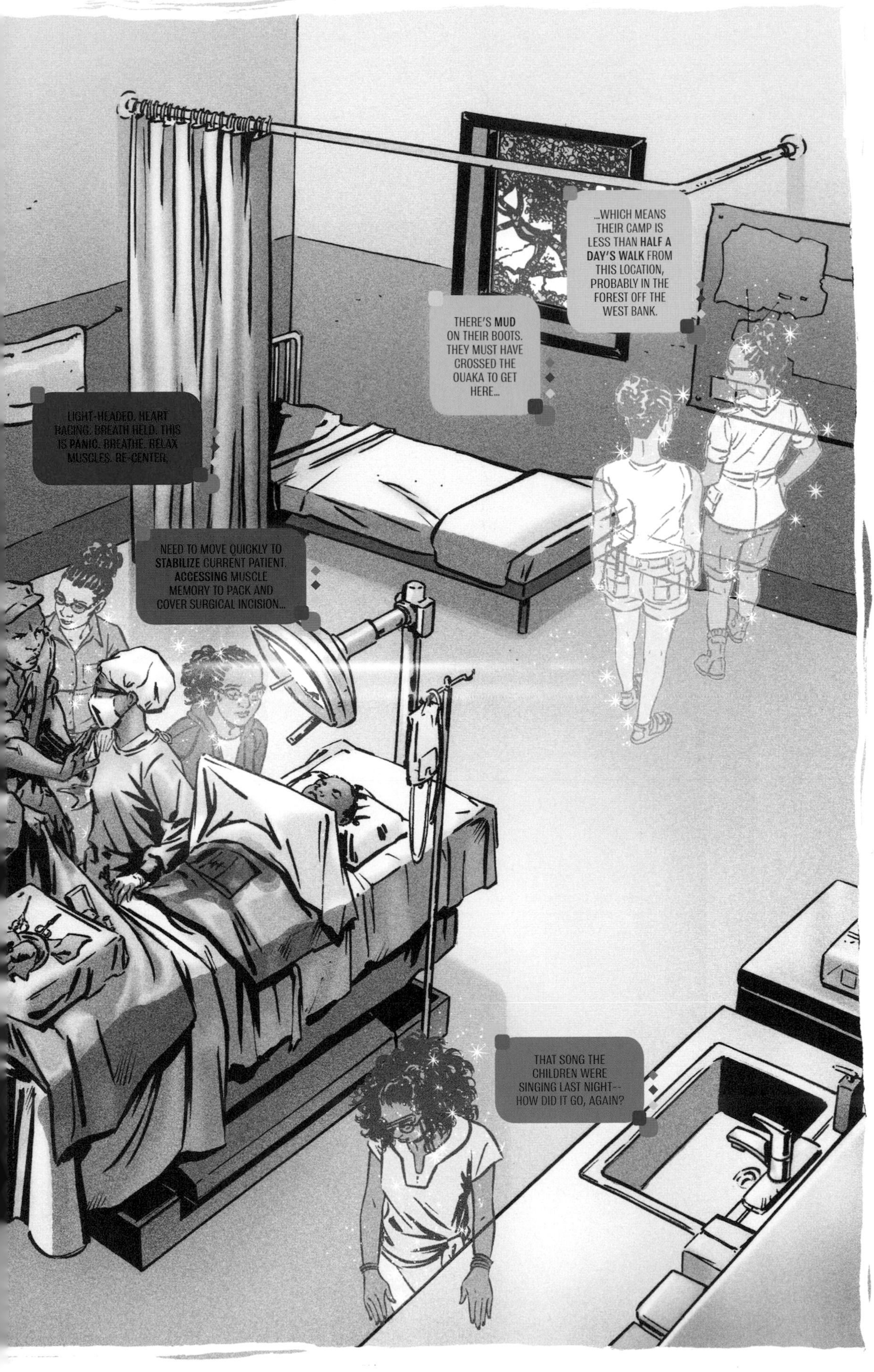

...WHICH MEANS THEIR CAMP IS LESS THAN **HALF A DAY'S WALK** FROM THIS LOCATION, PROBABLY IN THE FOREST OFF THE WEST BANK.
THERE'S **MUD** ON THEIR BOOTS. THEY MUST HAVE CROSSED THE OUAKA TO GET HERE...
LIGHT-HEADED. HEART RACING. BREATH HELD. THIS IS **PANIC**. BREATHE. RELAX MUSCLES. RE-CENTER.
NEED TO MOVE QUICKLY TO **STABILIZE** CURRENT PATIENT. **ACCESSING** MUSCLE MEMORY TO PACK AND COVER SURGICAL INCISION...
THAT SONG THE CHILDREN WERE SINGING LAST NIGHT-- HOW DID IT GO, AGAIN?

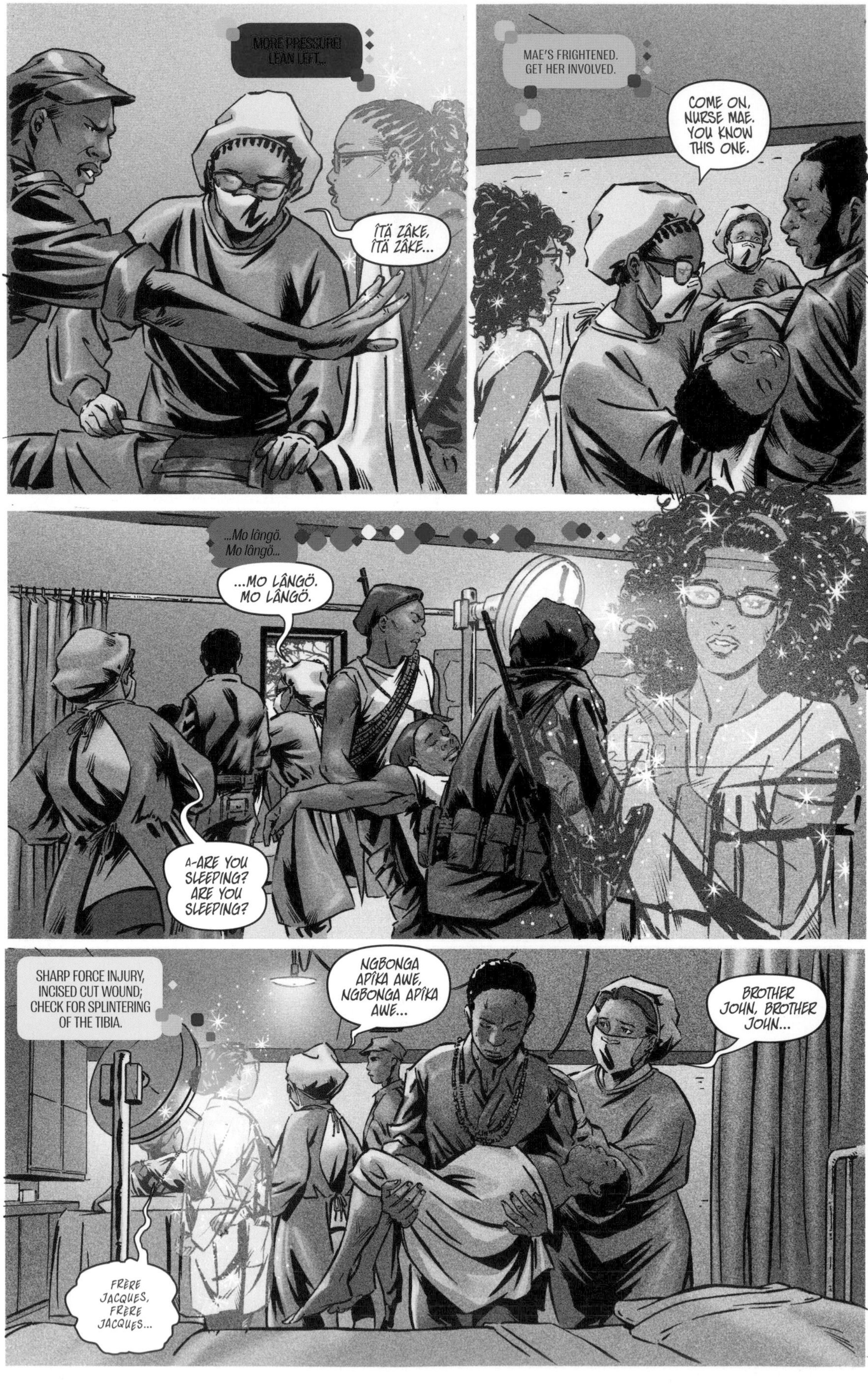
MORE PRESSURE! LEAN LEFT...
ÎTÄ ZÂKE, ÎTÄ ZÂKE...
MAE'S FRIGHTENED. GET HER INVOLVED.
COME ON, NURSE MAE. YOU KNOW THIS ONE.
...Mo lângö. Mo lângö...
...MO LÂNGÖ. MO LÂNGÖ.
A-ARE YOU SLEEPING? ARE YOU SLEEPING?
SHARP FORCE INJURY, INCISED CUT WOUND; CHECK FOR SPLINTERING OF THE TIBIA.
NGBONGA APÏKA AWE, NGBONGA APÏKA AWE...
BROTHER JOHN, BROTHER JOHN...
FRÈRE JACQUES, FRÈRE JACQUES...

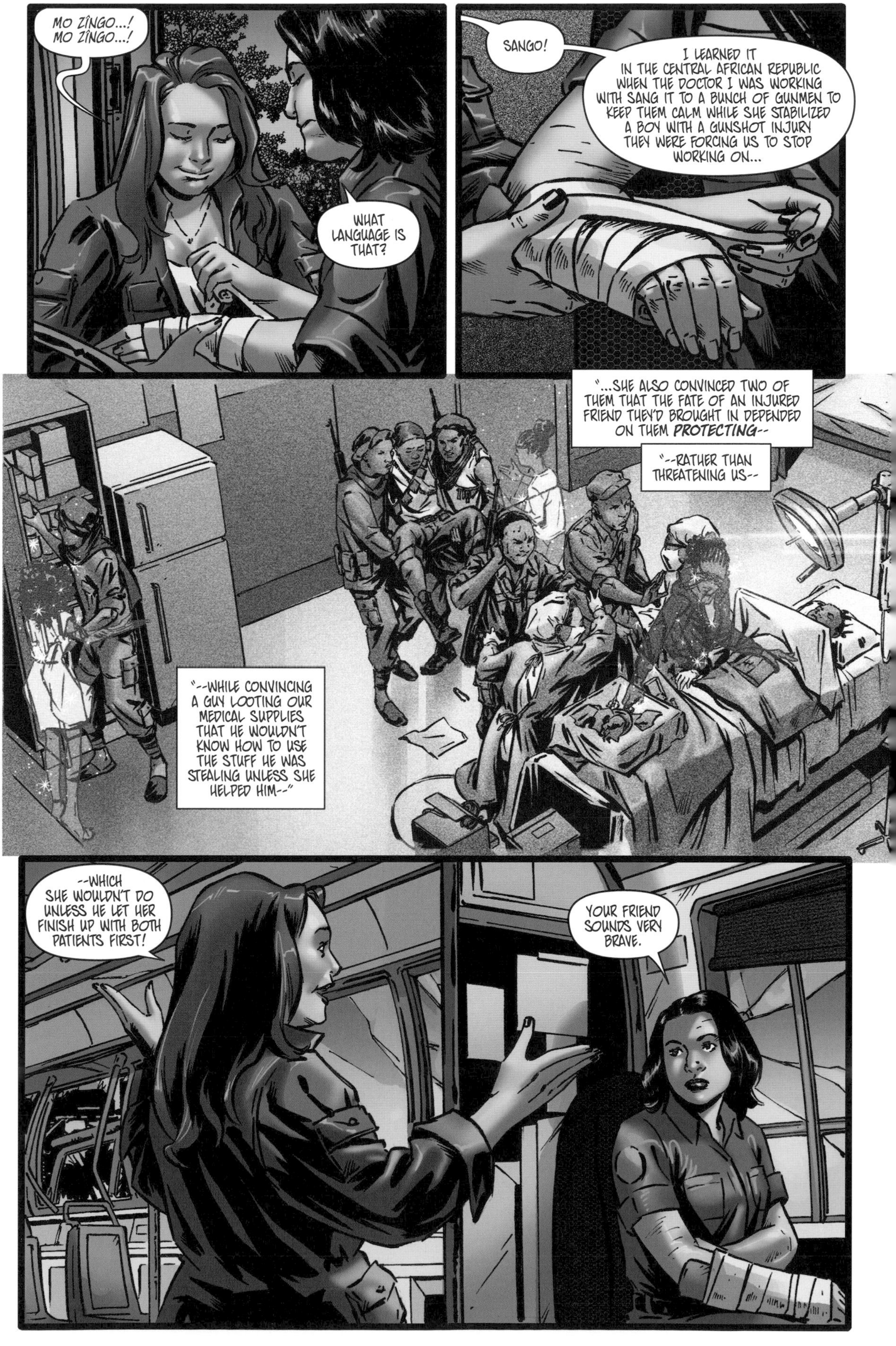
MO ZÎNGO...! MO ZÎNGO...!
WHAT LANGUAGE IS THAT?
SANGO!
I LEARNED IT IN THE CENTRAL AFRICAN REPUBLIC WHEN THE DOCTOR I WAS WORKING WITH SANG IT TO A BUNCH OF GUNMEN TO KEEP THEM CALM WHILE SHE STABILIZED A BOY WITH A GUNSHOT INJURY THEY WERE FORCING US TO STOP WORKING ON...
"...SHE ALSO CONVINCED TWO OF THEM THAT THE FATE OF AN INJURED FRIEND THEY'D BROUGHT IN DEPENDED ON THEM *PROTECTING*--
"--RATHER THAN THREATENING US--
"--WHILE CONVINCING A GUY LOOTING OUR MEDICAL SUPPLIES THAT HE WOULDN'T KNOW HOW TO USE THE STUFF HE WAS STEALING UNLESS SHE HELPED HIM--"
--WHICH SHE WOULDN'T DO UNLESS HE LET HER FINISH UP WITH BOTH PATIENTS FIRST!
YOUR FRIEND SOUNDS VERY BRAVE.

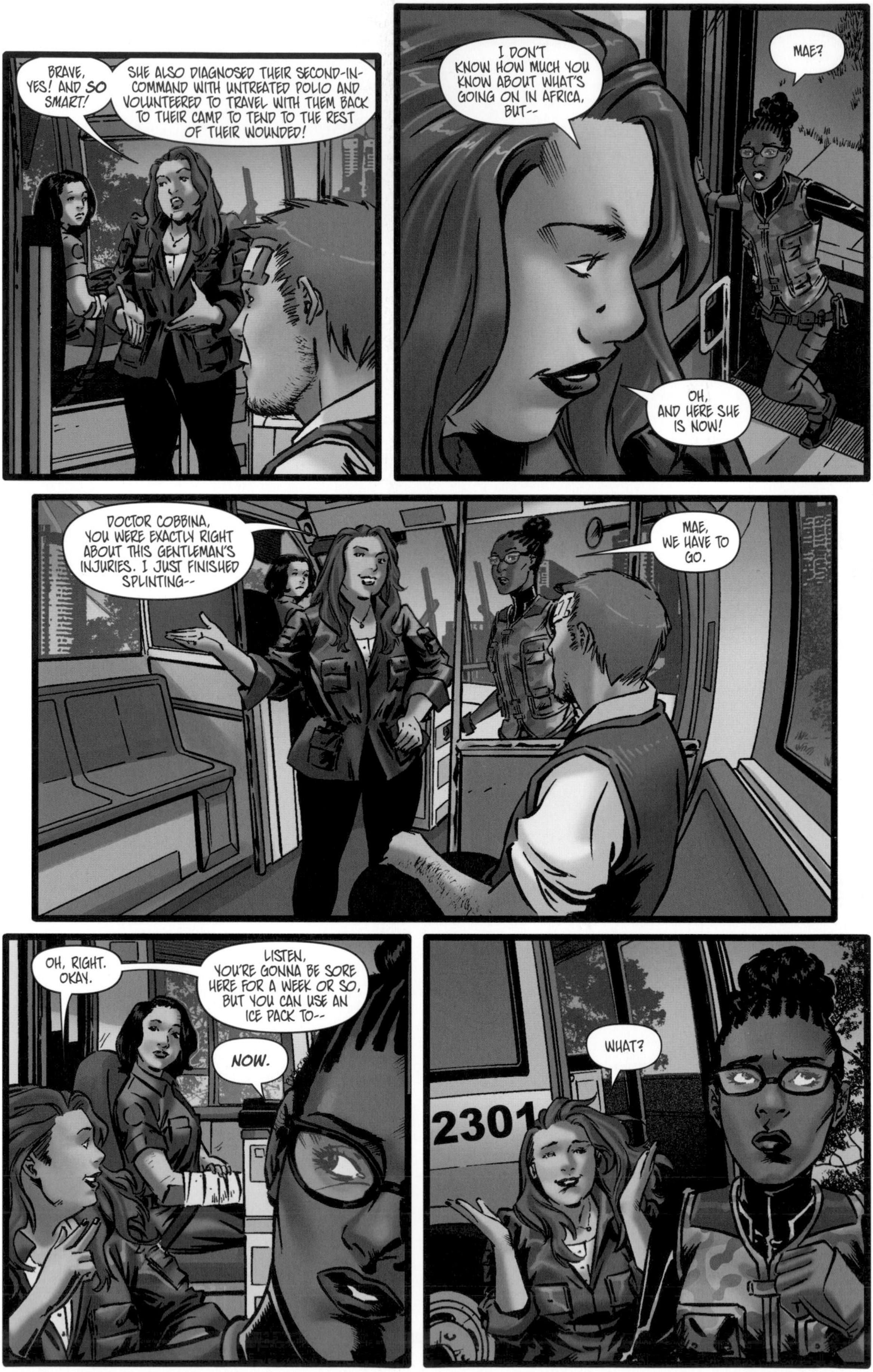
BRAVE, YES! AND SO SMART!
SHE ALSO DIAGNOSED THEIR SECOND-IN-COMMAND WITH UNTREATED POLIO AND VOLUNTEERED TO TRAVEL WITH THEM BACK TO THEIR CAMP TO TEND TO THE REST OF THEIR WOUNDED!
I DON'T KNOW HOW MUCH YOU KNOW ABOUT WHAT'S GOING ON IN AFRICA, BUT--
MAE?
OH, AND HERE SHE IS NOW!
DOCTOR COBBINA, YOU WERE EXACTLY RIGHT ABOUT THIS GENTLEMAN'S INJURIES. I JUST FINISHED SPLINTING--
MAE, WE HAVE TO GO.
OH, RIGHT. OKAY.
LISTEN, YOU'RE GONNA BE SORE HERE FOR A WEEK OR SO, BUT YOU CAN USE AN ICE PACK TO--
NOW.
WHAT?
2301

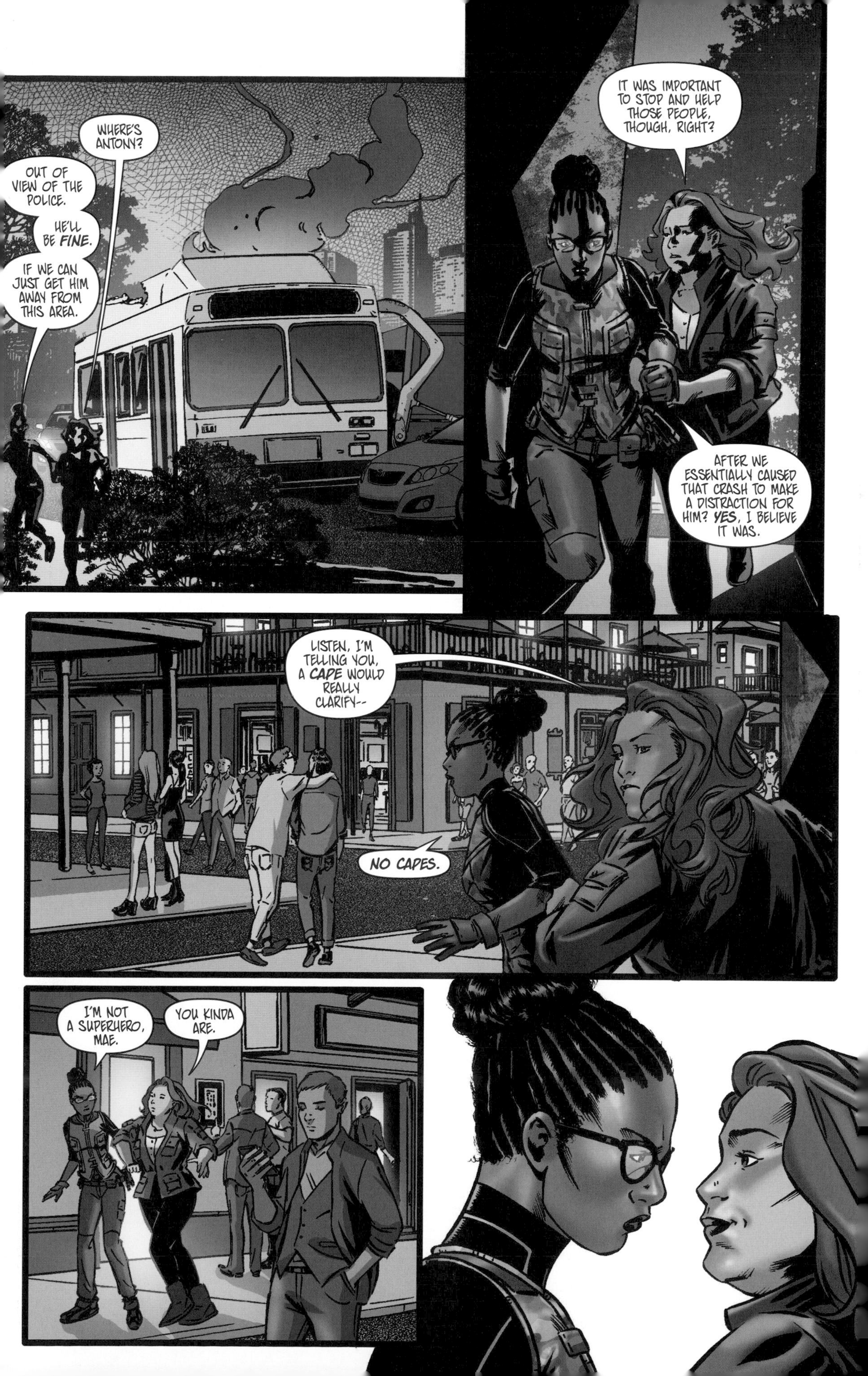
WHERE'S ANTONY?
OUT OF VIEW OF THE POLICE.
HE'LL BE FINE.
IF WE CAN JUST GET HIM AWAY FROM THIS AREA.
IT WAS IMPORTANT TO STOP AND HELP THOSE PEOPLE, THOUGH, RIGHT?
AFTER WE ESSENTIALLY CAUSED THAT CRASH TO MAKE A DISTRACTION FOR HIM? YES, I BELIEVE IT WAS.
LISTEN, I'M TELLING YOU, A CAPE WOULD REALLY CLARIFY--
NO CAPES.
I'M NOT A SUPERHERO, MAE.
YOU KINDA ARE.

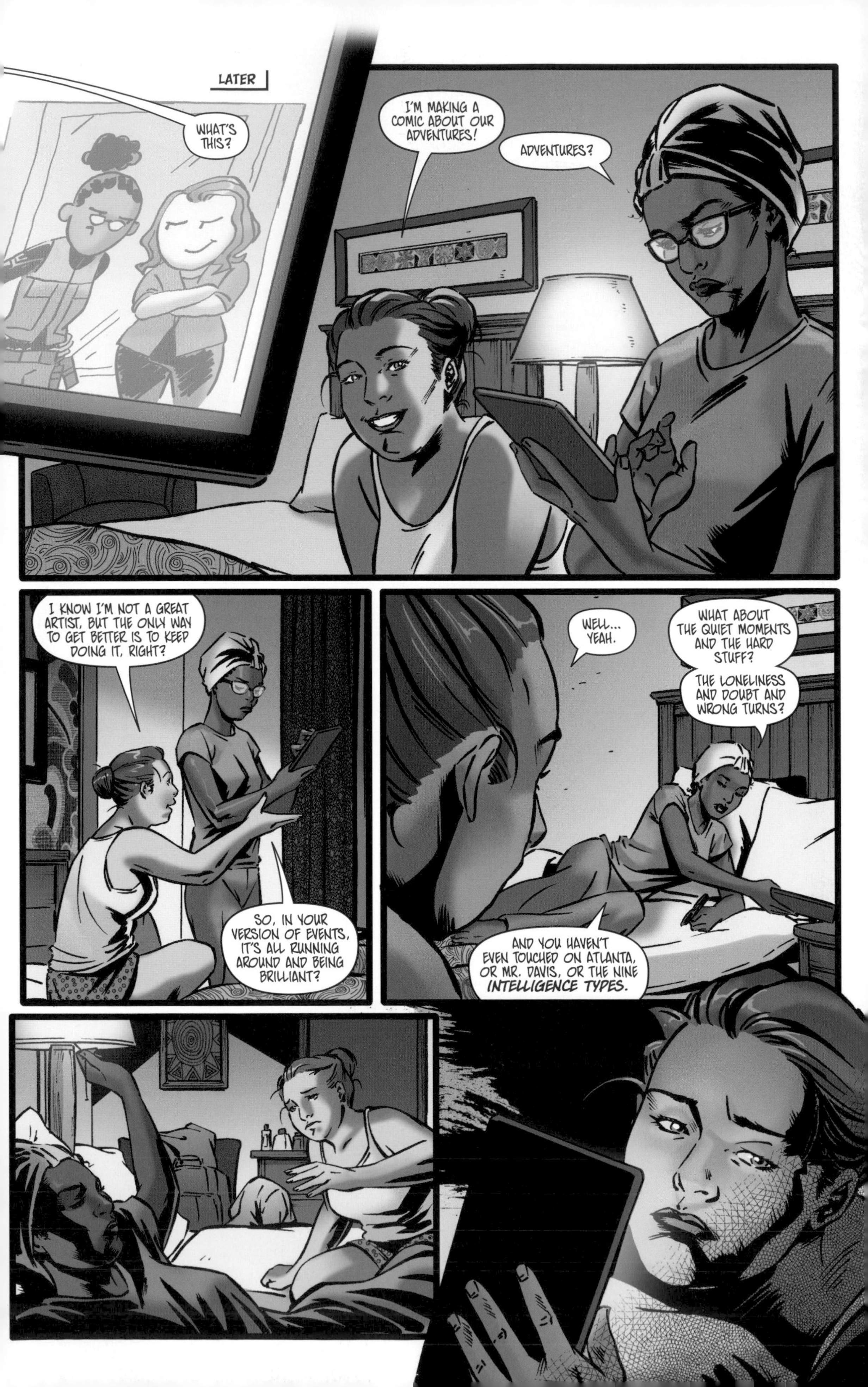
LATER
WHAT'S THIS?
I'M MAKING A COMIC ABOUT OUR ADVENTURES!
ADVENTURES?
I KNOW I'M NOT A GREAT ARTIST, BUT THE ONLY WAY TO GET BETTER IS TO KEEP DOING IT, RIGHT?
SO, IN YOUR VERSION OF EVENTS, IT'S ALL RUNNING AROUND AND BEING BRILLIANT?
WELL... YEAH.
WHAT ABOUT THE QUIET MOMENTS AND THE HARD STUFF?
THE LONELINESS AND DOUBT AND WRONG TURNS?
AND YOU HAVEN'T EVEN TOUCHED ON ATLANTA, OR MR. DAVIS, OR THE NINE **INTELLIGENCE TYPES.**

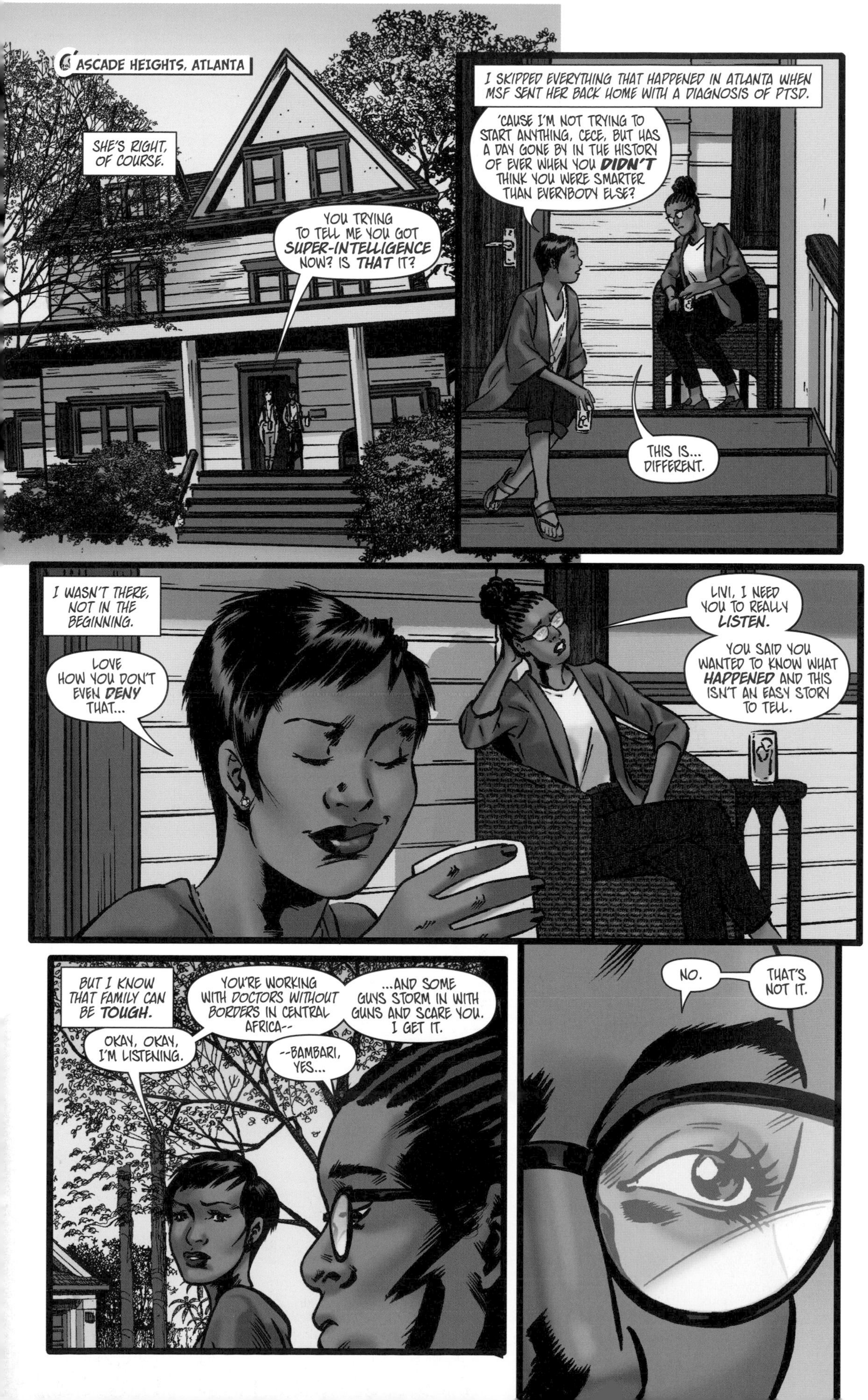
CASCADE HEIGHTS, ATLANTA
SHE'S RIGHT, OF COURSE.
YOU TRYING TO TELL ME YOU GOT SUPER-INTELLIGENCE NOW? IS THAT IT?
I SKIPPED EVERYTHING THAT HAPPENED IN ATLANTA WHEN MSF SENT HER BACK HOME WITH A DIAGNOSIS OF PTSD.
'CAUSE I'M NOT TRYING TO START ANYTHING, CECE, BUT HAS A DAY GONE BY IN THE HISTORY OF EVER WHEN YOU DIDN'T THINK YOU WERE SMARTER THAN EVERYBODY ELSE?
THIS IS... DIFFERENT.
I WASN'T THERE, NOT IN THE BEGINNING.
LOVE HOW YOU DON'T EVEN DENY THAT...
LIVI, I NEED YOU TO REALLY LISTEN.
YOU SAID YOU WANTED TO KNOW WHAT HAPPENED AND THIS ISN'T AN EASY STORY TO TELL.
BUT I KNOW THAT FAMILY CAN BE TOUGH.
OKAY, OKAY, I'M LISTENING.
YOU'RE WORKING WITH DOCTORS WITHOUT BORDERS IN CENTRAL AFRICA--
--BAMBARI, YES...
...AND SOME GUYS STORM IN WITH GUNS AND SCARE YOU. I GET IT.
NO.
THAT'S NOT IT.

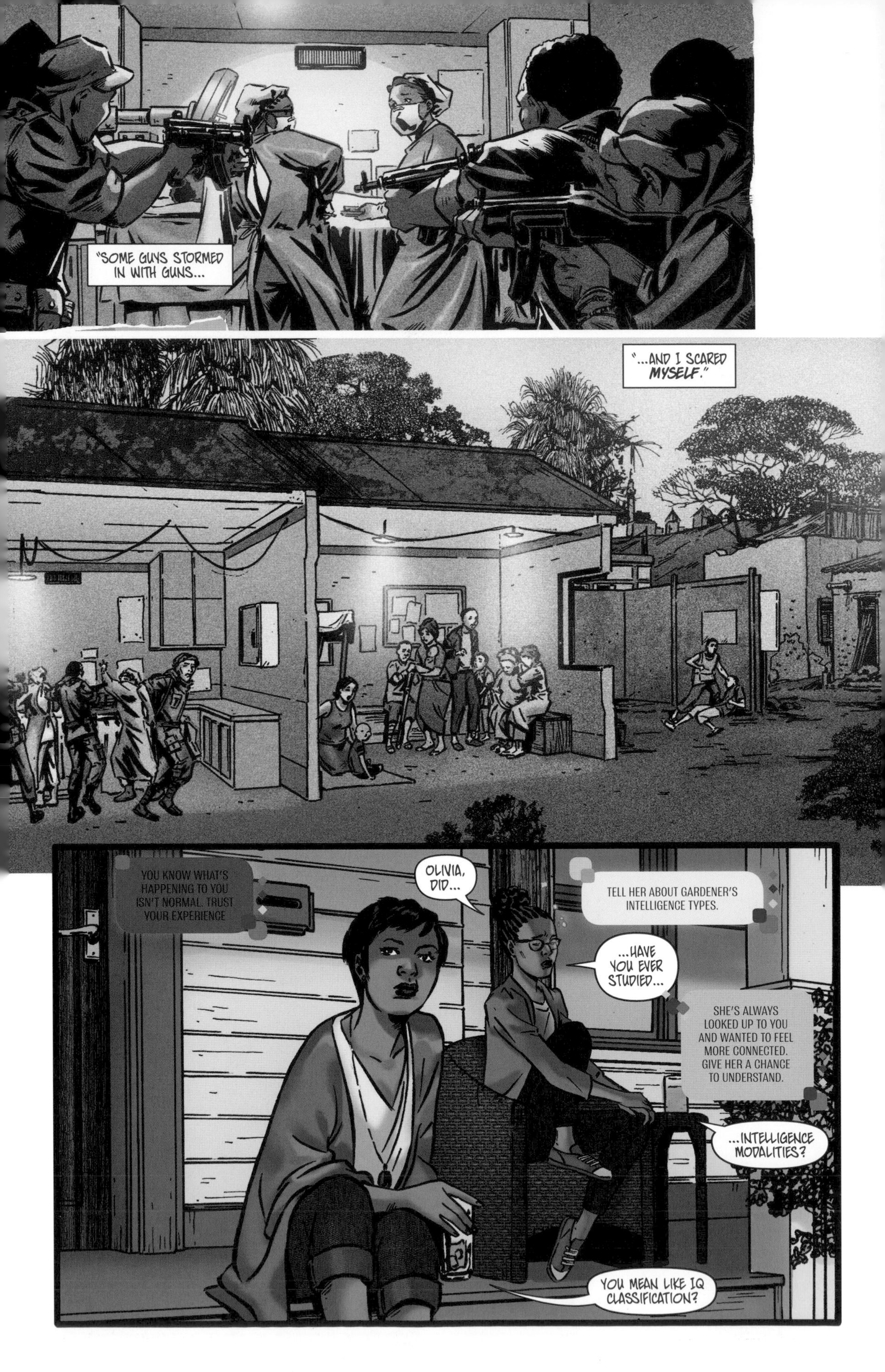
"SOME GUYS STORMED IN WITH GUNS...
"...AND I SCARED MYSELF."
YOU KNOW WHAT'S HAPPENING TO YOU ISN'T NORMAL. TRUST YOUR EXPERIENCE
OLIVIA, DID...
TELL HER ABOUT GARDENER'S INTELLIGENCE TYPES.
...HAVE YOU EVER STUDIED...
SHE'S ALWAYS LOOKED UP TO YOU AND WANTED TO FEEL MORE CONNECTED. GIVE HER A CHANCE TO UNDERSTAND.
...INTELLIGENCE MODALITIES?
YOU MEAN LIKE IQ CLASSIFICATION?

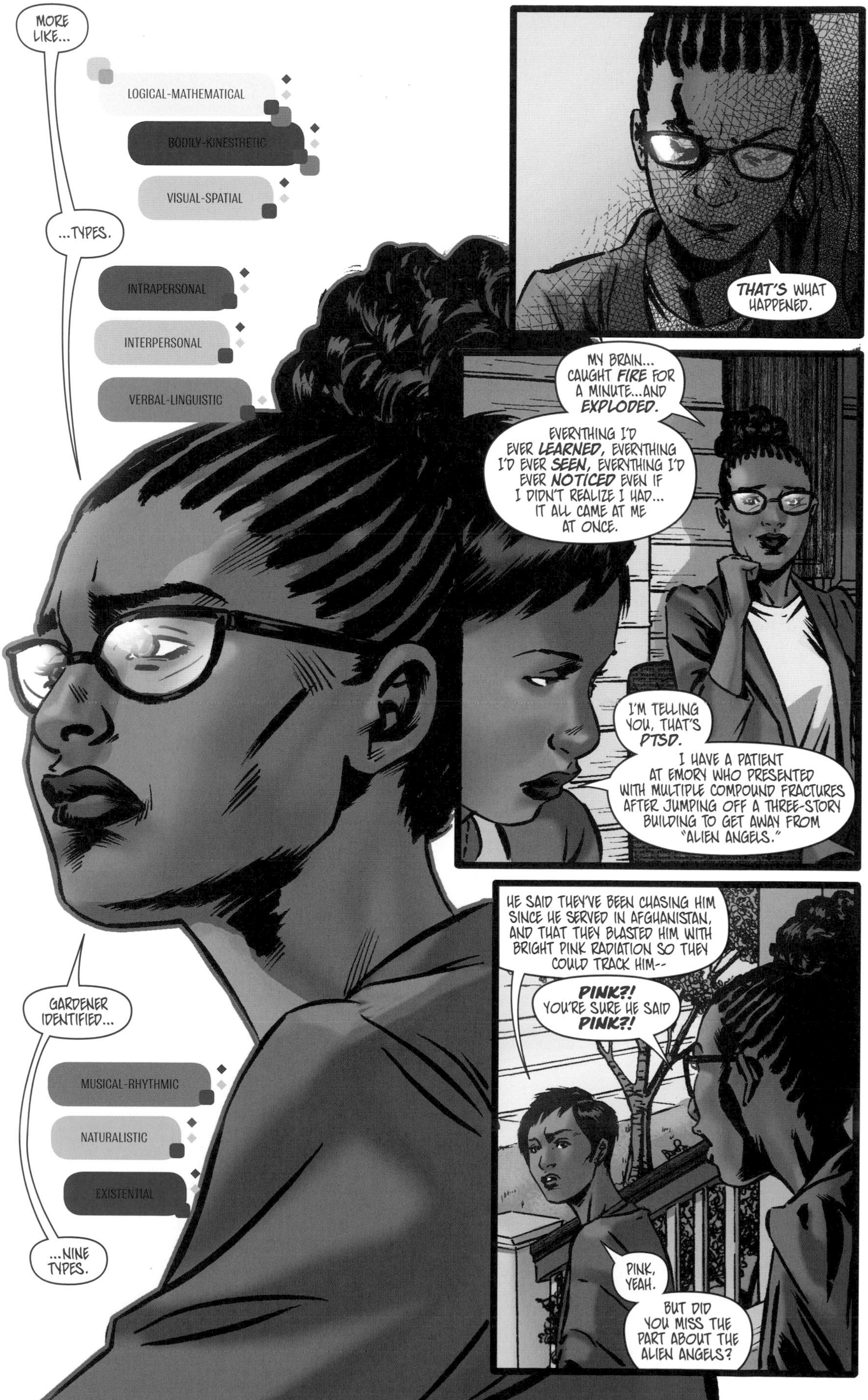

MORE LIKE...
LOGICAL-MATHEMATICAL
BODILY-KINESTHETIC
VISUAL-SPATIAL
...TYPES.
INTRAPERSONAL
INTERPERSONAL
VERBAL-LINGUISTIC
THAT'S WHAT HAPPENED.
MY BRAIN... CAUGHT FIRE FOR A MINUTE...AND EXPLODED.
EVERYTHING I'D EVER LEARNED, EVERYTHING I'D EVER SEEN, EVERYTHING I'D EVER NOTICED EVEN IF I DIDN'T REALIZE I HAD... IT ALL CAME AT ME AT ONCE.
I'M TELLING YOU, THAT'S PTSD.
I HAVE A PATIENT AT EMORY WHO PRESENTED WITH MULTIPLE COMPOUND FRACTURES AFTER JUMPING OFF A THREE-STORY BUILDING TO GET AWAY FROM "ALIEN ANGELS."
HE SAID THEY'VE BEEN CHASING HIM SINCE HE SERVED IN AFGHANISTAN, AND THAT THEY BLASTED HIM WITH BRIGHT PINK RADIATION SO THEY COULD TRACK HIM--
PINK?! YOU'RE SURE HE SAID PINK?!
PINK, YEAH.
BUT DID YOU MISS THE PART ABOUT THE ALIEN ANGELS?
GARDENER IDENTIFIED...
MUSICAL-RHYTHMIC
NATURALISTIC
EXISTENTIAL
...NINE TYPES.

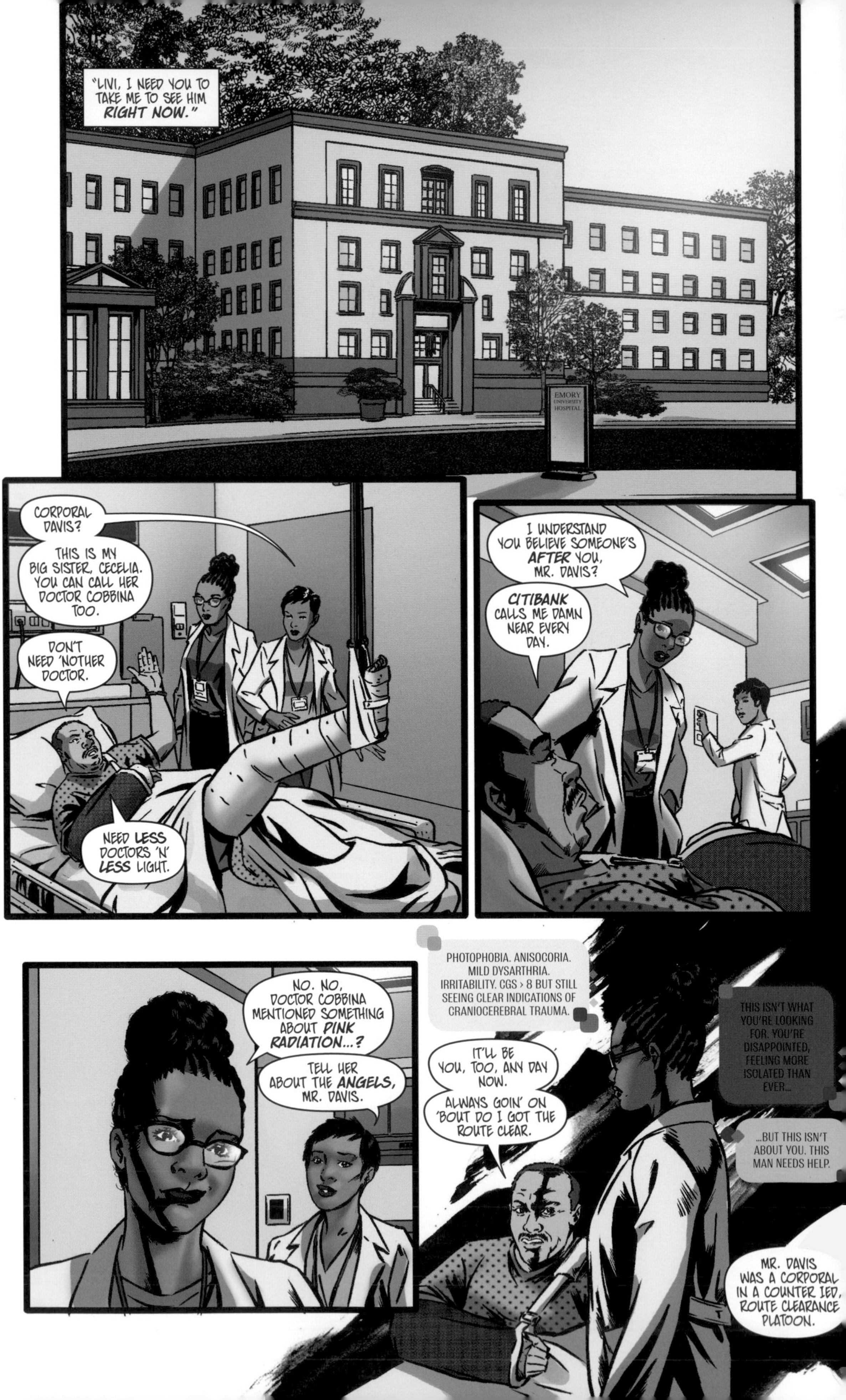
"LIVI, I NEED YOU TO TAKE ME TO SEE HIM RIGHT NOW."
EMORY UNIVERSITY HOSPITAL
CORPORAL DAVIS?
THIS IS MY BIG SISTER, CECELIA. YOU CAN CALL HER DOCTOR COBBINA TOO.
DON'T NEED 'NOTHER DOCTOR.
NEED LESS DOCTORS 'N' LESS LIGHT.
I UNDERSTAND YOU BELIEVE SOMEONE'S AFTER YOU, MR. DAVIS?
CITIBANK CALLS ME DAMN NEAR EVERY DAY.
NO. NO, DOCTOR COBBINA MENTIONED SOMETHING ABOUT PINK RADIATION...?
TELL HER ABOUT THE ANGELS, MR. DAVIS.
PHOTOPHOBIA. ANISOCORIA. MILD DYSARTHRIA. IRRITABILITY. CGS > 8 BUT STILL SEEING CLEAR INDICATIONS OF CRANIOCEREBRAL TRAUMA.
IT'LL BE YOU, TOO, ANY DAY NOW.
ALWAYS GOIN' ON 'BOUT DO I GOT THE ROUTE CLEAR.
THIS ISN'T WHAT YOU'RE LOOKING FOR. YOU'RE DISAPPOINTED, FEELING MORE ISOLATED THAN EVER...
...BUT THIS ISN'T ABOUT YOU. THIS MAN NEEDS HELP.
MR. DAVIS WAS A CORPORAL IN A COUNTER IED, ROUTE CLEARANCE PLATOON.

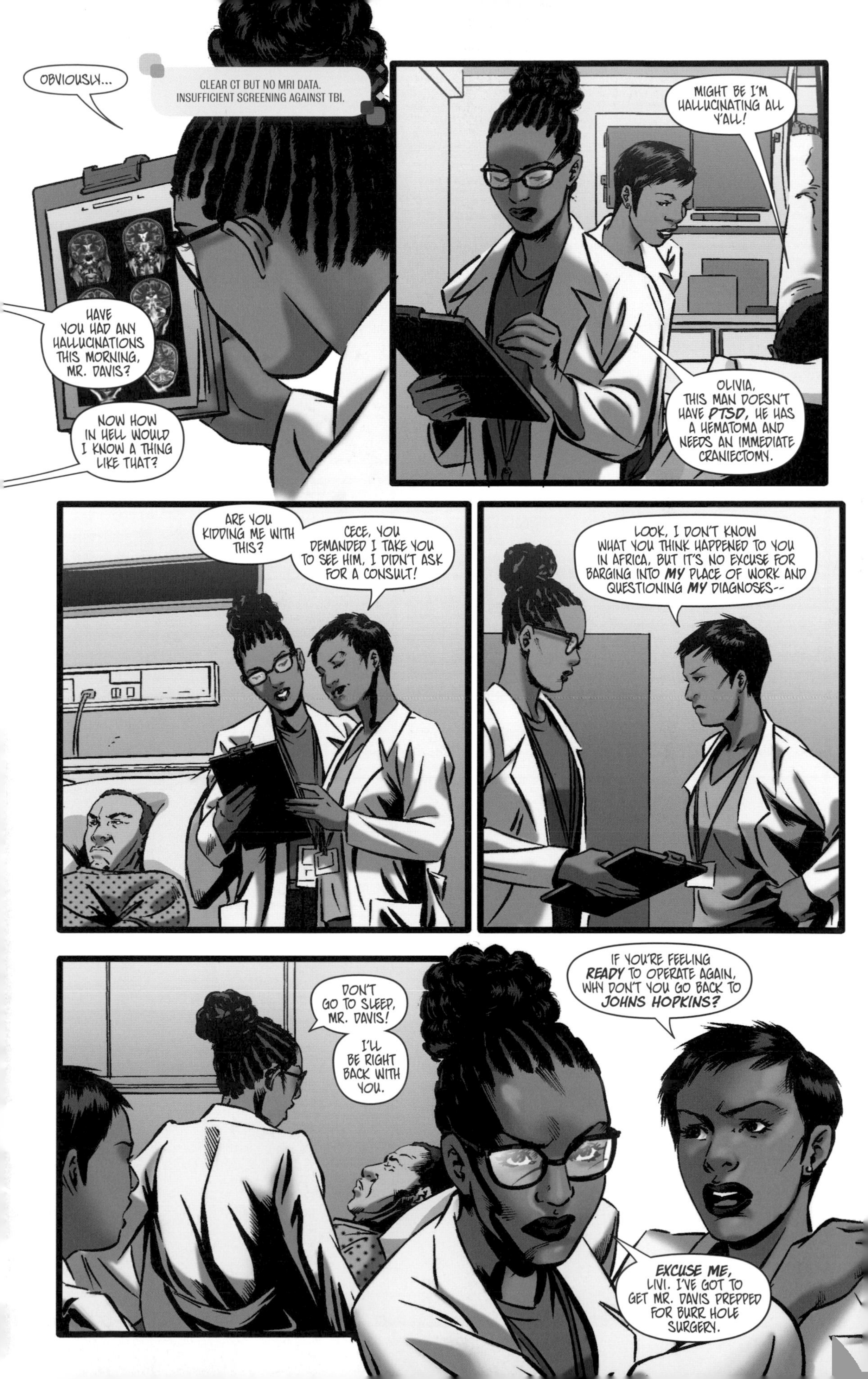
OBVIOUSLY...
CLEAR CT BUT NO MRI DATA. INSUFFICIENT SCREENING AGAINST TBI.
HAVE YOU HAD ANY HALLUCINATIONS THIS MORNING, MR. DAVIS?
NOW HOW IN HELL WOULD I KNOW A THING LIKE THAT?
MIGHT BE I'M HALLUCINATING ALL Y'ALL!
OLIVIA, THIS MAN DOESN'T HAVE PTSD, HE HAS A HEMATOMA AND NEEDS AN IMMEDIATE CRANIECTOMY.
ARE YOU KIDDING ME WITH THIS?
CECE, YOU DEMANDED I TAKE YOU TO SEE HIM, I DIDN'T ASK FOR A CONSULT!
LOOK, I DON'T KNOW WHAT YOU THINK HAPPENED TO YOU IN AFRICA, BUT IT'S NO EXCUSE FOR BARGING INTO MY PLACE OF WORK AND QUESTIONING MY DIAGNOSES--
IF YOU'RE FEELING READY TO OPERATE AGAIN, WHY DON'T YOU GO BACK TO JOHNS HOPKINS?
EXCUSE ME, LIVI. I'VE GOT TO GET MR. DAVIS PREPPED FOR BURR HOLE SURGERY.
DON'T GO TO SLEEP, MR. DAVIS!
I'LL BE RIGHT BACK WITH YOU.

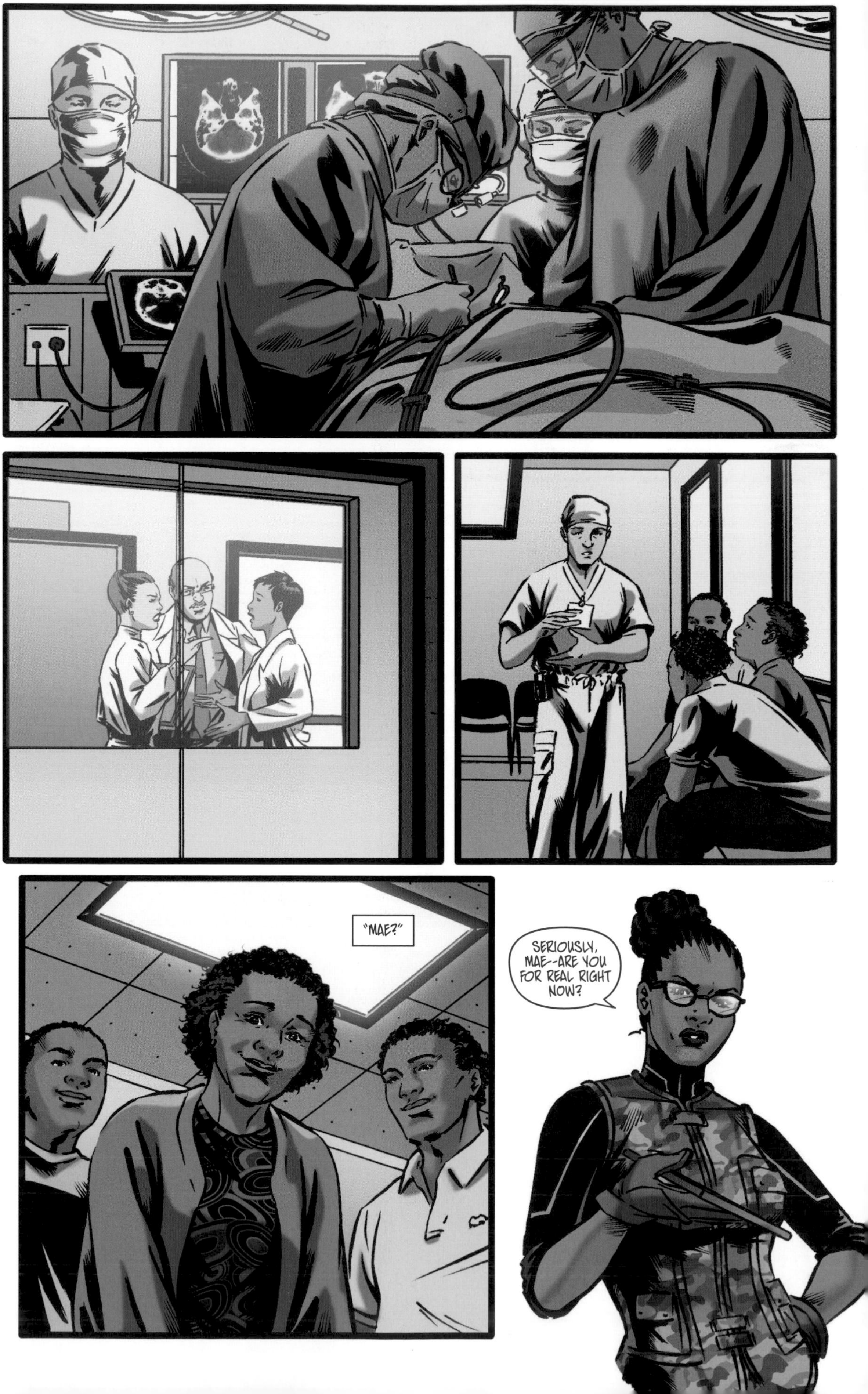
"MAE?"
SERIOUSLY, MAE--ARE YOU FOR REAL RIGHT NOW?

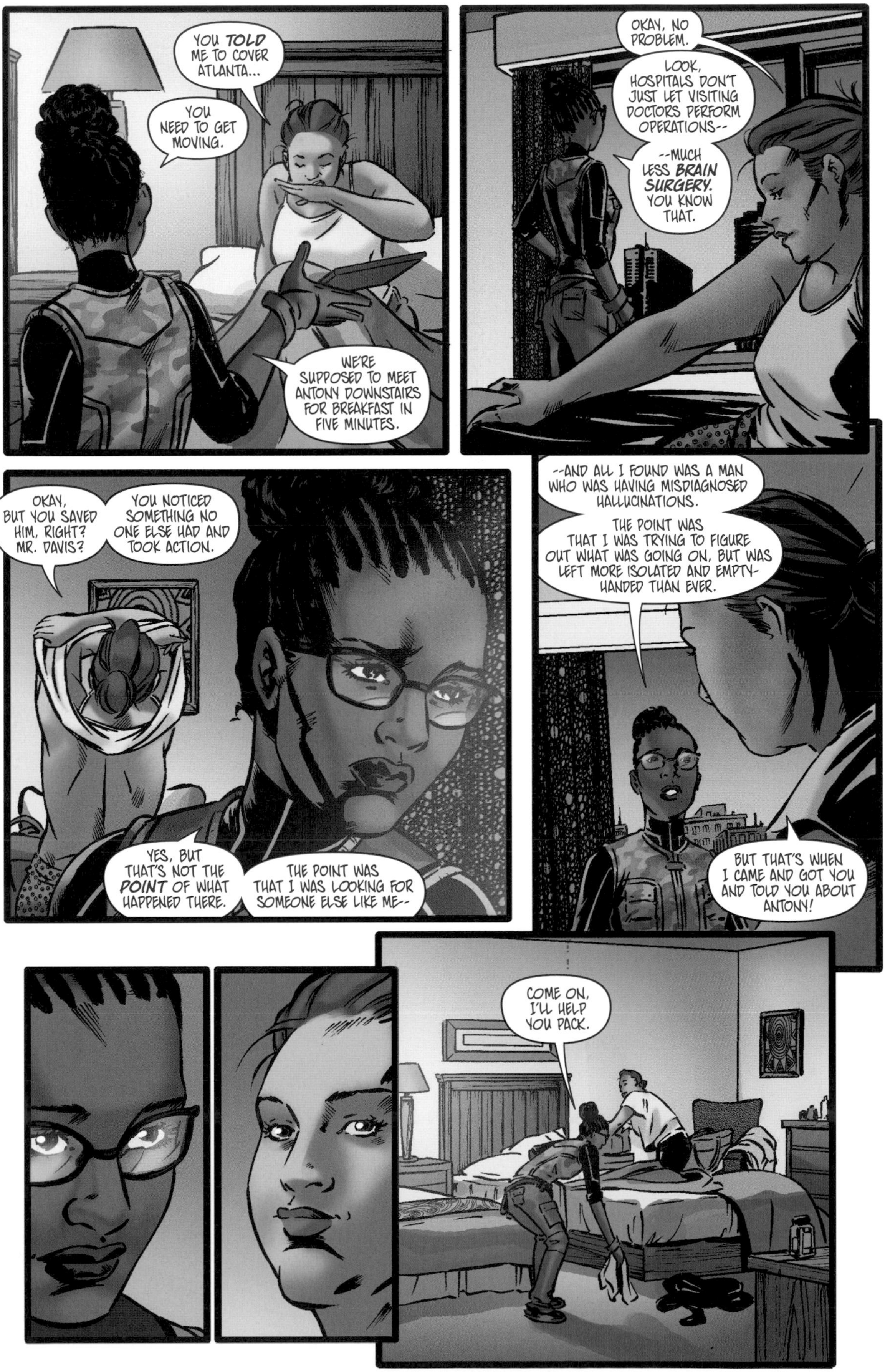
YOU **TOLD** ME TO COVER ATLANTA...
YOU NEED TO GET MOVING.
WE'RE SUPPOSED TO MEET ANTONY DOWNSTAIRS FOR BREAKFAST IN FIVE MINUTES.
OKAY, NO PROBLEM.
LOOK, HOSPITALS DON'T JUST LET VISITING DOCTORS PERFORM OPERATIONS--
--MUCH LESS **BRAIN SURGERY.** YOU KNOW THAT.
OKAY, BUT YOU SAVED HIM, RIGHT? MR. DAVIS?
YOU NOTICED SOMETHING NO ONE ELSE HAD AND TOOK ACTION.
YES, BUT THAT'S NOT THE ***POINT*** OF WHAT HAPPENED THERE.
THE POINT WAS THAT I WAS LOOKING FOR SOMEONE ELSE LIKE ME--
--AND ALL I FOUND WAS A MAN WHO WAS HAVING MISDIAGNOSED HALLUCINATIONS.
THE POINT WAS THAT I WAS TRYING TO FIGURE OUT WHAT WAS GOING ON, BUT WAS LEFT MORE ISOLATED AND EMPTY-HANDED THAN EVER.
BUT THAT'S WHEN I CAME AND GOT YOU AND TOLD YOU ABOUT ANTONY!
COME ON, I'LL HELP YOU PACK.

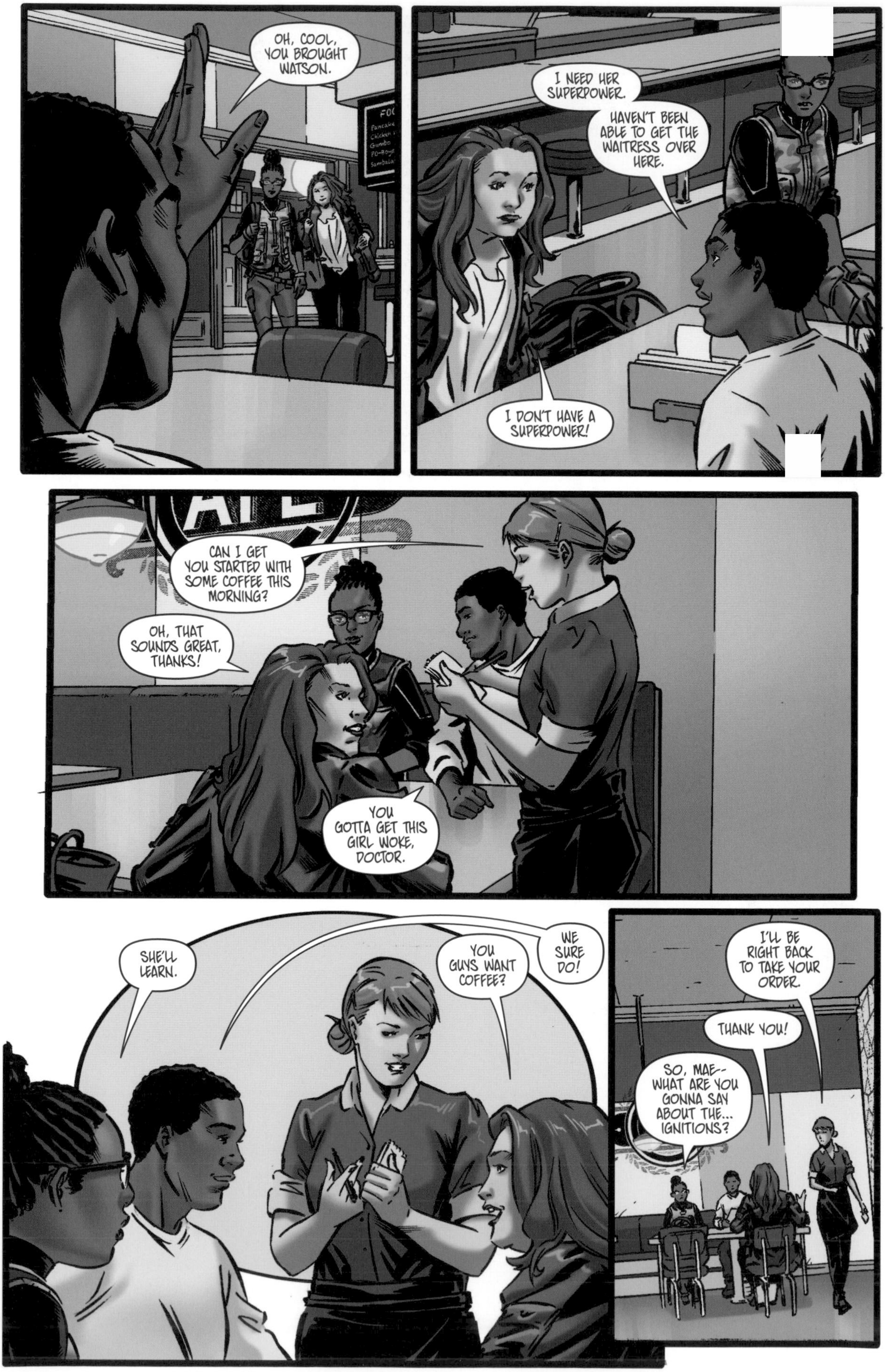
OH, COOL, YOU BROUGHT WATSON.
FOO
Pancake
Chicken
Gumbo
PO-Boys
Sambala
I NEED HER SUPERPOWER.
HAVEN'T BEEN ABLE TO GET THE WAITRESS OVER HERE.
I DON'T HAVE A SUPERPOWER!
CAN I GET YOU STARTED WITH SOME COFFEE THIS MORNING?
OH, THAT SOUNDS GREAT, THANKS!
YOU GOTTA GET THIS GIRL WOKE, DOCTOR.
SHE'LL LEARN.
YOU GUYS WANT COFFEE?
WE SURE DO!
I'LL BE RIGHT BACK TO TAKE YOUR ORDER.
THANK YOU!
SO, MAE-- WHAT ARE YOU GONNA SAY ABOUT THE... IGNITIONS?

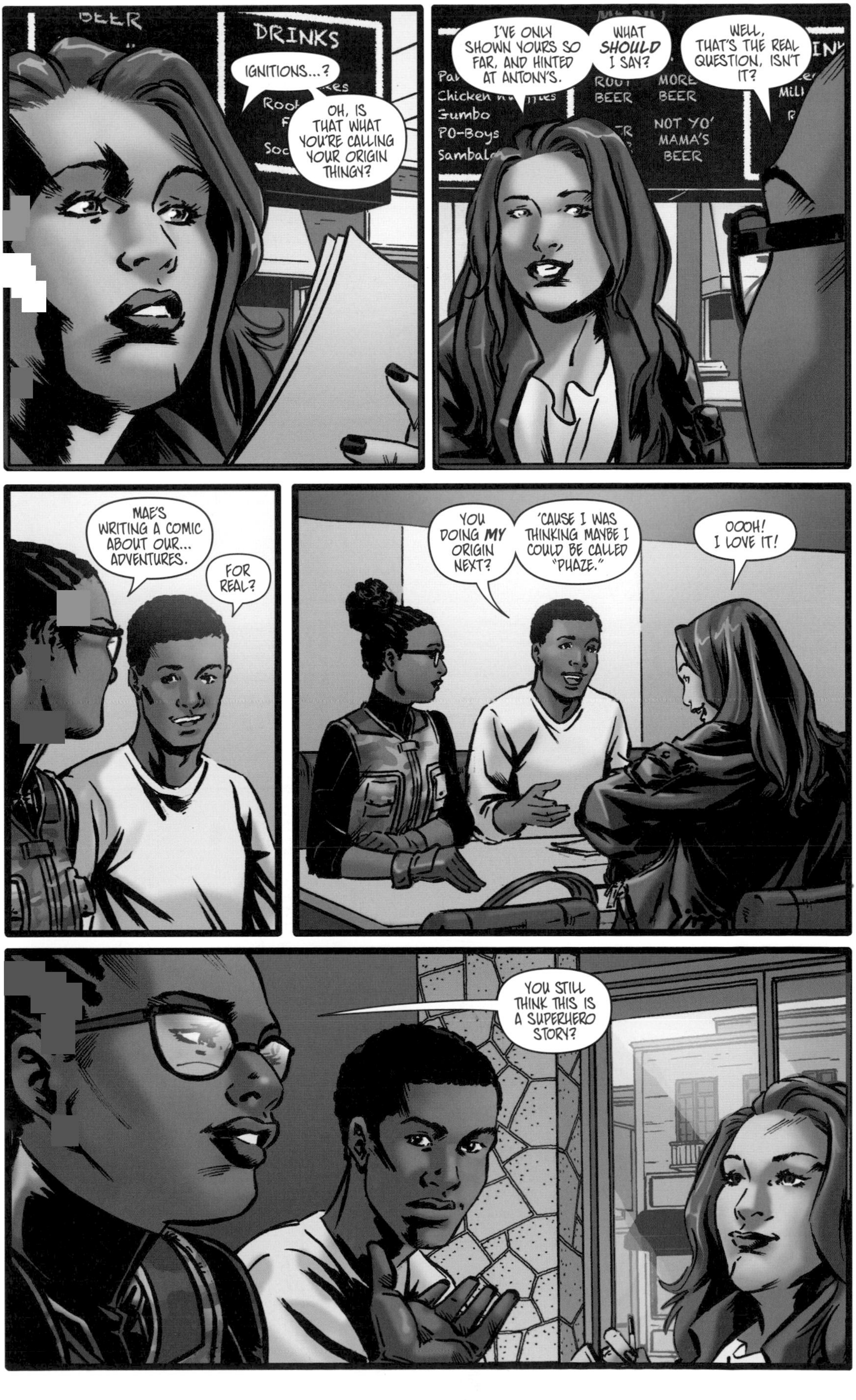
DRINKS
IGNITIONS...?
OH, IS THAT WHAT YOU'RE CALLING YOUR ORIGIN THINGY?
Gumbo
PO-Boys
ROOT BEER
MORE BEER
NOT YO' MAMA'S BEER
I'VE ONLY SHOWN YOURS SO FAR, AND HINTED AT ANTONY'S.
WHAT *SHOULD* I SAY?
WELL, THAT'S THE REAL QUESTION, ISN'T IT?
MAE'S WRITING A COMIC ABOUT OUR... ADVENTURES.
FOR REAL?
YOU DOING *MY* ORIGIN NEXT?
'CAUSE I WAS THINKING MAYBE I COULD BE CALLED "PHAZE."
OOOH! I LOVE IT!
YOU STILL THINK THIS IS A SUPERHERO STORY?

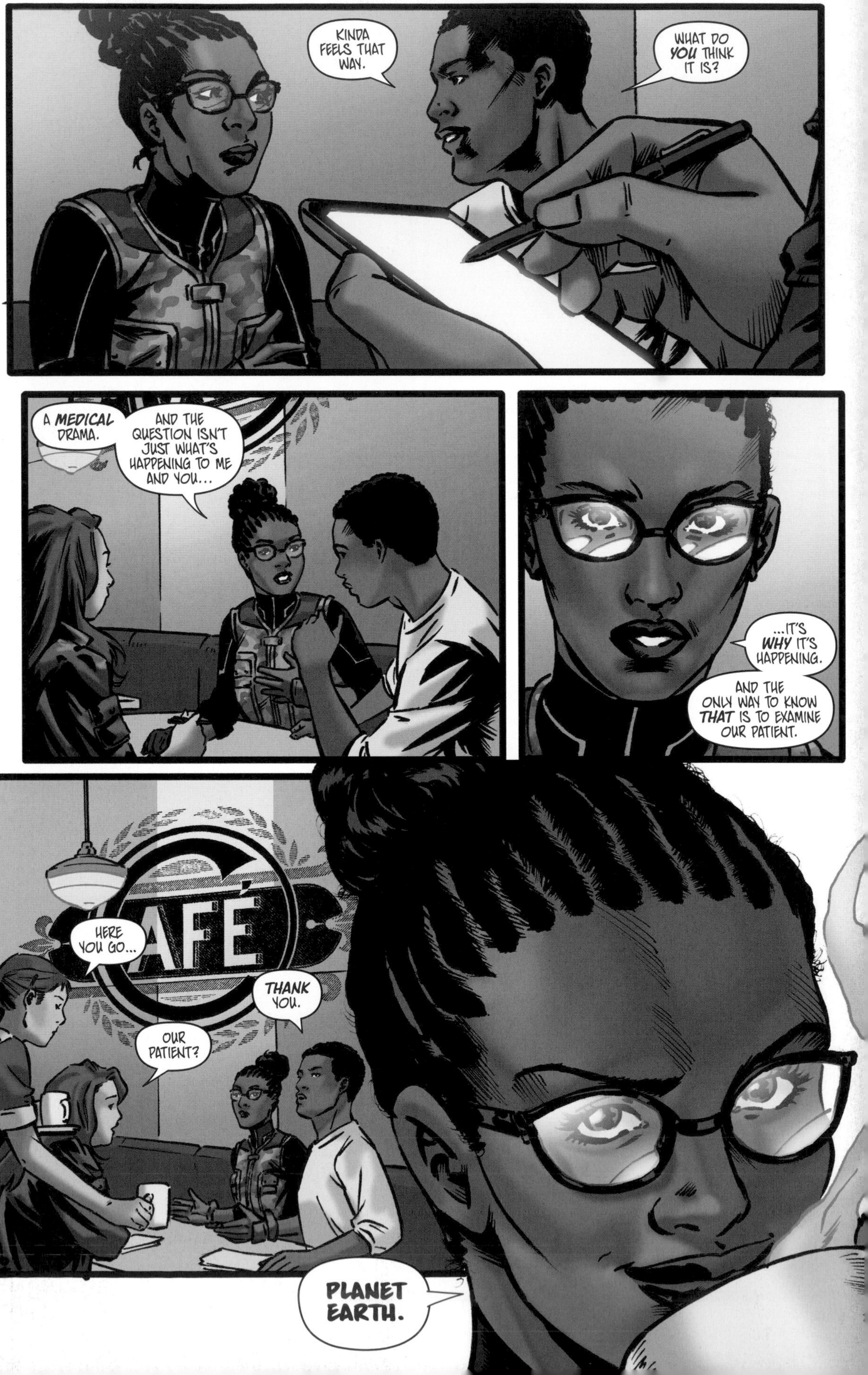
KINDA FEELS THAT WAY.
WHAT DO YOU THINK IT IS?
A MEDICAL DRAMA.
AND THE QUESTION ISN'T JUST WHAT'S HAPPENING TO ME AND YOU...
...IT'S WHY IT'S HAPPENING.
AND THE ONLY WAY TO KNOW THAT IS TO EXAMINE OUR PATIENT.
AFÉ
HERE YOU GO...
THANK YOU.
OUR PATIENT?
PLANET EARTH.

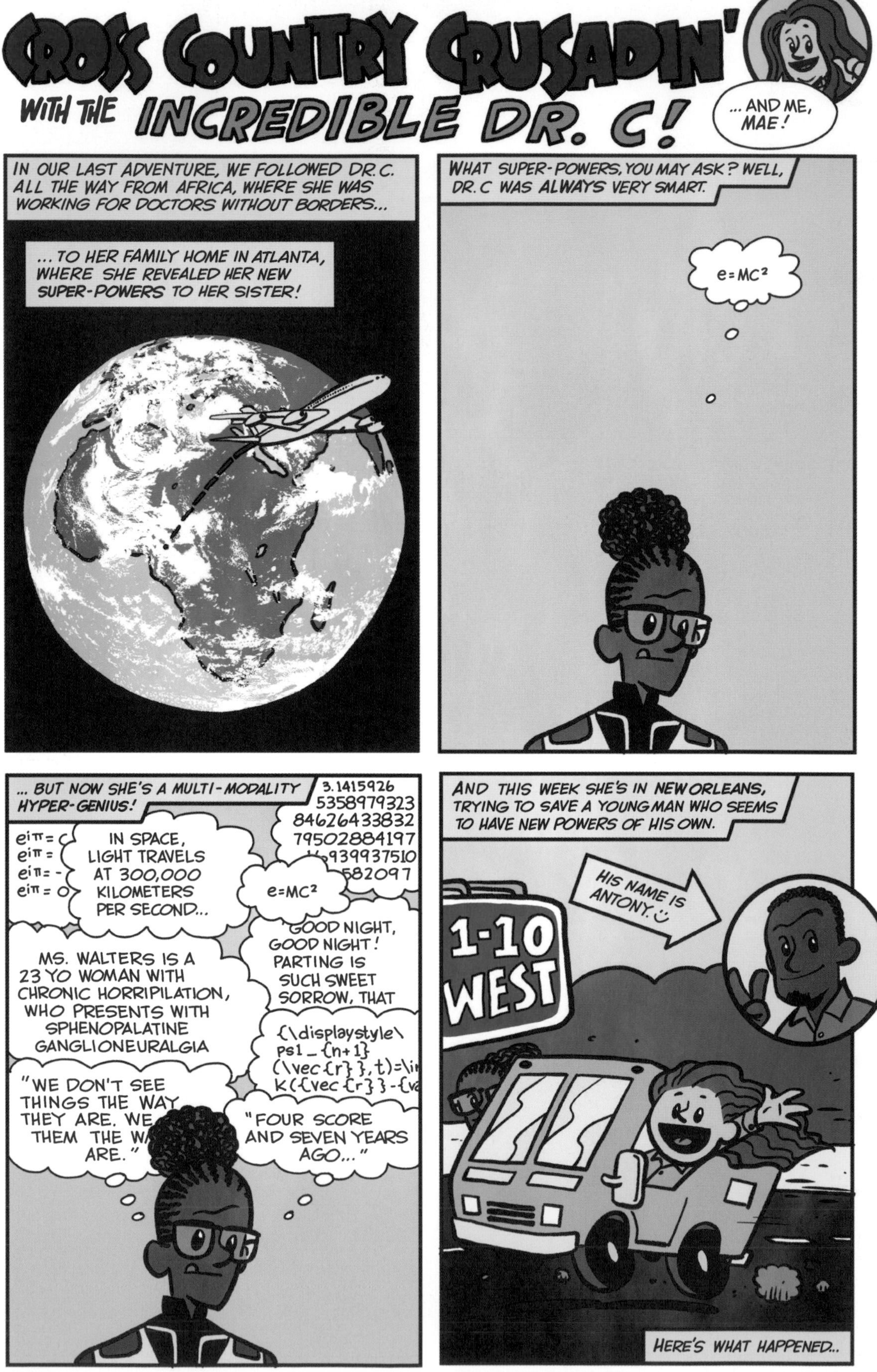
CROSS COUNTRY CRUSADIN'
WITH THE INCREDIBLE DR. C!
... AND ME, MAE!
IN OUR LAST ADVENTURE, WE FOLLOWED DR. C. ALL THE WAY FROM AFRICA, WHERE SHE WAS WORKING FOR DOCTORS WITHOUT BORDERS...
... TO HER FAMILY HOME IN ATLANTA, WHERE SHE REVEALED HER NEW SUPER-POWERS TO HER SISTER!
WHAT SUPER-POWERS, YOU MAY ASK? WELL, DR. C WAS ALWAYS VERY SMART.
e=MC²
... BUT NOW SHE'S A MULTI-MODALITY HYPER-GENIUS!
3.1415926
5358979323
84626433832
79502884197
IN SPACE, LIGHT TRAVELS AT 300,000 KILOMETERS PER SECOND...
e=MC²
"GOOD NIGHT, GOOD NIGHT! PARTING IS SUCH SWEET SORROW, THAT
MS. WALTERS IS A 23 YO WOMAN WITH CHRONIC HORRIPILATION, WHO PRESENTS WITH SPHENOPALATINE GANGLIONEURALGIA
"WE DON'T SEE THINGS THE WAY THEY ARE. WE
"FOUR SCORE AND SEVEN YEARS AGO..."
AND THIS WEEK SHE'S IN NEW ORLEANS, TRYING TO SAVE A YOUNG MAN WHO SEEMS TO HAVE NEW POWERS OF HIS OWN.
HIS NAME IS ANTONY. :)
I-10 WEST
HERE'S WHAT HAPPENED...

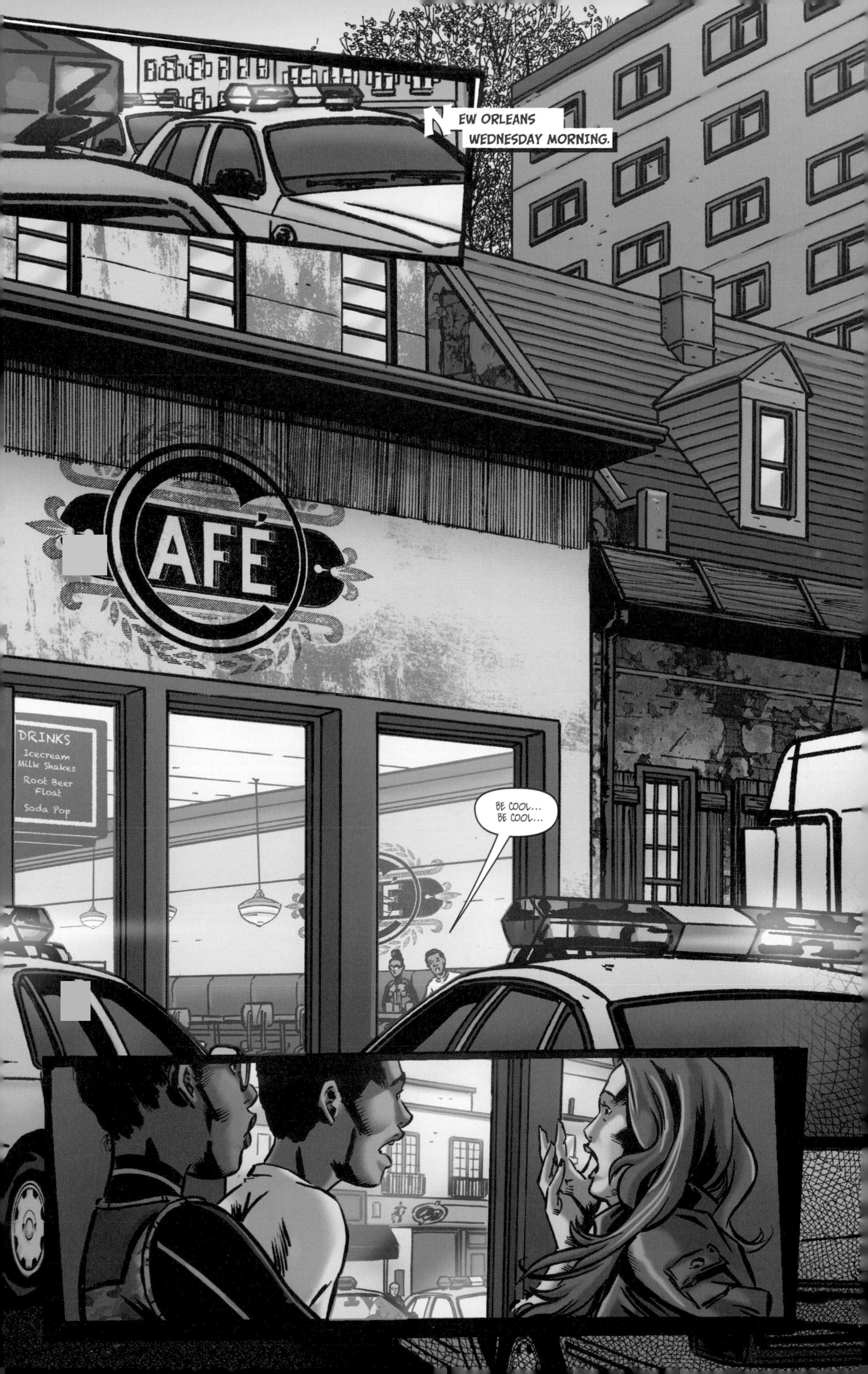
NEW ORLEANS
WEDNESDAY MORNING.
CAFÉ
DRINKS
Icecream
Milk Shakes
Root Beer
Float
Soda Pop
BE COOL...
BE COOL...

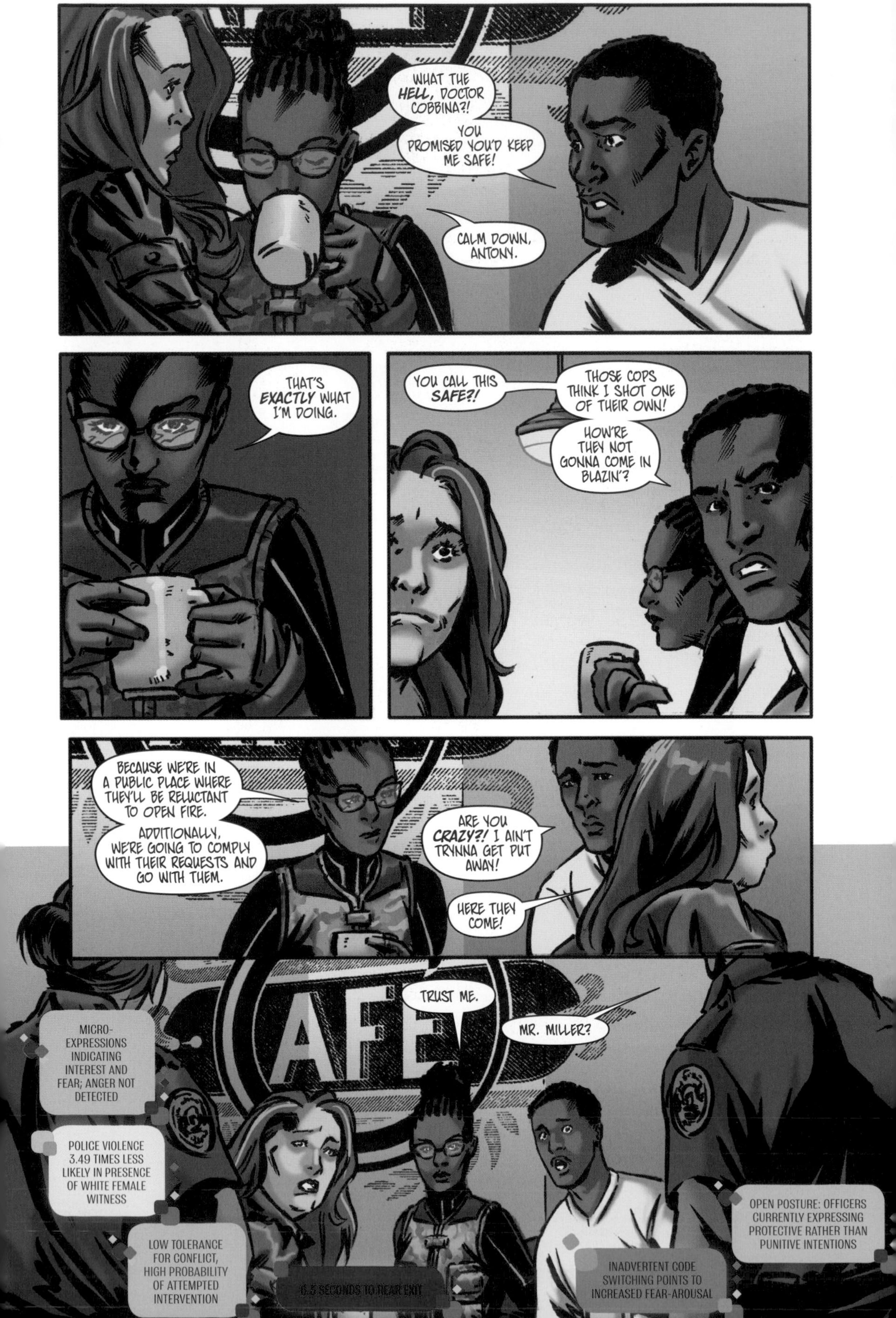
WHAT THE HELL, DOCTOR COBBINA?!
YOU PROMISED YOU'D KEEP ME SAFE!
CALM DOWN, ANTONY.
THAT'S EXACTLY WHAT I'M DOING.
YOU CALL THIS SAFE?!
THOSE COPS THINK I SHOT ONE OF THEIR OWN!
HOW'RE THEY NOT GONNA COME IN BLAZIN'?
BECAUSE WE'RE IN A PUBLIC PLACE WHERE THEY'LL BE RELUCTANT TO OPEN FIRE.
ADDITIONALLY, WE'RE GOING TO COMPLY WITH THEIR REQUESTS AND GO WITH THEM.
ARE YOU CRAZY?! I AIN'T TRYNNA GET PUT AWAY!
HERE THEY COME!
AFE
TRUST ME.
MR. MILLER?
MICRO-EXPRESSIONS INDICATING INTEREST AND FEAR; ANGER NOT DETECTED
POLICE VIOLENCE 3.49 TIMES LESS LIKELY IN PRESENCE OF WHITE FEMALE WITNESS
LOW TOLERANCE FOR CONFLICT, HIGH PROBABILITY OF ATTEMPTED INTERVENTION
0.5 SECONDS TO REAR EXIT
INADVERTENT CODE SWITCHING POINTS TO INCREASED FEAR-AROUSAL
OPEN POSTURE: OFFICERS CURRENTLY EXPRESSING PROTECTIVE RATHER THAN PUNITIVE INTENTIONS

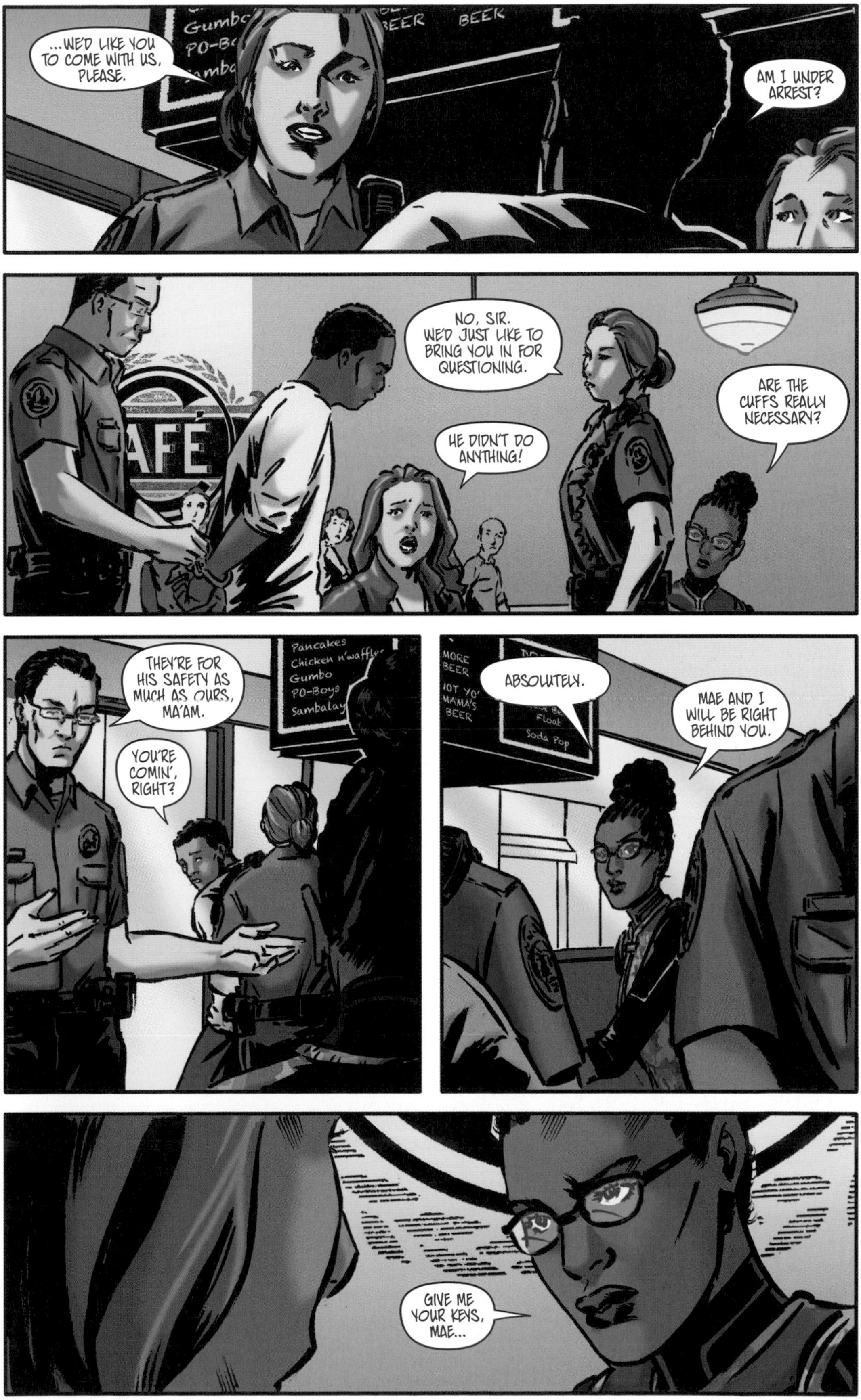
...WE'D LIKE YOU TO COME WITH US, PLEASE.
AM I UNDER ARREST?
NO, SIR. WE'D JUST LIKE TO BRING YOU IN FOR QUESTIONING.
HE DIDN'T DO ANYTHING!
ARE THE CUFFS REALLY NECESSARY?
THEY'RE FOR HIS SAFETY AS MUCH AS OURS, MA'AM.
YOU'RE COMIN', RIGHT?
ABSOLUTELY.
MAE AND I WILL BE RIGHT BEHIND YOU.
GIVE ME YOUR KEYS, MAE...

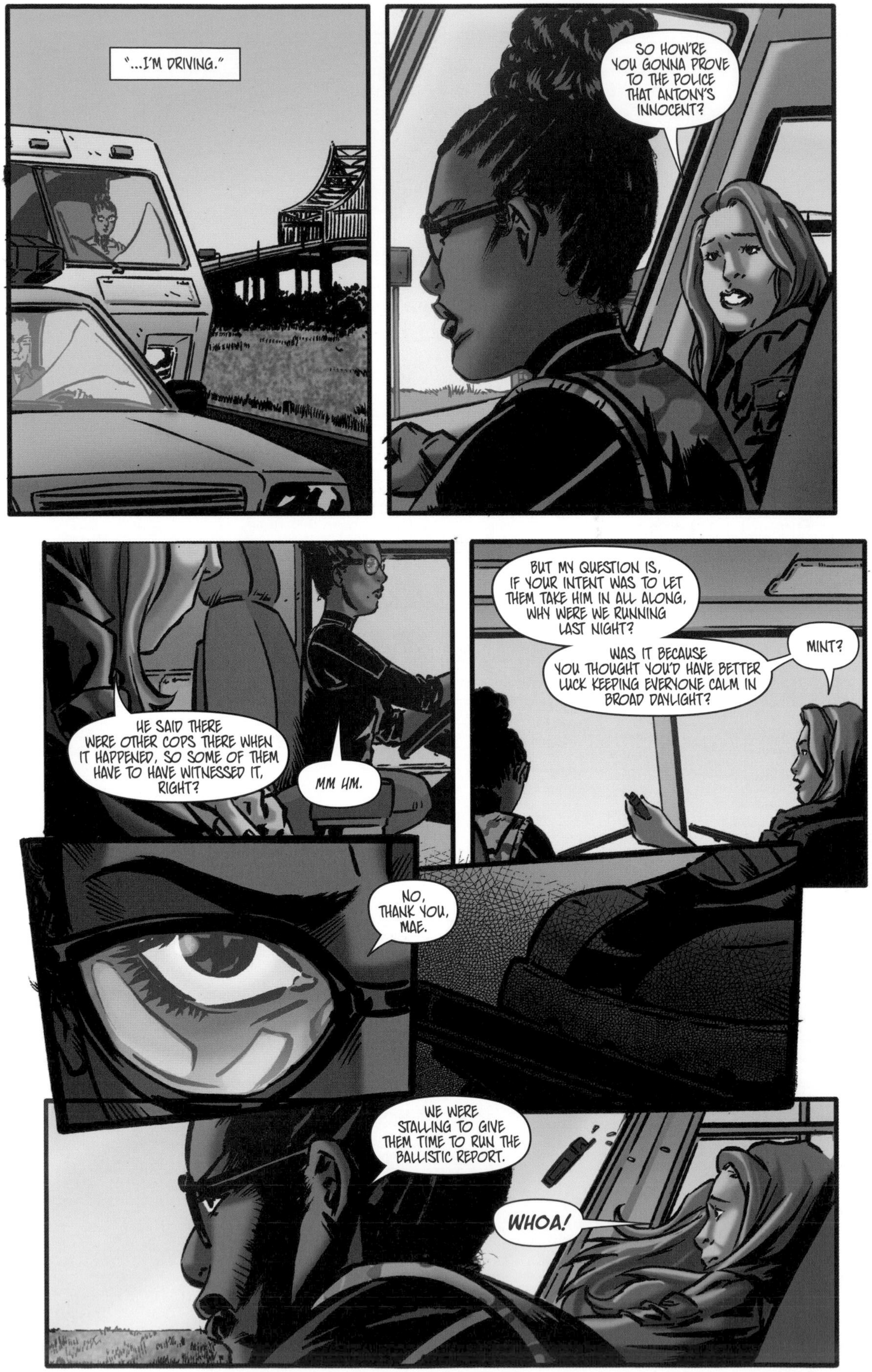
"...I'M DRIVING."
SO HOW'RE YOU GONNA PROVE TO THE POLICE THAT ANTONY'S INNOCENT?
HE SAID THERE WERE OTHER COPS THERE WHEN IT HAPPENED, SO SOME OF THEM HAVE TO HAVE WITNESSED IT, RIGHT?
MM HM.
BUT MY QUESTION IS, IF YOUR INTENT WAS TO LET THEM TAKE HIM IN ALL ALONG, WHY WERE WE RUNNING LAST NIGHT?
WAS IT BECAUSE YOU THOUGHT YOU'D HAVE BETTER LUCK KEEPING EVERYONE CALM IN BROAD DAYLIGHT?
MINT?
NO, THANK YOU, MAE.
WE WERE STALLING TO GIVE THEM TIME TO RUN THE BALLISTIC REPORT.
WHOA!

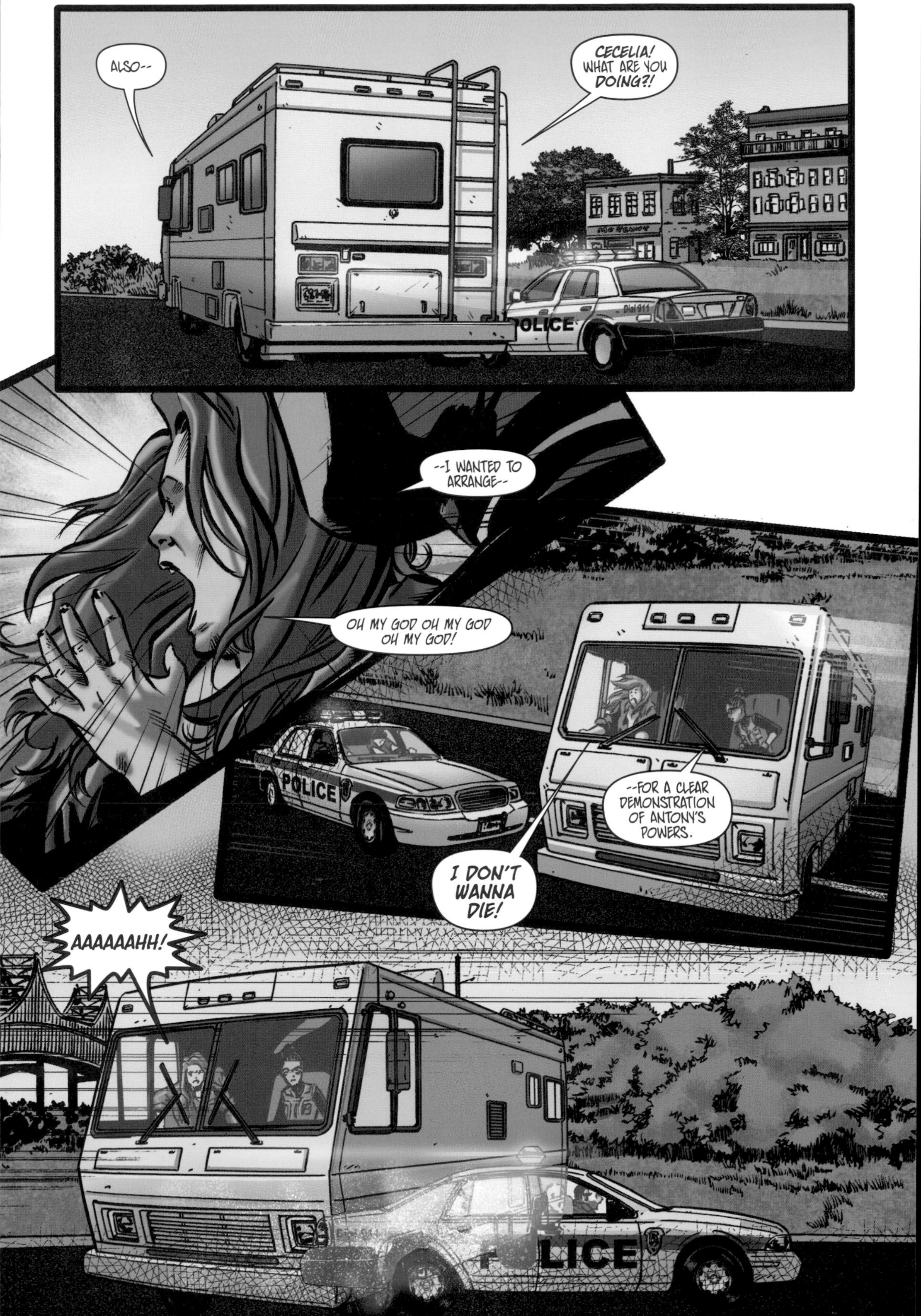
ALSO--
CECELIA! WHAT ARE YOU DOING?!
--I WANTED TO ARRANGE--
OH MY GOD OH MY GOD OH MY GOD!
--FOR A CLEAR DEMONSTRATION OF ANTONY'S POWERS.
I DON'T WANNA DIE!
AAAAAAHH!
POLICE

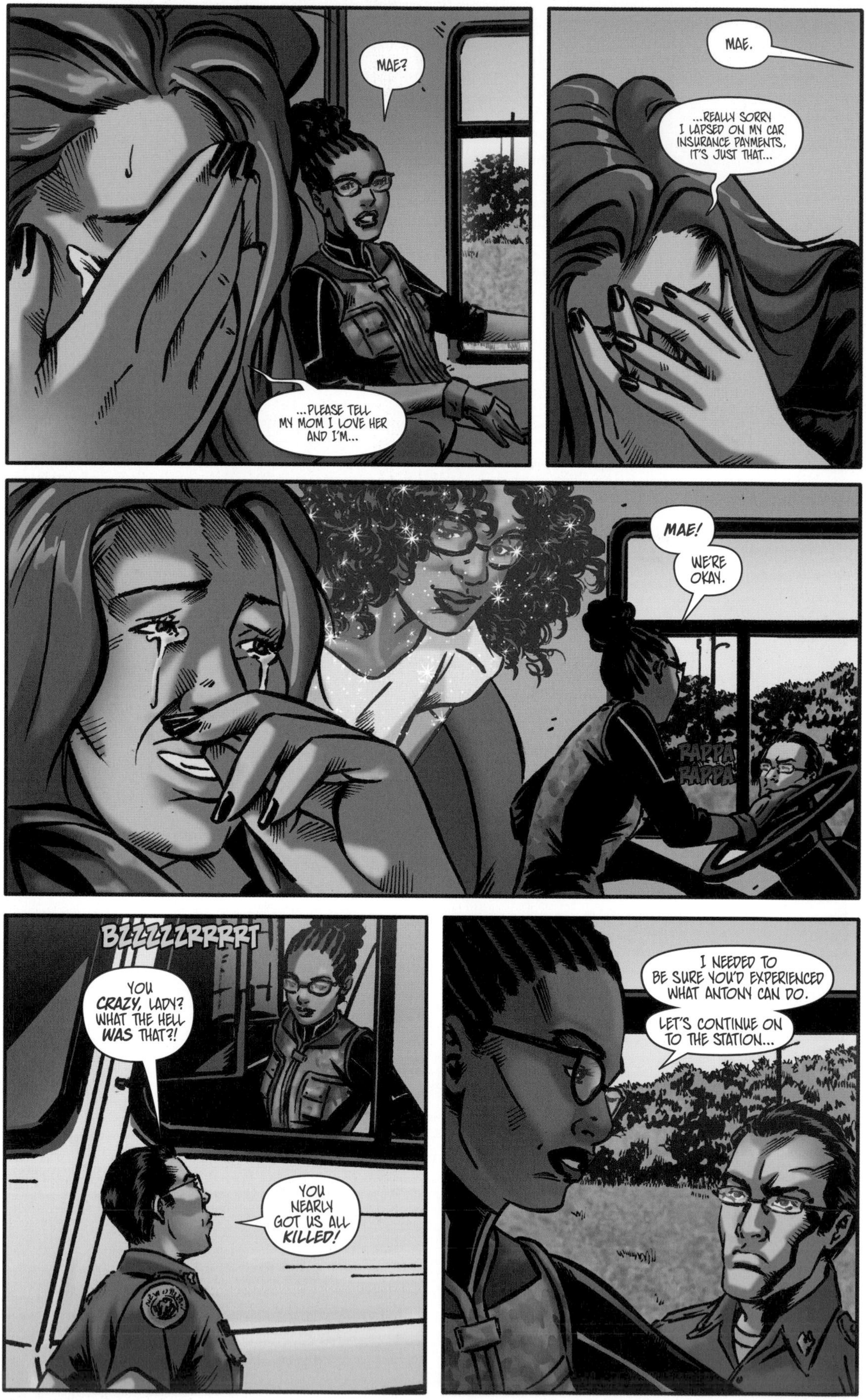
MAE?
...PLEASE TELL MY MOM I LOVE HER AND I'M...
MAE.
...REALLY SORRY I LAPSED ON MY CAR INSURANCE PAYMENTS, IT'S JUST THAT...
MAE!
WE'RE OKAY.
RAPPA RAPPA
BZZZZZRRRRT
YOU CRAZY, LADY? WHAT THE HELL WAS THAT?!
YOU NEARLY GOT US ALL KILLED!
I NEEDED TO BE SURE YOU'D EXPERIENCED WHAT ANTONY CAN DO.
LET'S CONTINUE ON TO THE STATION...

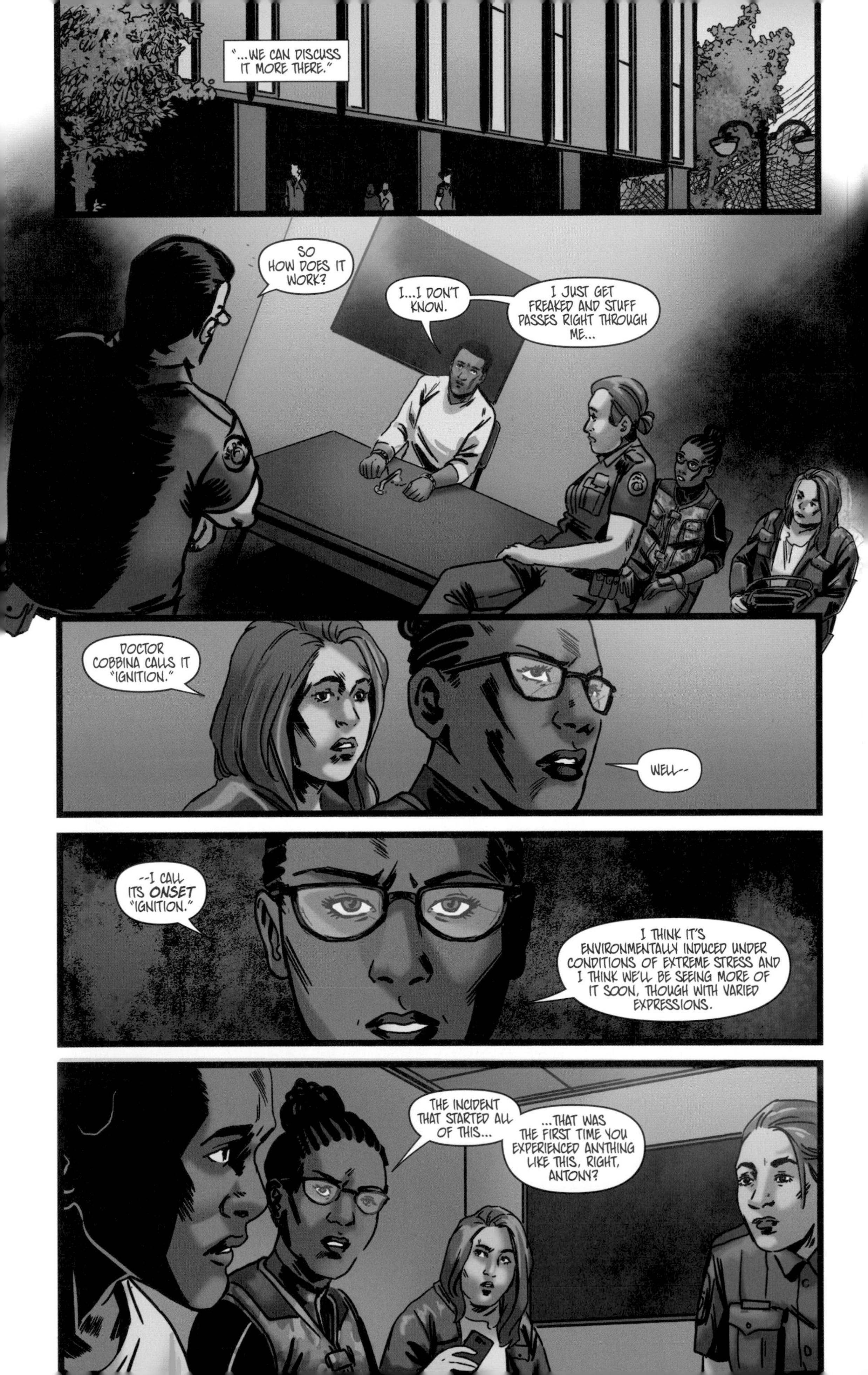
"...WE CAN DISCUSS IT MORE THERE."
SO HOW DOES IT WORK?
I...I DON'T KNOW.
I JUST GET FREAKED AND STUFF PASSES RIGHT THROUGH ME...
DOCTOR COBBINA CALLS IT "IGNITION."
WELL--
--I CALL ITS **ONSET** "IGNITION."
I THINK IT'S ENVIRONMENTALLY INDUCED UNDER CONDITIONS OF EXTREME STRESS AND I THINK WE'LL BE SEEING MORE OF IT SOON, THOUGH WITH VARIED EXPRESSIONS.
THE INCIDENT THAT STARTED ALL OF THIS...
...THAT WAS THE FIRST TIME YOU EXPERIENCED ANYTHING LIKE THIS, RIGHT, ANTONY?

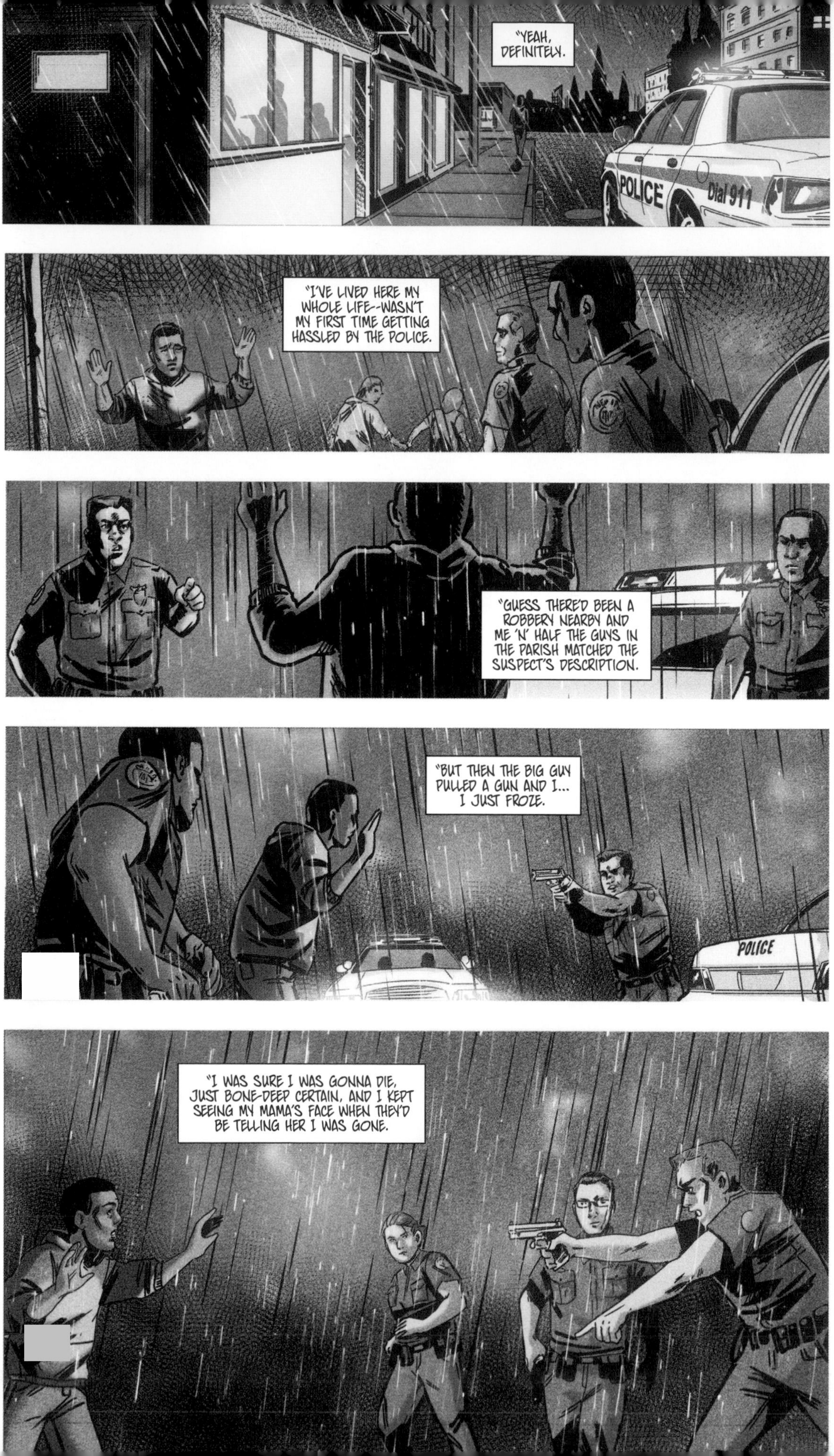
"YEAH, DEFINITELY.
POLICE
Dial 911
"I'VE LIVED HERE MY WHOLE LIFE--WASN'T MY FIRST TIME GETTING HASSLED BY THE POLICE.
"GUESS THERE'D BEEN A ROBBERY NEARBY AND ME 'N' HALF THE GUYS IN THE PARISH MATCHED THE SUSPECT'S DESCRIPTION.
"BUT THEN THE BIG GUY PULLED A GUN AND I... I JUST FROZE.
POLICE
"I WAS SURE I WAS GONNA DIE, JUST BONE-DEEP CERTAIN, AND I KEPT SEEING MY MAMA'S FACE WHEN THEY'D BE TELLING HER I WAS GONE.

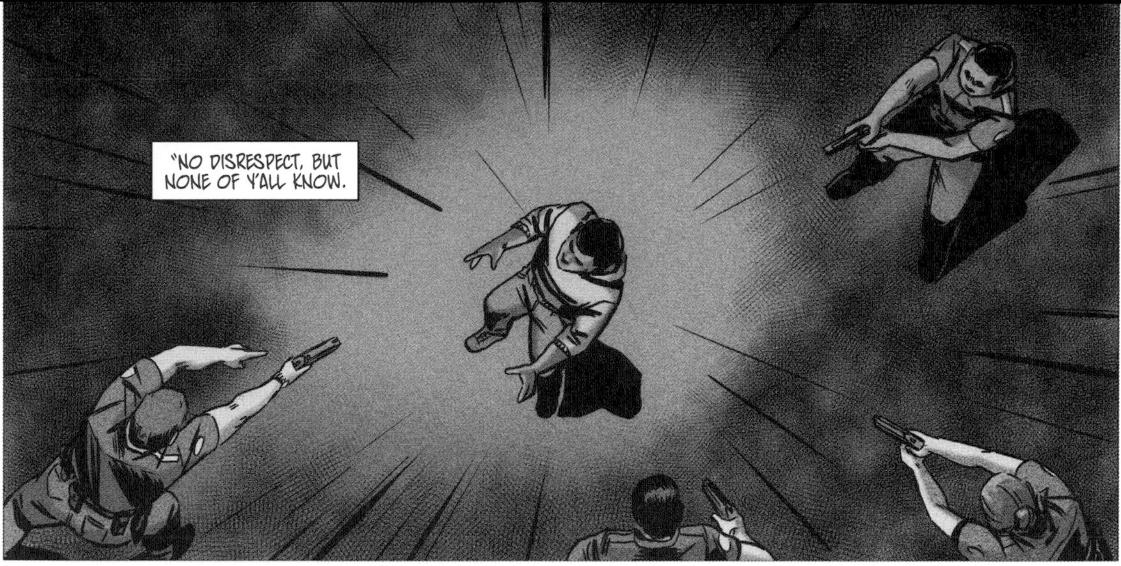
"NO DISRESPECT, BUT NONE OF Y'ALL KNOW.

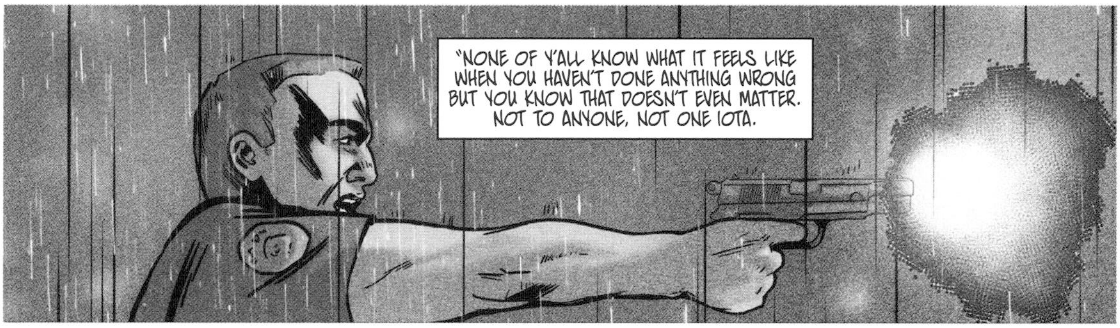
"NONE OF Y'ALL KNOW WHAT IT FEELS LIKE WHEN YOU HAVEN'T DONE ANYTHING WRONG BUT YOU KNOW THAT DOESN'T EVEN MATTER. NOT TO ANYONE, NOT ONE IOTA.

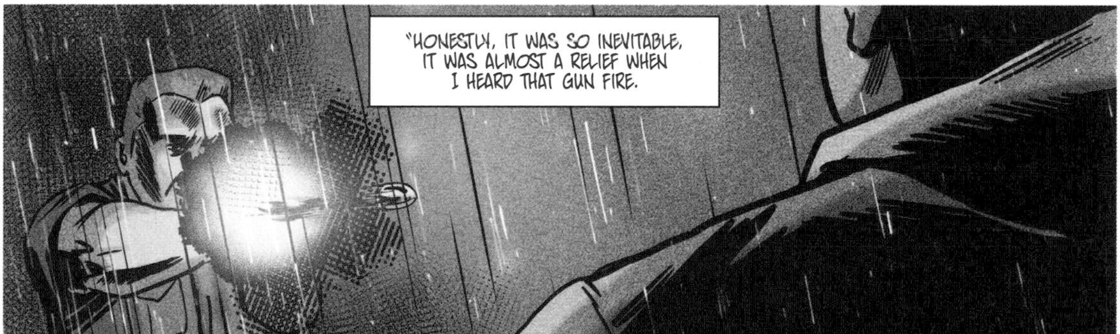
"HONESTLY, IT WAS SO INEVITABLE, IT WAS ALMOST A RELIEF WHEN I HEARD THAT GUN FIRE.

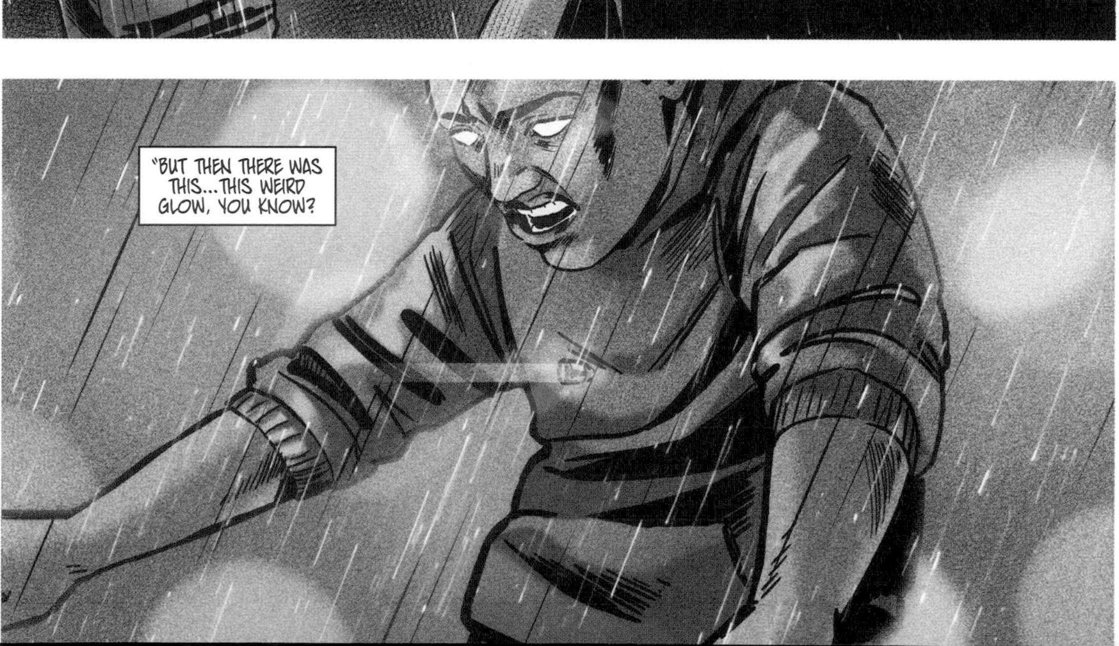
"BUT THEN THERE WAS THIS...THIS WEIRD GLOW, YOU KNOW?

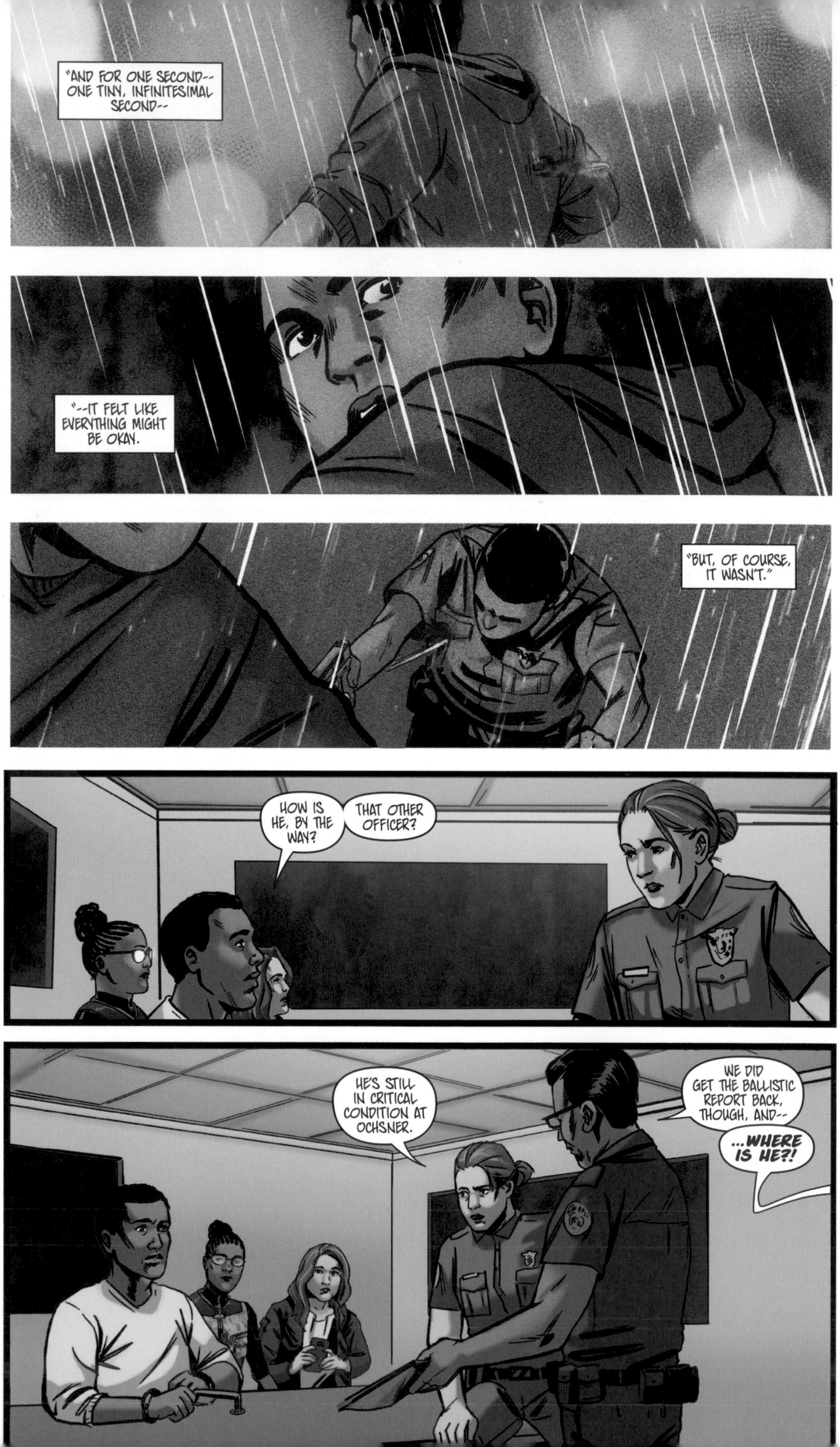
"AND FOR ONE SECOND-- ONE TINY, INFINITESIMAL SECOND--
"--IT FELT LIKE EVERYTHING MIGHT BE OKAY.
"BUT, OF COURSE, IT WASN'T."
HOW IS HE, BY THE WAY?
THAT OTHER OFFICER?
HE'S STILL IN CRITICAL CONDITION AT OCHSNER.
WE DID GET THE BALLISTIC REPORT BACK, THOUGH, AND--
...WHERE IS HE?!

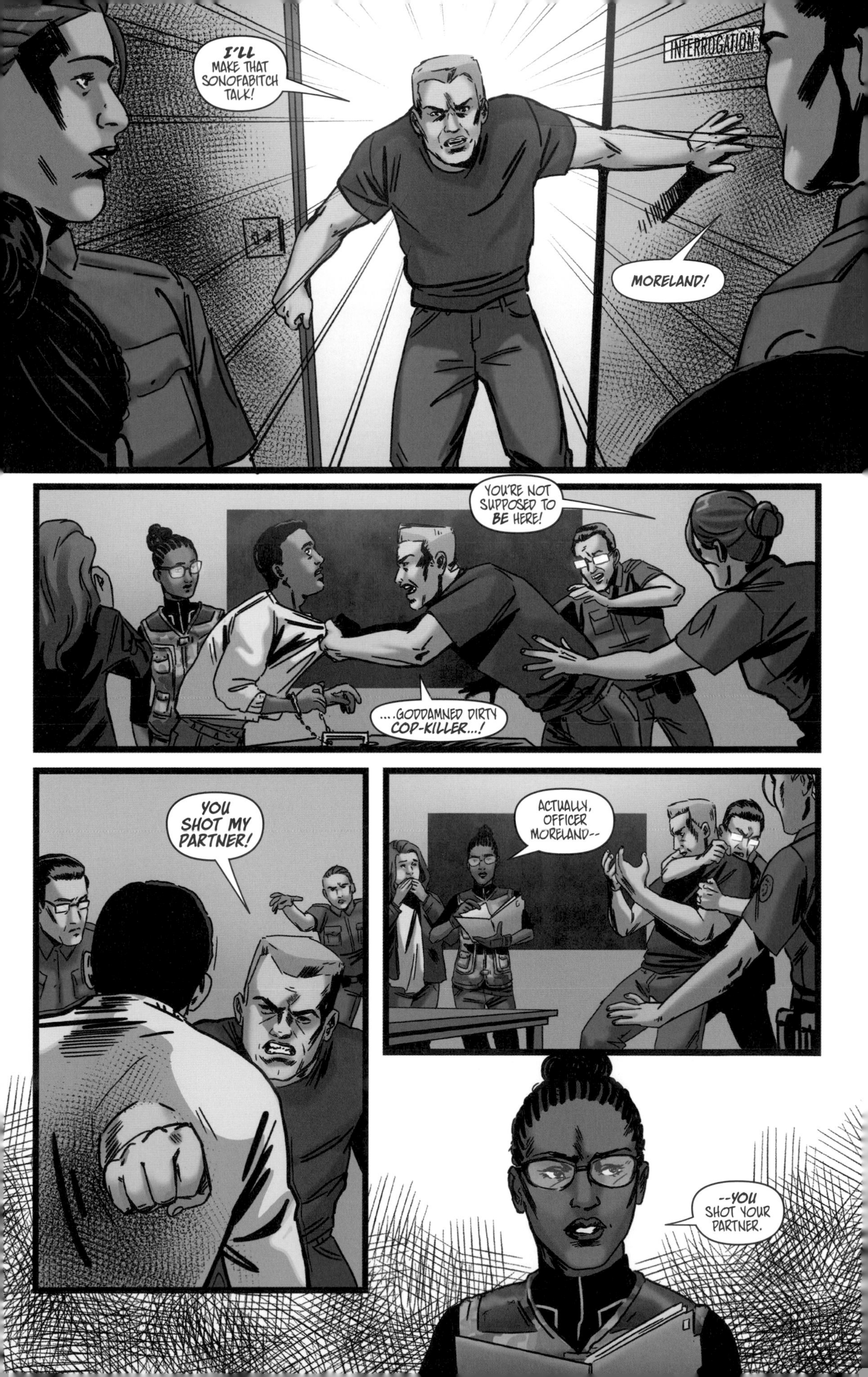
INTERROGATION
I'LL MAKE THAT SONOFABITCH TALK!
MORELAND!
YOU'RE NOT SUPPOSED TO BE HERE!
....GODDAMNED DIRTY COP-KILLER...!
YOU SHOT MY PARTNER!
ACTUALLY, OFFICER MORELAND--
--YOU SHOT YOUR PARTNER.

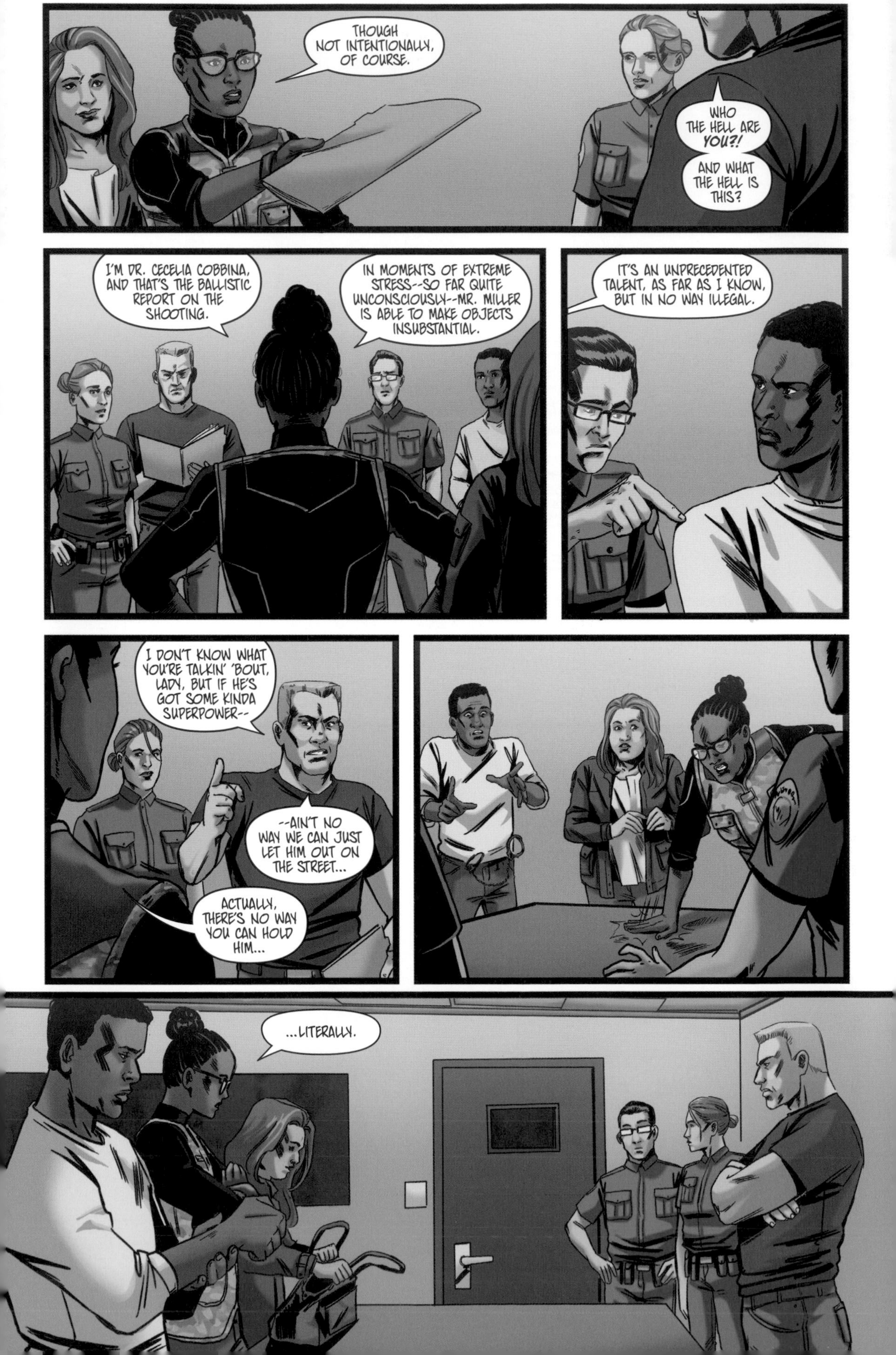
THOUGH NOT INTENTIONALLY, OF COURSE.
WHO THE HELL ARE YOU?!
AND WHAT THE HELL IS THIS?
I'M DR. CECELIA COBBINA, AND THAT'S THE BALLISTIC REPORT ON THE SHOOTING.
IN MOMENTS OF EXTREME STRESS--SO FAR QUITE UNCONSCIOUSLY--MR. MILLER IS ABLE TO MAKE OBJECTS INSUBSTANTIAL.
IT'S AN UNPRECEDENTED TALENT, AS FAR AS I KNOW, BUT IN NO WAY ILLEGAL.
I DON'T KNOW WHAT YOU'RE TALKIN' 'BOUT, LADY, BUT IF HE'S GOT SOME KINDA SUPERPOWER--
--AIN'T NO WAY WE CAN JUST LET HIM OUT ON THE STREET...
ACTUALLY, THERE'S NO WAY YOU CAN HOLD HIM...
...LITERALLY.

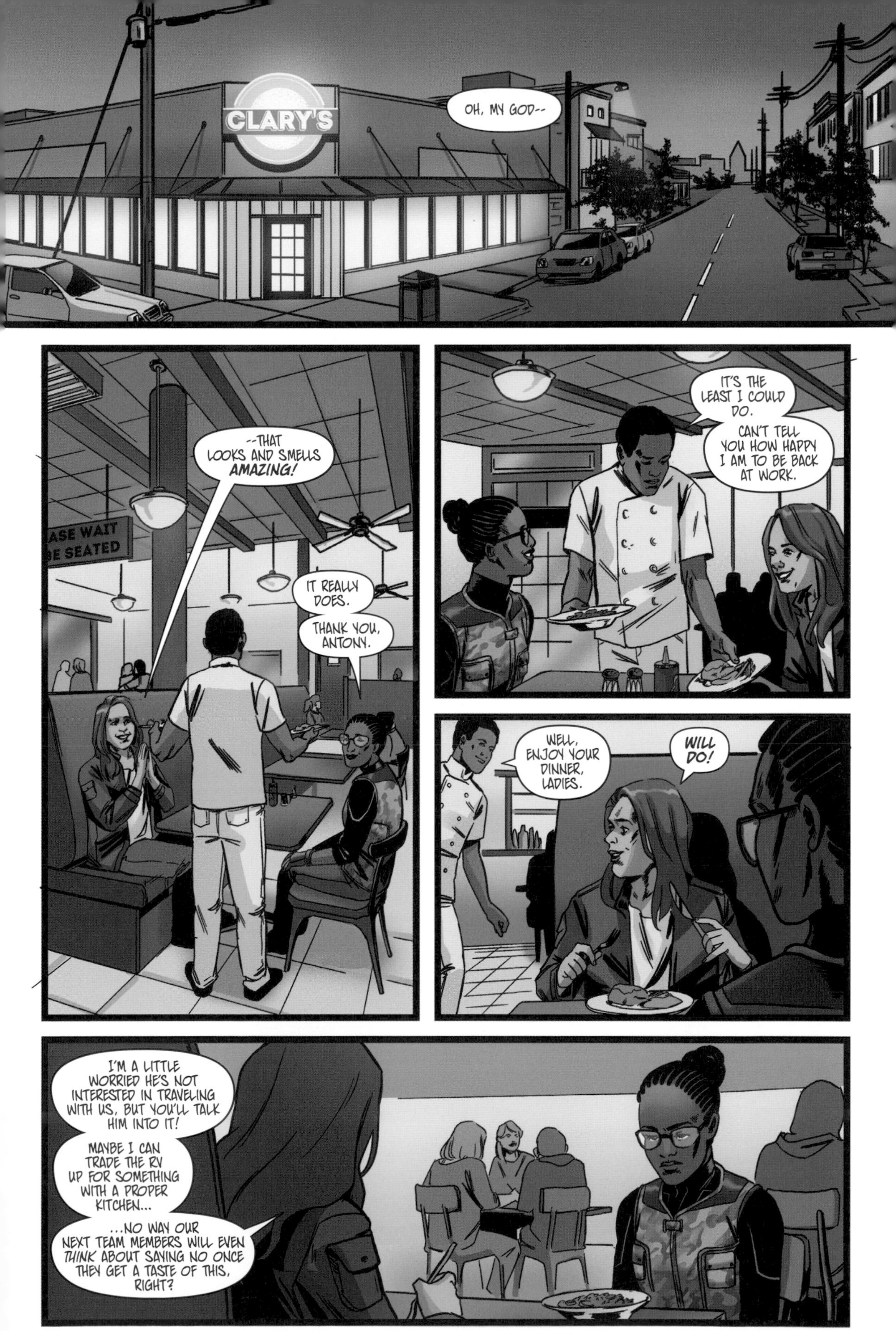
CLARY'S
OH, MY GOD--
--THAT LOOKS AND SMELLS AMAZING!
ASE WAIT
BE SEATED
IT REALLY DOES.
THANK YOU, ANTONY.
IT'S THE LEAST I COULD DO.
CAN'T TELL YOU HOW HAPPY I AM TO BE BACK AT WORK.
WELL, ENJOY YOUR DINNER, LADIES.
WILL DO!
I'M A LITTLE WORRIED HE'S NOT INTERESTED IN TRAVELING WITH US, BUT YOU'LL TALK HIM INTO IT!
MAYBE I CAN TRADE THE RV UP FOR SOMETHING WITH A PROPER KITCHEN...
...NO WAY OUR NEXT TEAM MEMBERS WILL EVEN THINK ABOUT SAYING NO ONCE THEY GET A TASTE OF THIS, RIGHT?

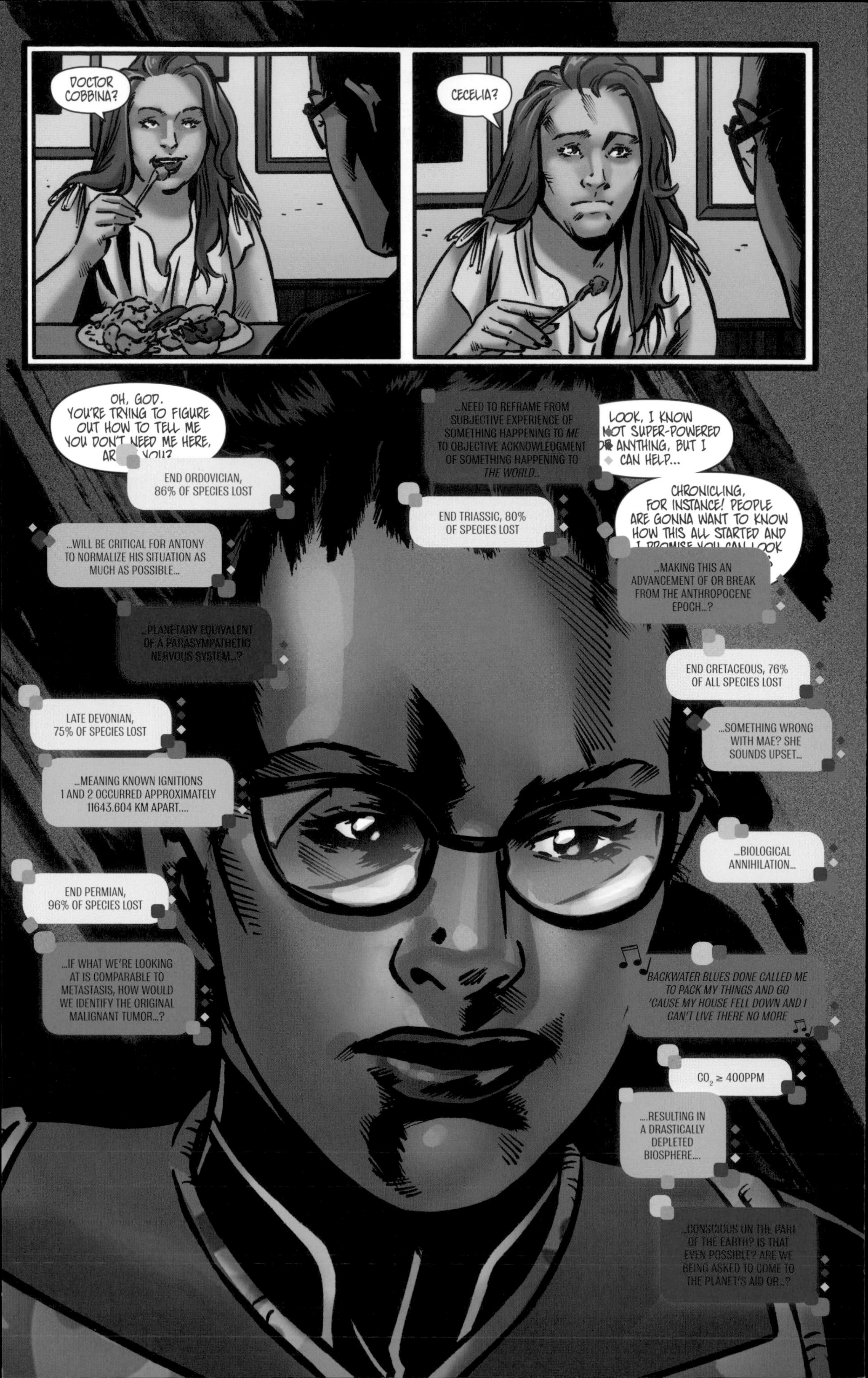

DOCTOR COBBINA?
CECELIA?
OH, GOD. YOU'RE TRYING TO FIGURE OUT HOW TO TELL ME YOU DON'T NEED ME HERE,
END ORDOVICIAN, 86% OF SPECIES LOST
...NEED TO REFRAME FROM SUBJECTIVE EXPERIENCE OF SOMETHING HAPPENING TO *ME* TO OBJECTIVE ACKNOWLEDGMENT OF SOMETHING HAPPENING TO *THE WORLD*...
LOOK, I KNOW SUPER-POWERED ANYTHING, BUT I CAN HELP...
END TRIASSIC, 80% OF SPECIES LOST
CHRONICLING, FOR INSTANCE! PEOPLE ARE GONNA WANT TO KNOW HOW THIS ALL STARTED AND
...WILL BE CRITICAL FOR ANTONY TO NORMALIZE HIS SITUATION AS MUCH AS POSSIBLE...
...MAKING THIS AN ADVANCEMENT OF OR BREAK FROM THE ANTHROPOCENE EPOCH...?
...PLANETARY EQUIVALENT OF A PARASYMPATHETIC NERVOUS SYSTEM...?
END CRETACEOUS, 76% OF ALL SPECIES LOST
LATE DEVONIAN, 75% OF SPECIES LOST
...SOMETHING WRONG WITH MAE? SHE SOUNDS UPSET...
...MEANING KNOWN IGNITIONS 1 AND 2 OCCURRED APPROXIMATELY 11643.604 KM APART....
...BIOLOGICAL ANNIHILATION...
END PERMIAN, 96% OF SPECIES LOST
...IF WHAT WE'RE LOOKING AT IS COMPARABLE TO METASTASIS, HOW WOULD WE IDENTIFY THE ORIGINAL MALIGNANT TUMOR...?
BACKWATER BLUES DONE CALLED ME TO PACK MY THINGS AND GO 'CAUSE MY HOUSE FELL DOWN AND I CAN'T LIVE THERE NO MORE
$CO_2 \geq$ 400PPM
....RESULTING IN A DRASTICALLY DEPLETED BIOSPHERE....
...CONSCIOUS ON THE PART OF THE EARTH? IS THAT EVEN POSSIBLE? ARE WE BEING ASKED TO COME TO THE PLANET'S AID OR...?

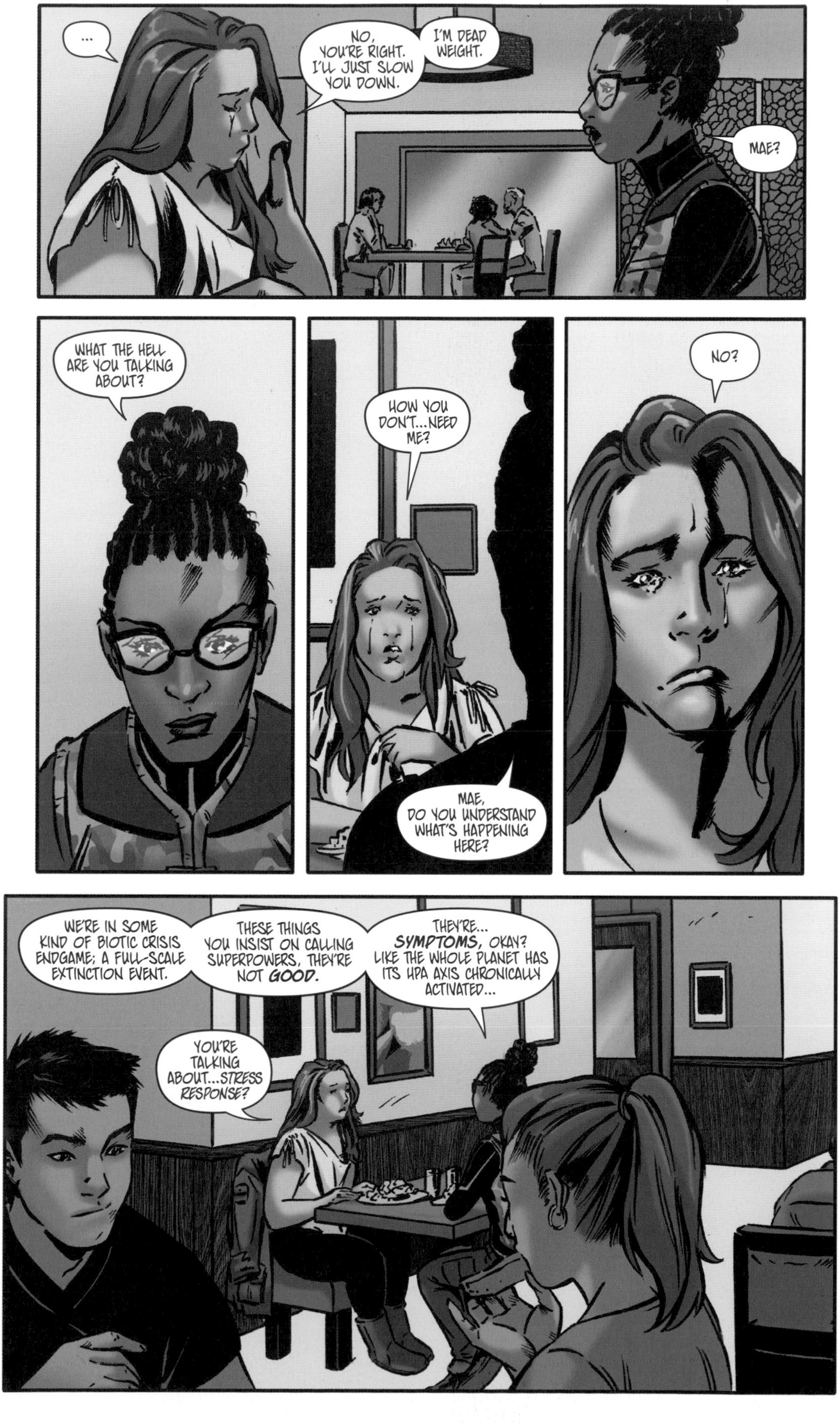
...
NO, YOU'RE RIGHT. I'LL JUST SLOW YOU DOWN.
I'M DEAD WEIGHT.
MAE?
WHAT THE HELL ARE YOU TALKING ABOUT?
HOW YOU DON'T...NEED ME?
MAE, DO YOU UNDERSTAND WHAT'S HAPPENING HERE?
NO?
WE'RE IN SOME KIND OF BIOTIC CRISIS ENDGAME; A FULL-SCALE EXTINCTION EVENT.
THESE THINGS YOU INSIST ON CALLING SUPERPOWERS, THEY'RE NOT GOOD.
THEY'RE... SYMPTOMS, OKAY? LIKE THE WHOLE PLANET HAS ITS HPA AXIS CHRONICALLY ACTIVATED...
YOU'RE TALKING ABOUT...STRESS RESPONSE?

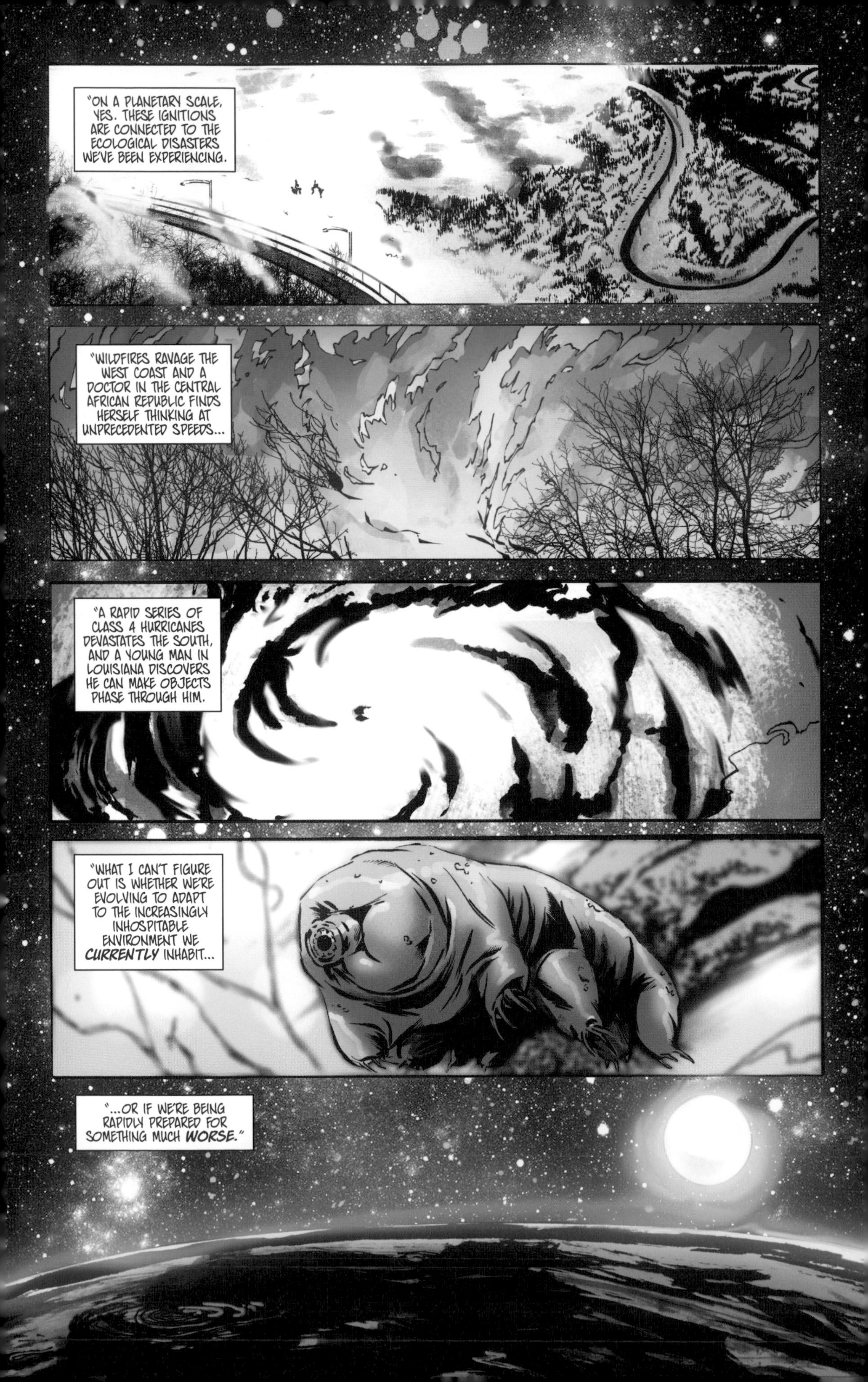
"ON A PLANETARY SCALE, YES. THESE IGNITIONS ARE CONNECTED TO THE ECOLOGICAL DISASTERS WE'VE BEEN EXPERIENCING.
"WILDFIRES RAVAGE THE WEST COAST AND A DOCTOR IN THE CENTRAL AFRICAN REPUBLIC FINDS HERSELF THINKING AT UNPRECEDENTED SPEEDS...
"A RAPID SERIES OF CLASS 4 HURRICANES DEVASTATES THE SOUTH, AND A YOUNG MAN IN LOUISIANA DISCOVERS HE CAN MAKE OBJECTS PHASE THROUGH HIM.
"WHAT I CAN'T FIGURE OUT IS WHETHER WE'RE EVOLVING TO ADAPT TO THE INCREASINGLY INHOSPITABLE ENVIRONMENT WE *CURRENTLY* INHABIT...
"...OR IF WE'RE BEING RAPIDLY PREPARED FOR SOMETHING MUCH *WORSE*."

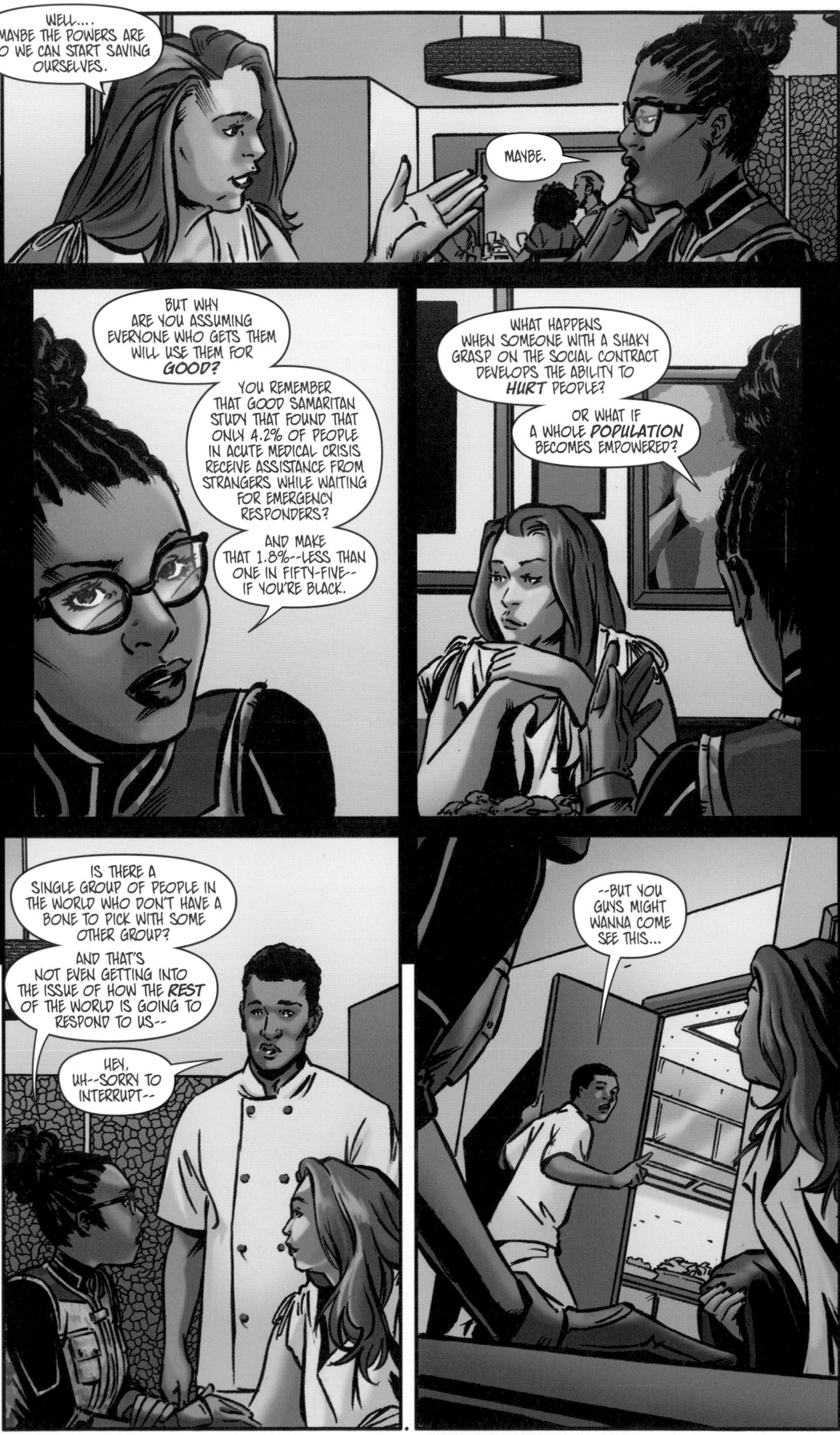
WELL.... MAYBE THE POWERS ARE SO WE CAN START SAVING OURSELVES.
MAYBE.
BUT WHY ARE YOU ASSUMING EVERYONE WHO GETS THEM WILL USE THEM FOR GOOD?
YOU REMEMBER THAT GOOD SAMARITAN STUDY THAT FOUND THAT ONLY 4.2% OF PEOPLE IN ACUTE MEDICAL CRISIS RECEIVE ASSISTANCE FROM STRANGERS WHILE WAITING FOR EMERGENCY RESPONDERS?
AND MAKE THAT 1.8%--LESS THAN ONE IN FIFTY-FIVE--IF YOU'RE BLACK.
WHAT HAPPENS WHEN SOMEONE WITH A SHAKY GRASP ON THE SOCIAL CONTRACT DEVELOPS THE ABILITY TO HURT PEOPLE?
OR WHAT IF A WHOLE POPULATION BECOMES EMPOWERED?
IS THERE A SINGLE GROUP OF PEOPLE IN THE WORLD WHO DON'T HAVE A BONE TO PICK WITH SOME OTHER GROUP?
AND THAT'S NOT EVEN GETTING INTO THE ISSUE OF HOW THE REST OF THE WORLD IS GOING TO RESPOND TO US--
HEY, UH--SORRY TO INTERRUPT--
--BUT YOU GUYS MIGHT WANNA COME SEE THIS...

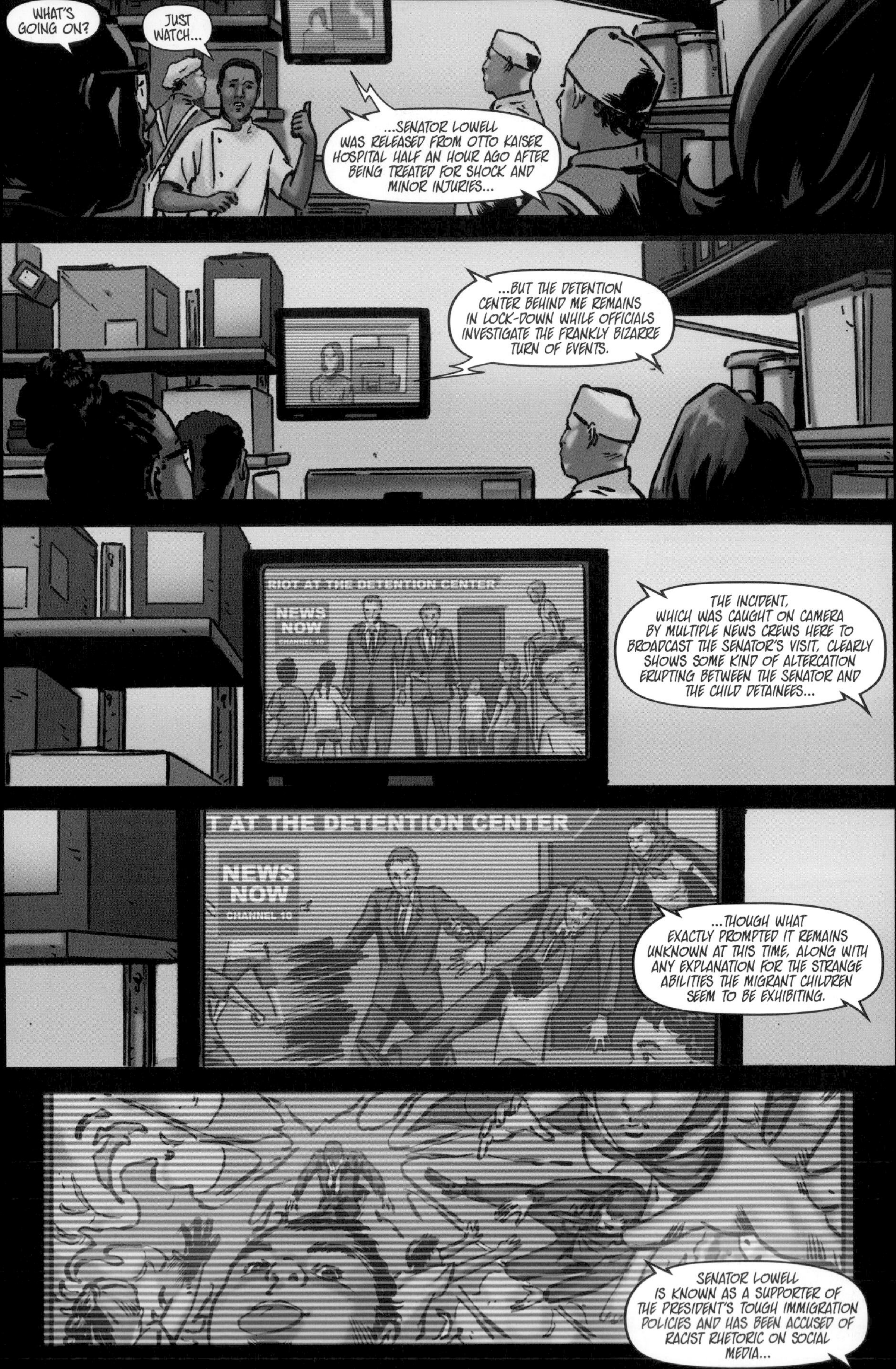
WHAT'S GOING ON?
JUST WATCH...
...SENATOR LOWELL WAS RELEASED FROM OTTO KAISER HOSPITAL HALF AN HOUR AGO AFTER BEING TREATED FOR SHOCK AND MINOR INJURIES...
...BUT THE DETENTION CENTER BEHIND ME REMAINS IN LOCK-DOWN WHILE OFFICIALS INVESTIGATE THE FRANKLY BIZARRE TURN OF EVENTS.
RIOT AT THE DETENTION CENTER
NEWS NOW
CHANNEL 10
THE INCIDENT, WHICH WAS CAUGHT ON CAMERA BY MULTIPLE NEWS CREWS HERE TO BROADCAST THE SENATOR'S VISIT, CLEARLY SHOWS SOME KIND OF ALTERCATION ERUPTING BETWEEN THE SENATOR AND THE CHILD DETAINEES...
T AT THE DETENTION CENTER
NEWS NOW
CHANNEL 10
...THOUGH WHAT EXACTLY PROMPTED IT REMAINS UNKNOWN AT THIS TIME, ALONG WITH ANY EXPLANATION FOR THE STRANGE ABILITIES THE MIGRANT CHILDREN SEEM TO BE EXHIBITING.
SENATOR LOWELL IS KNOWN AS A SUPPORTER OF THE PRESIDENT'S TOUGH IMMIGRATION POLICIES AND HAS BEEN ACCUSED OF RACIST RHETORIC ON SOCIAL MEDIA...

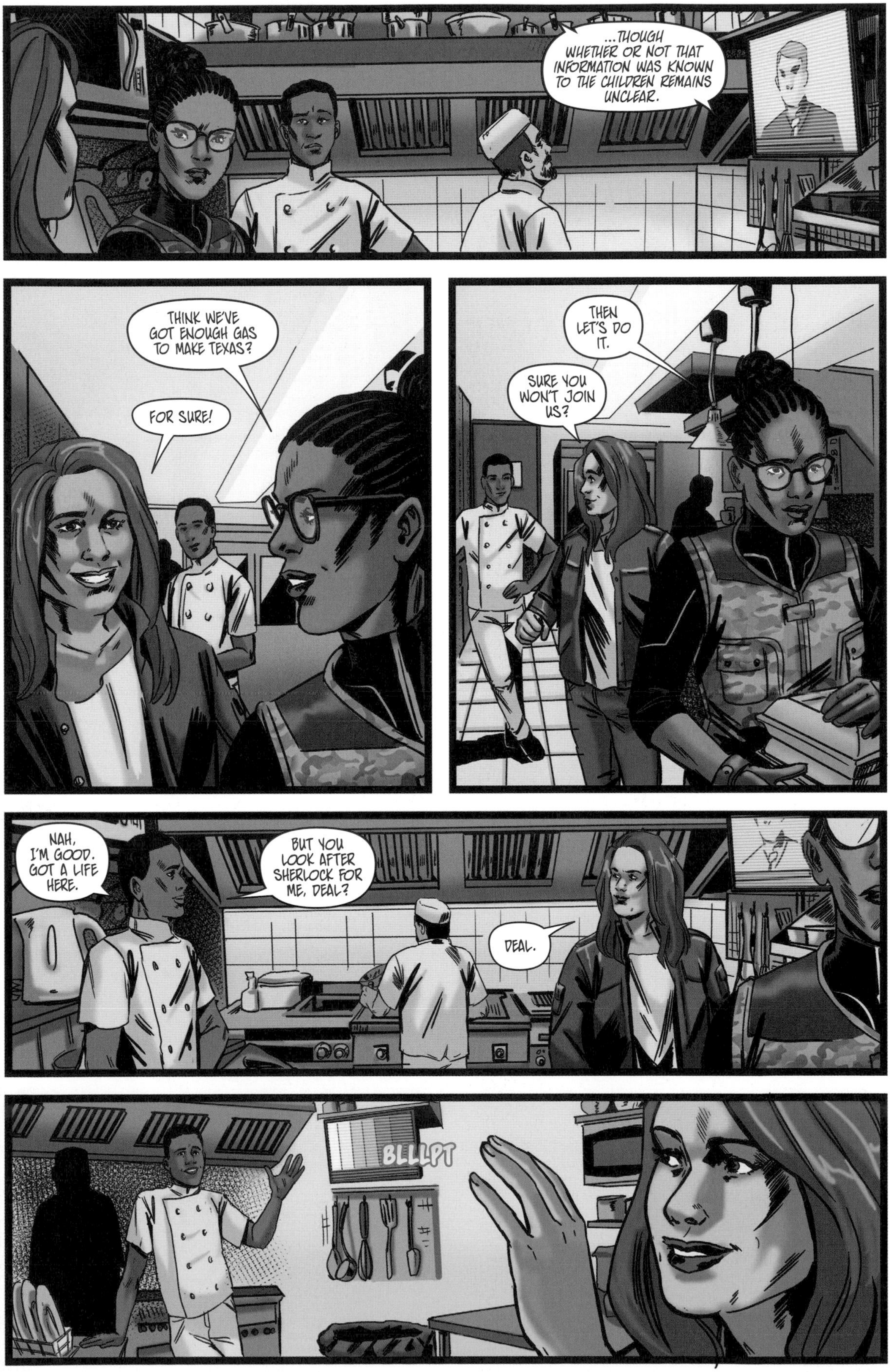
...THOUGH WHETHER OR NOT THAT INFORMATION WAS KNOWN TO THE CHILDREN REMAINS UNCLEAR.
THINK WE'VE GOT ENOUGH GAS TO MAKE TEXAS?
FOR SURE!
THEN LET'S DO IT.
SURE YOU WON'T JOIN US?
NAH, I'M GOOD. GOT A LIFE HERE.
BUT YOU LOOK AFTER SHERLOCK FOR ME, DEAL?
DEAL.
BLLLPT

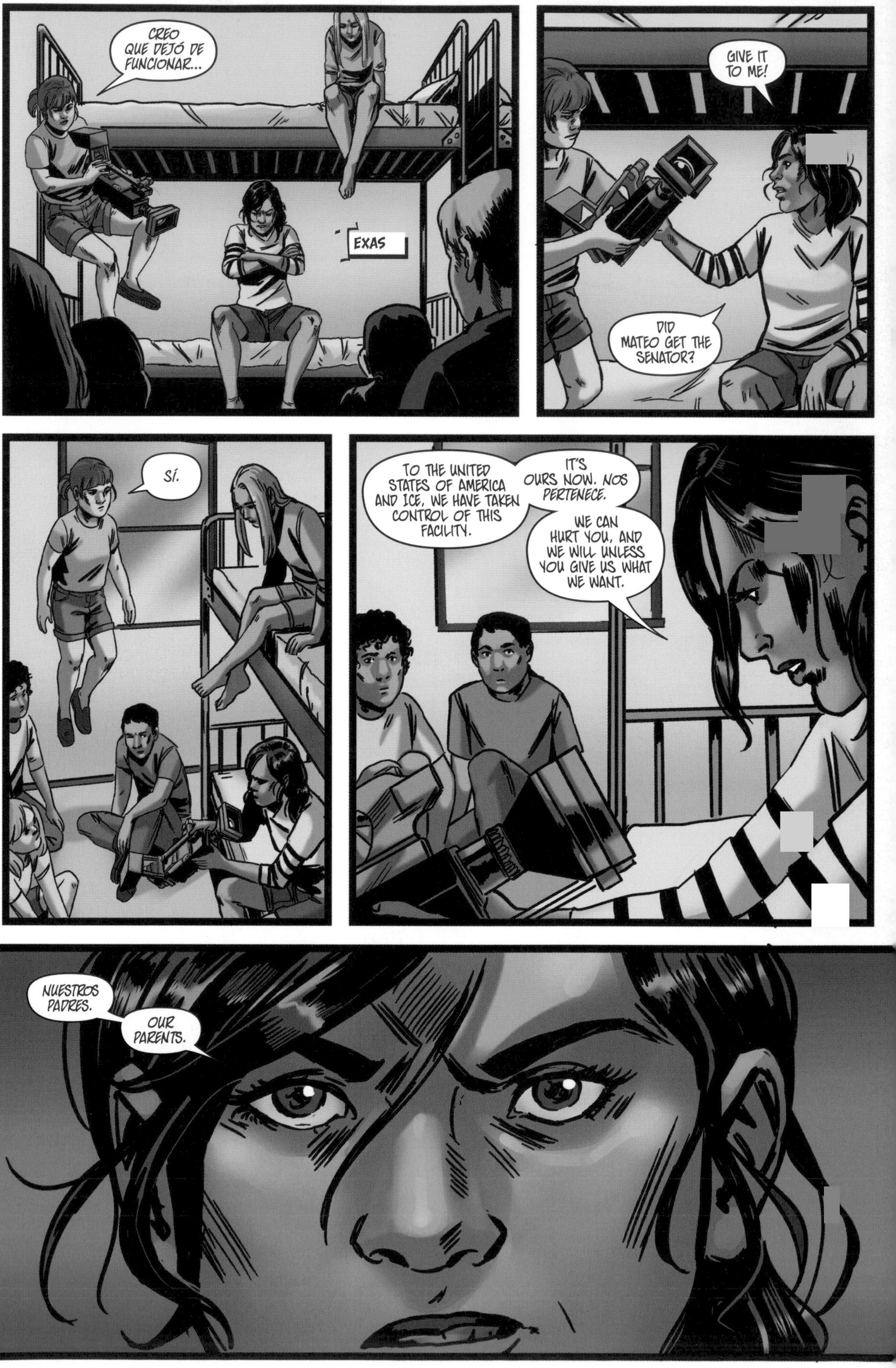
CREO QUE DEJÓ DE FUNCIONAR...
EXAS
GIVE IT TO ME!
DID MATEO GET THE SENATOR?
SÍ.
TO THE UNITED STATES OF AMERICA AND ICE, WE HAVE TAKEN CONTROL OF THIS FACILITY.
IT'S OURS NOW. NOS PERTENECE.
WE CAN HURT YOU, AND WE WILL UNLESS YOU GIVE US WHAT WE WANT.
NUESTROS PADRES.
OUR PARENTS.

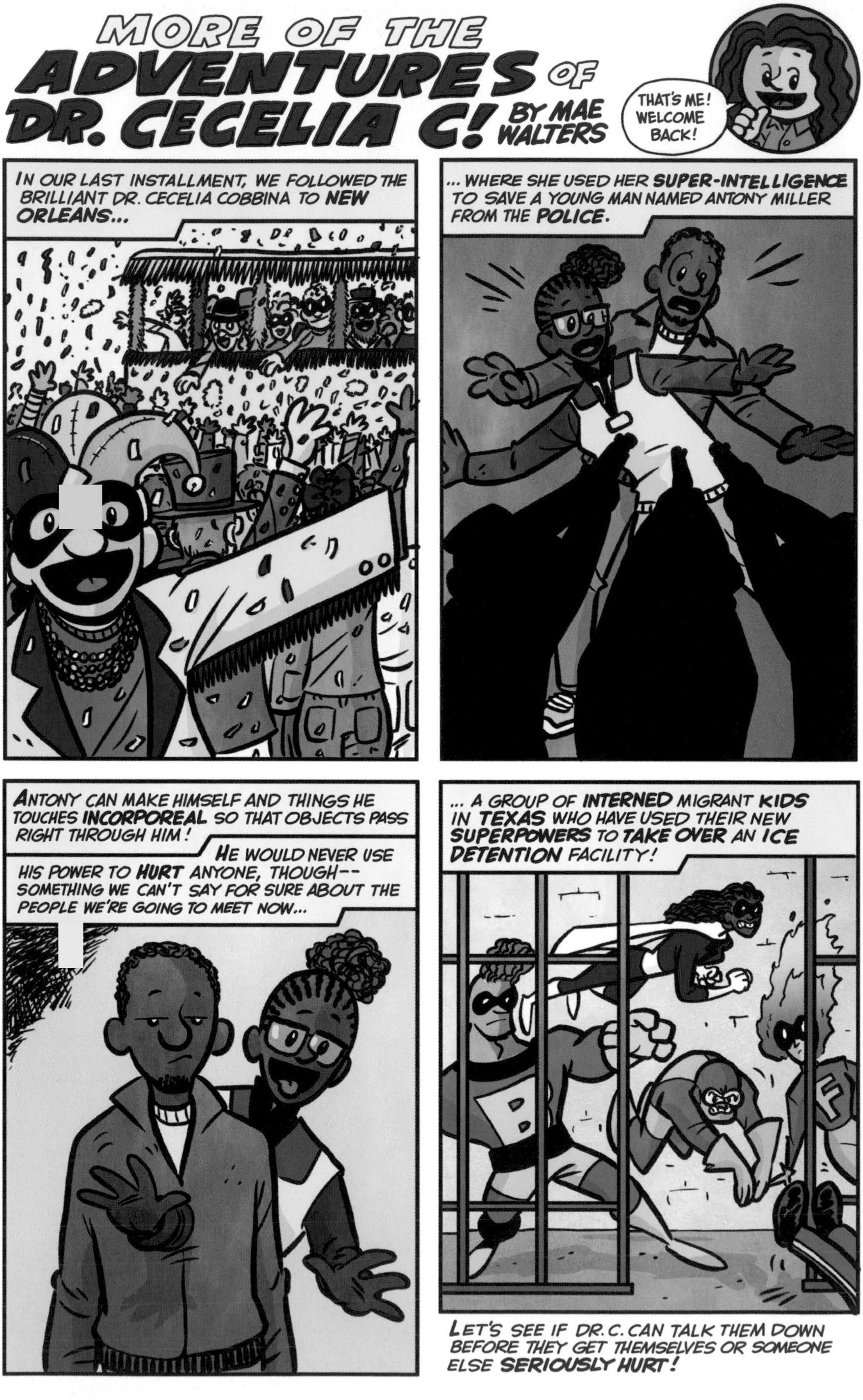
MORE OF THE ADVENTURES OF DR. CECELIA C!
BY MAE WALTERS
THAT'S ME! WELCOME BACK!
IN OUR LAST INSTALLMENT, WE FOLLOWED THE BRILLIANT DR. CECELIA COBBINA TO NEW ORLEANS...
... WHERE SHE USED HER SUPER-INTELLIGENCE TO SAVE A YOUNG MAN NAMED ANTONY MILLER FROM THE POLICE.
ANTONY CAN MAKE HIMSELF AND THINGS HE TOUCHES INCORPOREAL SO THAT OBJECTS PASS RIGHT THROUGH HIM!
HE WOULD NEVER USE HIS POWER TO HURT ANYONE, THOUGH-- SOMETHING WE CAN'T SAY FOR SURE ABOUT THE PEOPLE WE'RE GOING TO MEET NOW...
... A GROUP OF INTERNED MIGRANT KIDS IN TEXAS WHO HAVE USED THEIR NEW SUPERPOWERS TO TAKE OVER AN ICE DETENTION FACILITY!
LET'S SEE IF DR. C. CAN TALK THEM DOWN BEFORE THEY GET THEMSELVES OR SOMEONE ELSE SERIOUSLY HURT!

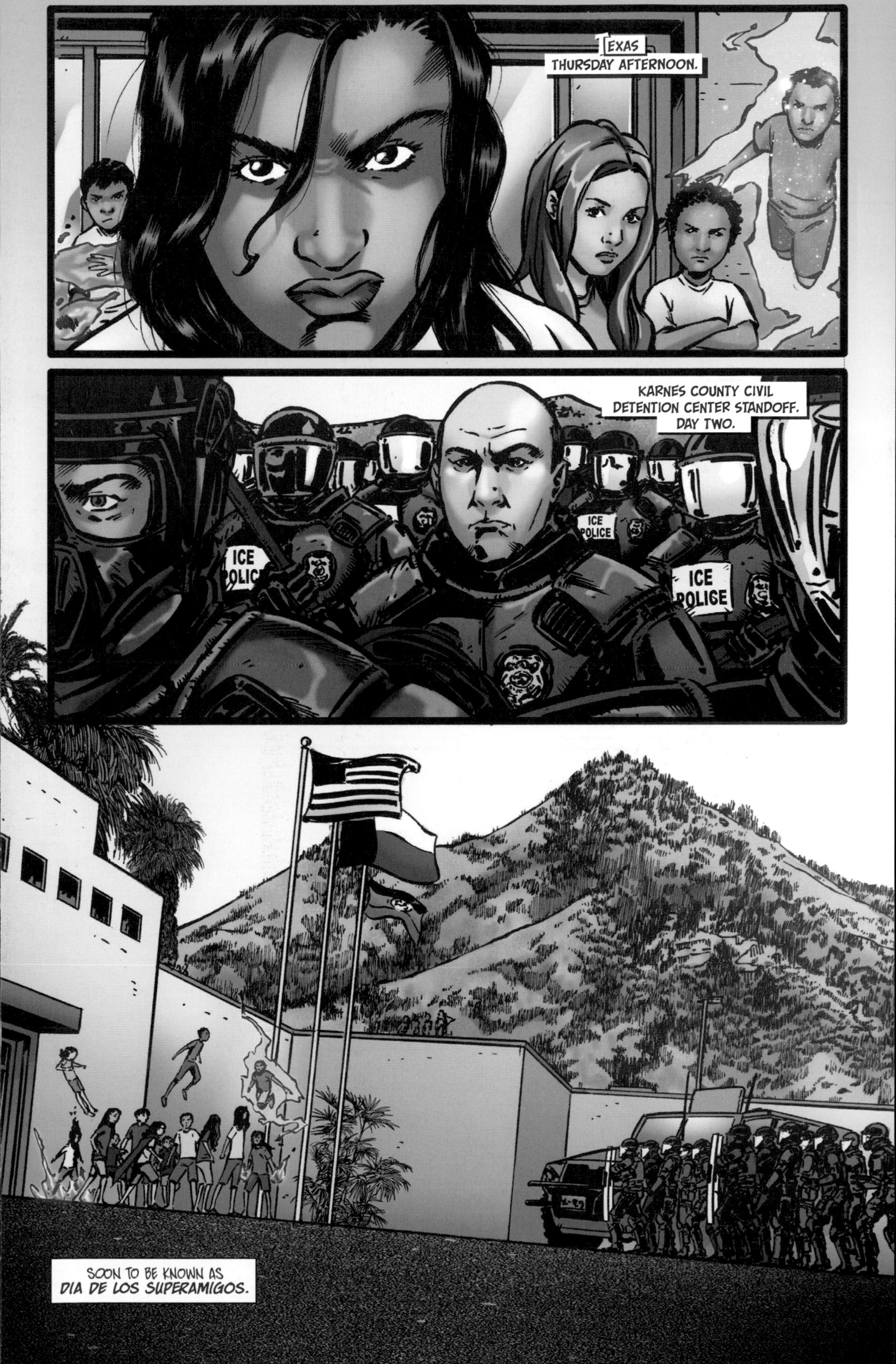
TEXAS
THURSDAY AFTERNOON.
KARNES COUNTY CIVIL DETENTION CENTER STANDOFF. DAY TWO.
ICE POLICE
ICE POLICE
ICE POLICE
SOON TO BE KNOWN AS
DIA DE LOS SUPERAMIGOS.

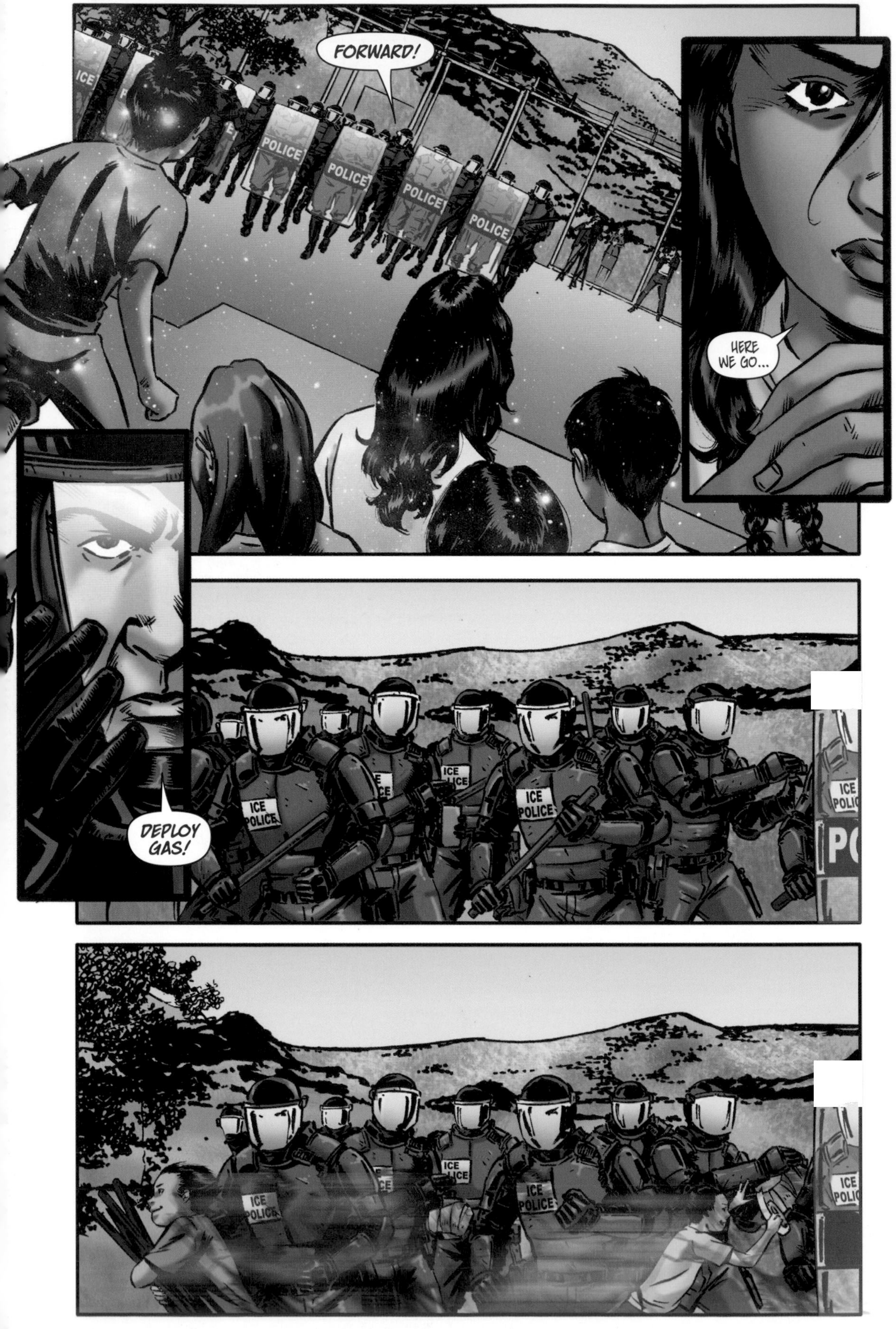

FORWARD!
ICE
POLICE
POLICE
POLICE
POLICE
HERE WE GO...
DEPLOY GAS!
ICE POLICE
ICE POLICE
ICE POLICE
ICE POLICE
POL
ICE POLICE
ICE POLICE
ICE POLICE
ICE POLICE

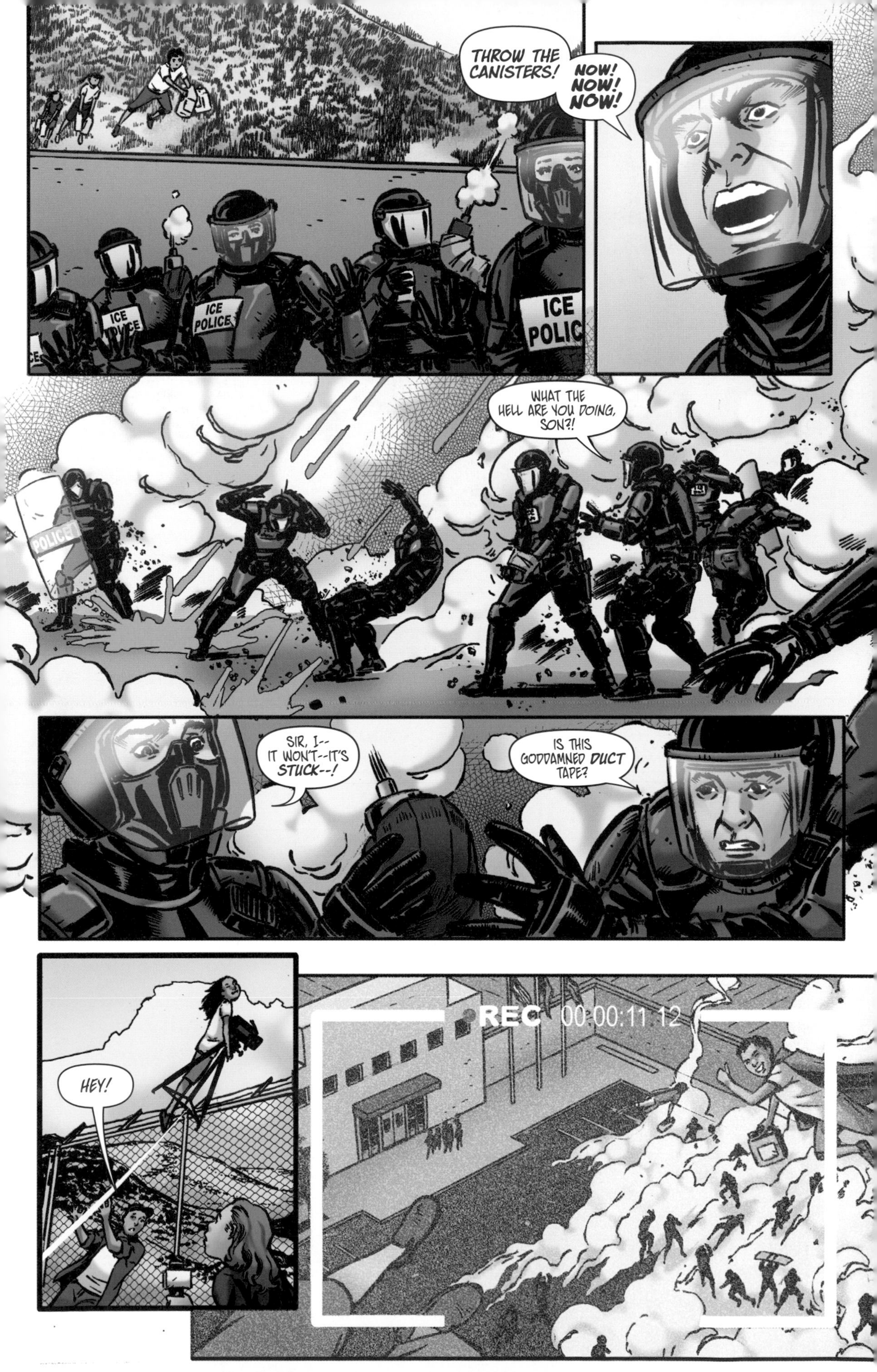
THROW THE CANISTERS!
NOW! NOW! NOW!
ICE POLICE
ICE POLICE
ICE POLICE
WHAT THE HELL ARE YOU DOING, SON?!
POLICE
SIR, I-- IT WON'T--IT'S STUCK--!
IS THIS GODDAMNED DUCT TAPE?
HEY!
REC 00:00:11:12

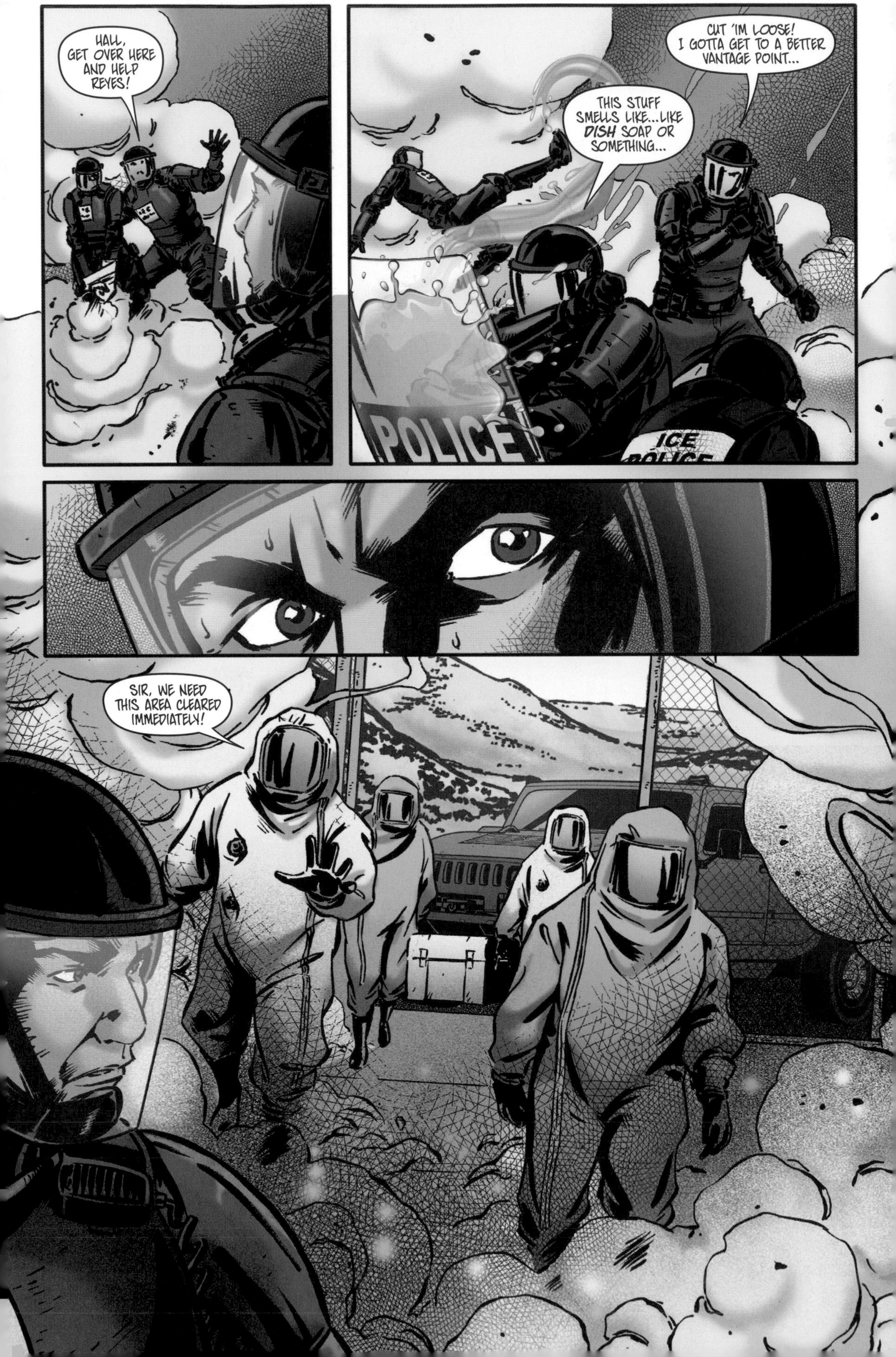
HALL, GET OVER HERE AND HELP REYES!
CUT 'IM LOOSE! I GOTTA GET TO A BETTER VANTAGE POINT...
THIS STUFF SMELLS LIKE...LIKE DISH SOAP OR SOMETHING...
POLICE
ICE
SIR, WE NEED THIS AREA CLEARED IMMEDIATELY!

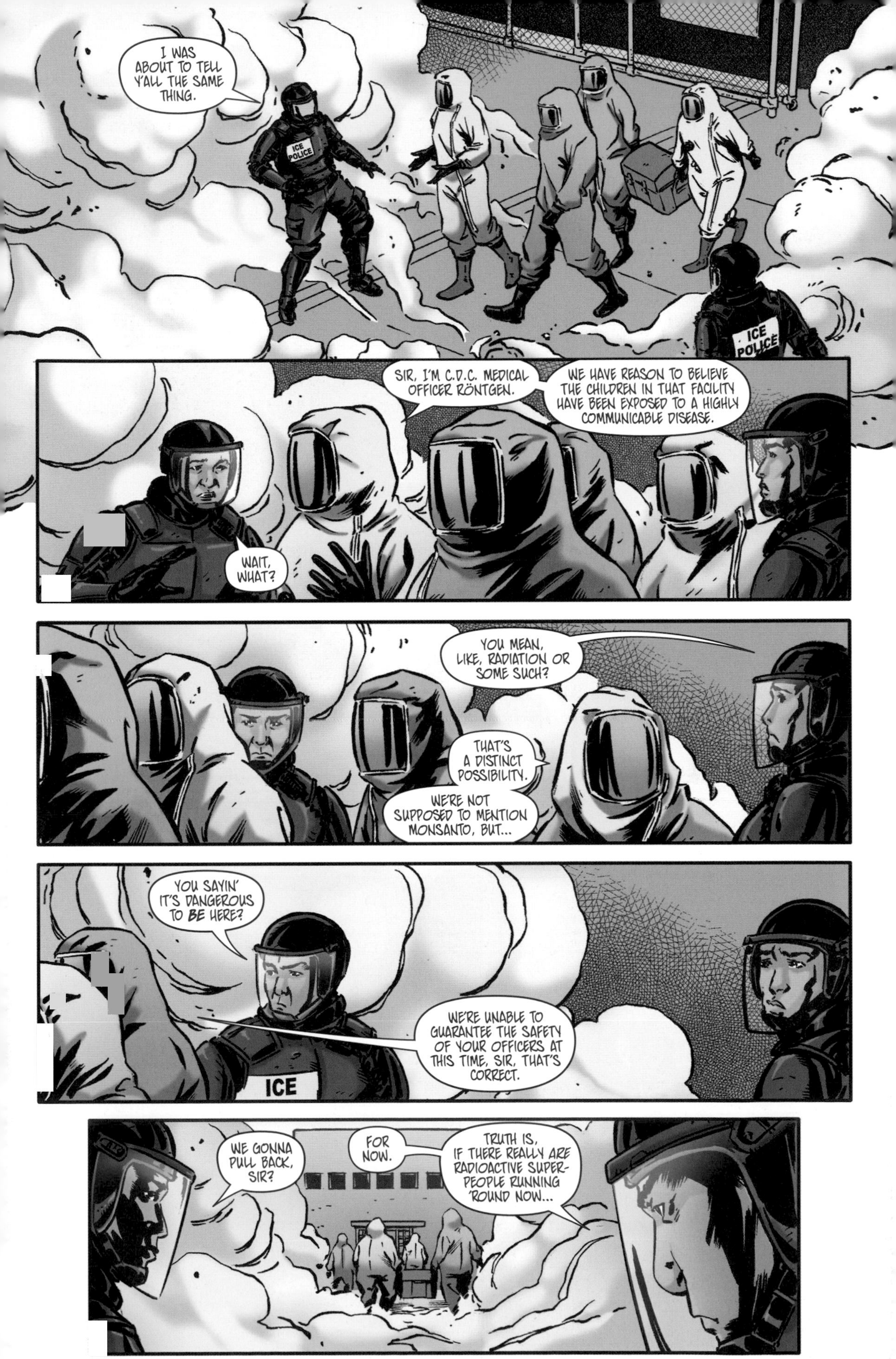
I WAS ABOUT TO TELL Y'ALL THE SAME THING.
ICE POLICE
ICE POLICE
SIR, I'M C.D.C. MEDICAL OFFICER RÖNTGEN.
WE HAVE REASON TO BELIEVE THE CHILDREN IN THAT FACILITY HAVE BEEN EXPOSED TO A HIGHLY COMMUNICABLE DISEASE.
WAIT, WHAT?
YOU MEAN, LIKE, RADIATION OR SOME SUCH?
THAT'S A DISTINCT POSSIBILITY.
WE'RE NOT SUPPOSED TO MENTION MONSANTO, BUT...
YOU SAYIN' IT'S DANGEROUS TO **BE** HERE?
WE'RE UNABLE TO GUARANTEE THE SAFETY OF YOUR OFFICERS AT THIS TIME, SIR, THAT'S CORRECT.
ICE
WE GONNA PULL BACK, SIR?
FOR NOW.
TRUTH IS, IF THERE REALLY ARE RADIOACTIVE SUPER-PEOPLE RUNNING 'ROUND NOW...

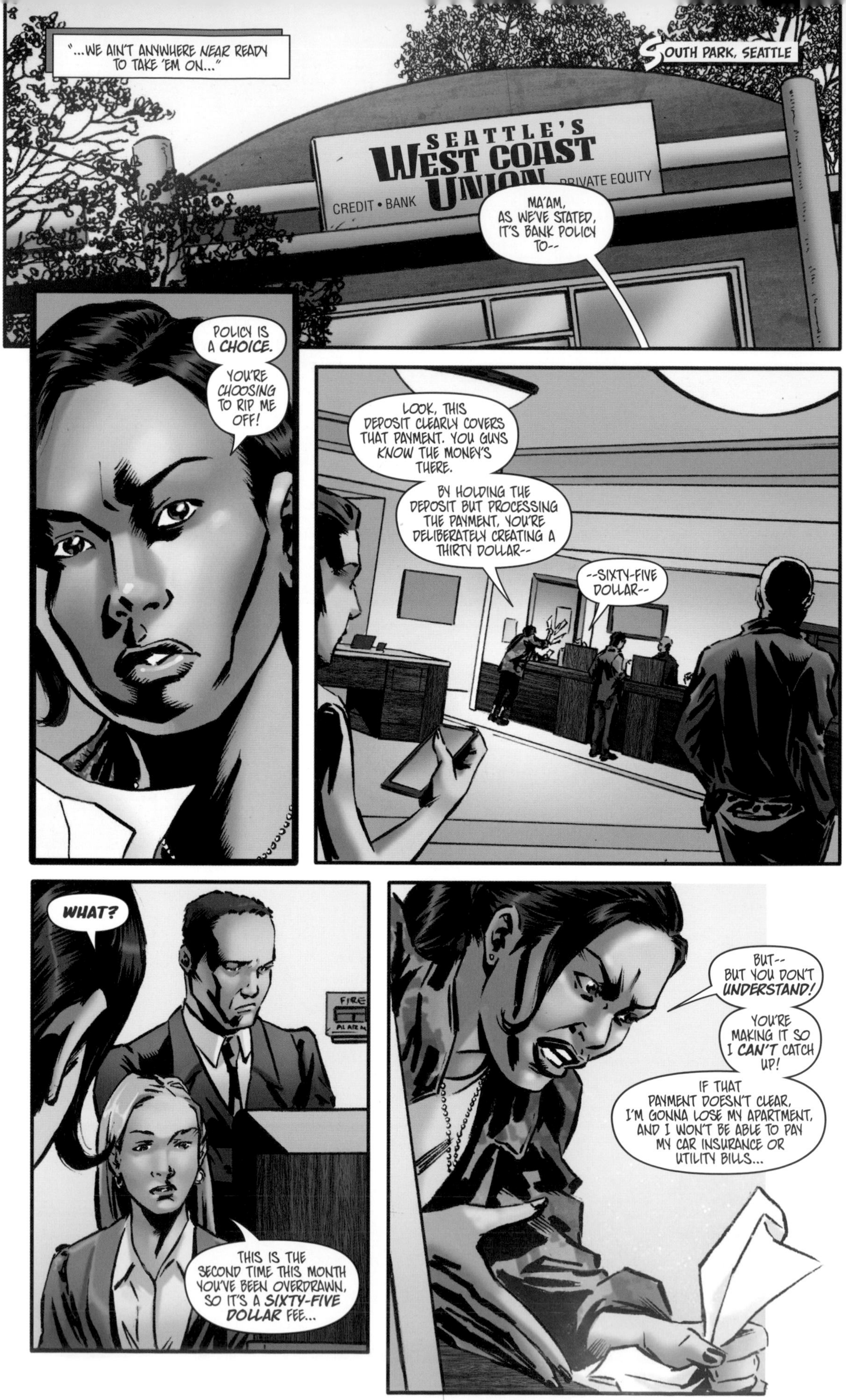
"...WE AIN'T ANYWHERE NEAR READY TO TAKE 'EM ON..."
SOUTH PARK, SEATTLE
SEATTLE'S WEST COAST UNION
CREDIT • BANK
PRIVATE EQUITY
MA'AM, AS WE'VE STATED, IT'S BANK POLICY TO--
POLICY IS A CHOICE.
YOU'RE CHOOSING TO RIP ME OFF!
LOOK, THIS DEPOSIT CLEARLY COVERS THAT PAYMENT. YOU GUYS KNOW THE MONEY'S THERE.
BY HOLDING THE DEPOSIT BUT PROCESSING THE PAYMENT, YOU'RE DELIBERATELY CREATING A THIRTY DOLLAR--
--SIXTY-FIVE DOLLAR--
WHAT?
THIS IS THE SECOND TIME THIS MONTH YOU'VE BEEN OVERDRAWN, SO IT'S A SIXTY-FIVE DOLLAR FEE...
BUT-- BUT YOU DON'T UNDERSTAND!
YOU'RE MAKING IT SO I CAN'T CATCH UP!
IF THAT PAYMENT DOESN'T CLEAR, I'M GONNA LOSE MY APARTMENT, AND I WON'T BE ABLE TO PAY MY CAR INSURANCE OR UTILITY BILLS...

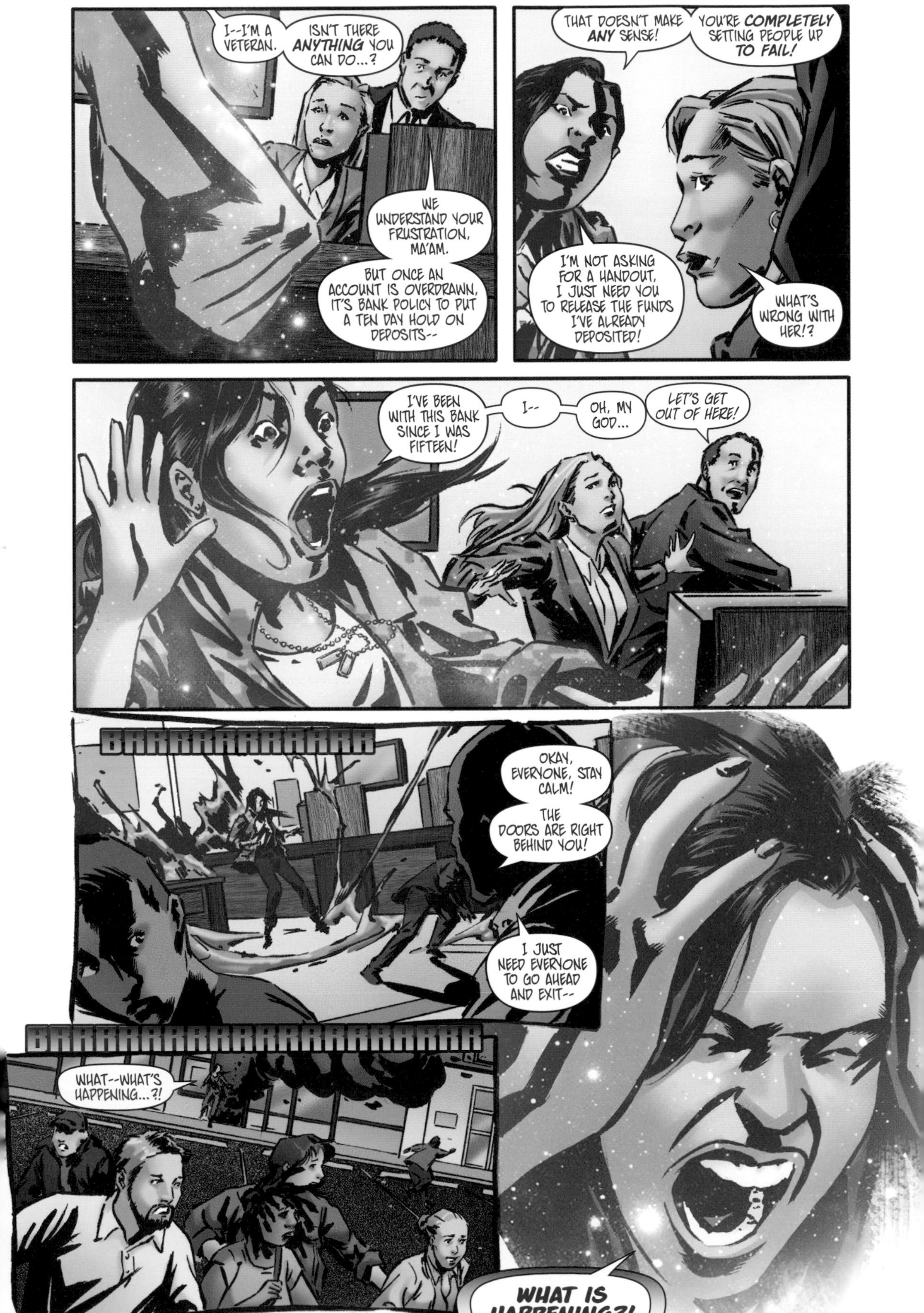

I--I'M A VETERAN.
ISN'T THERE ANYTHING YOU CAN DO...?
WE UNDERSTAND YOUR FRUSTRATION, MA'AM.
BUT ONCE AN ACCOUNT IS OVERDRAWN, IT'S BANK POLICY TO PUT A TEN DAY HOLD ON DEPOSITS--
THAT DOESN'T MAKE ANY SENSE!
YOU'RE COMPLETELY SETTING PEOPLE UP TO FAIL!
I'M NOT ASKING FOR A HANDOUT, I JUST NEED YOU TO RELEASE THE FUNDS I'VE ALREADY DEPOSITED!
WHAT'S WRONG WITH HER!?
I'VE BEEN WITH THIS BANK SINCE I WAS FIFTEEN!
I--
OH, MY GOD...
LET'S GET OUT OF HERE!
BRRRRRRRRRRRR
OKAY, EVERYONE, STAY CALM!
THE DOORS ARE RIGHT BEHIND YOU!
I JUST NEED EVERYONE TO GO AHEAD AND EXIT--
BRRRRRRRRRRRRRRRRRRRR
WHAT--WHAT'S HAPPENING...?!
WHAT IS HAPPENING?!

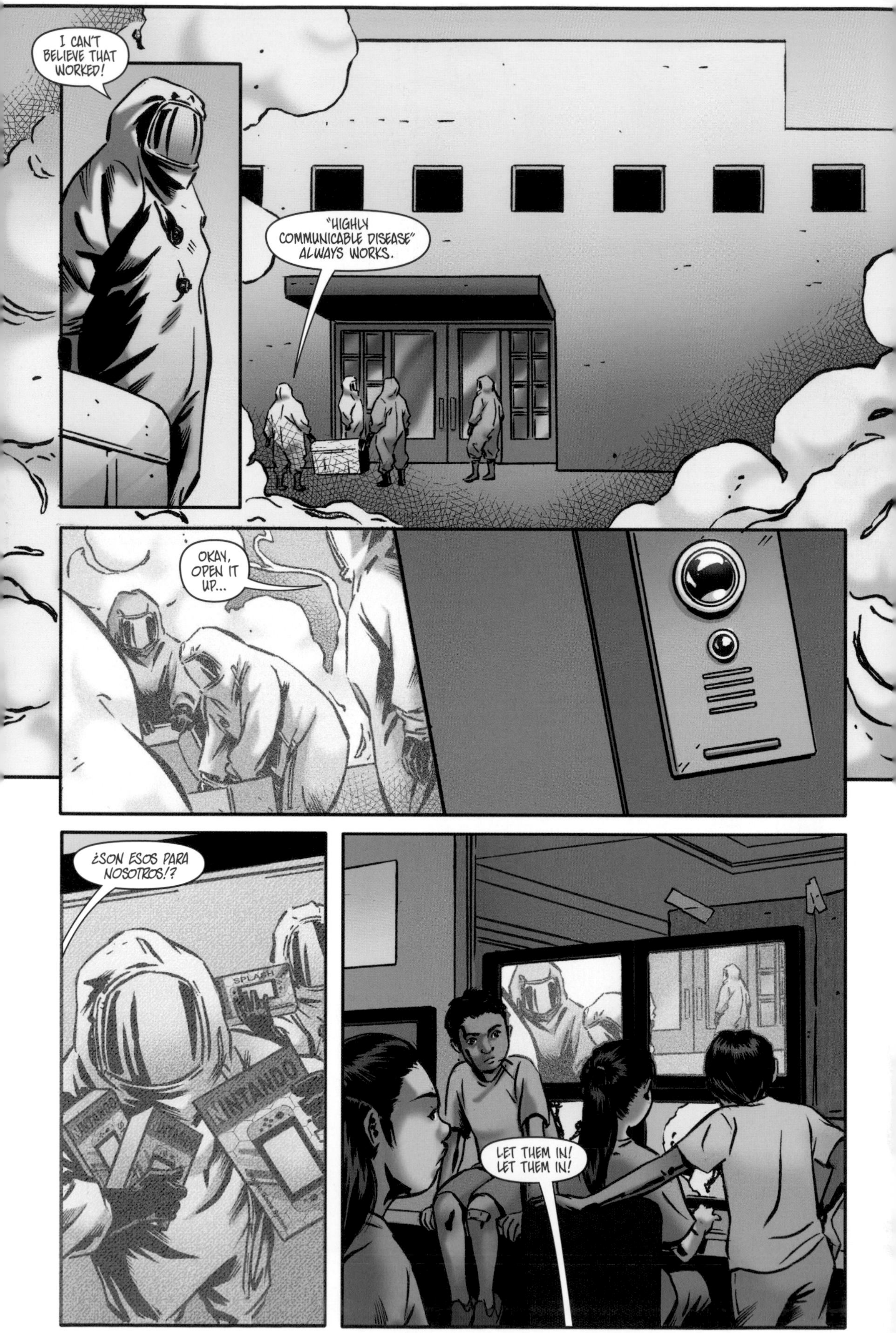
I CAN'T BELIEVE THAT WORKED!
"HIGHLY COMMUNICABLE DISEASE" ALWAYS WORKS.
OKAY, OPEN IT UP...
¿SON ESOS PARA NOSOTROS!?
SPLASH
LET THEM IN! LET THEM IN!

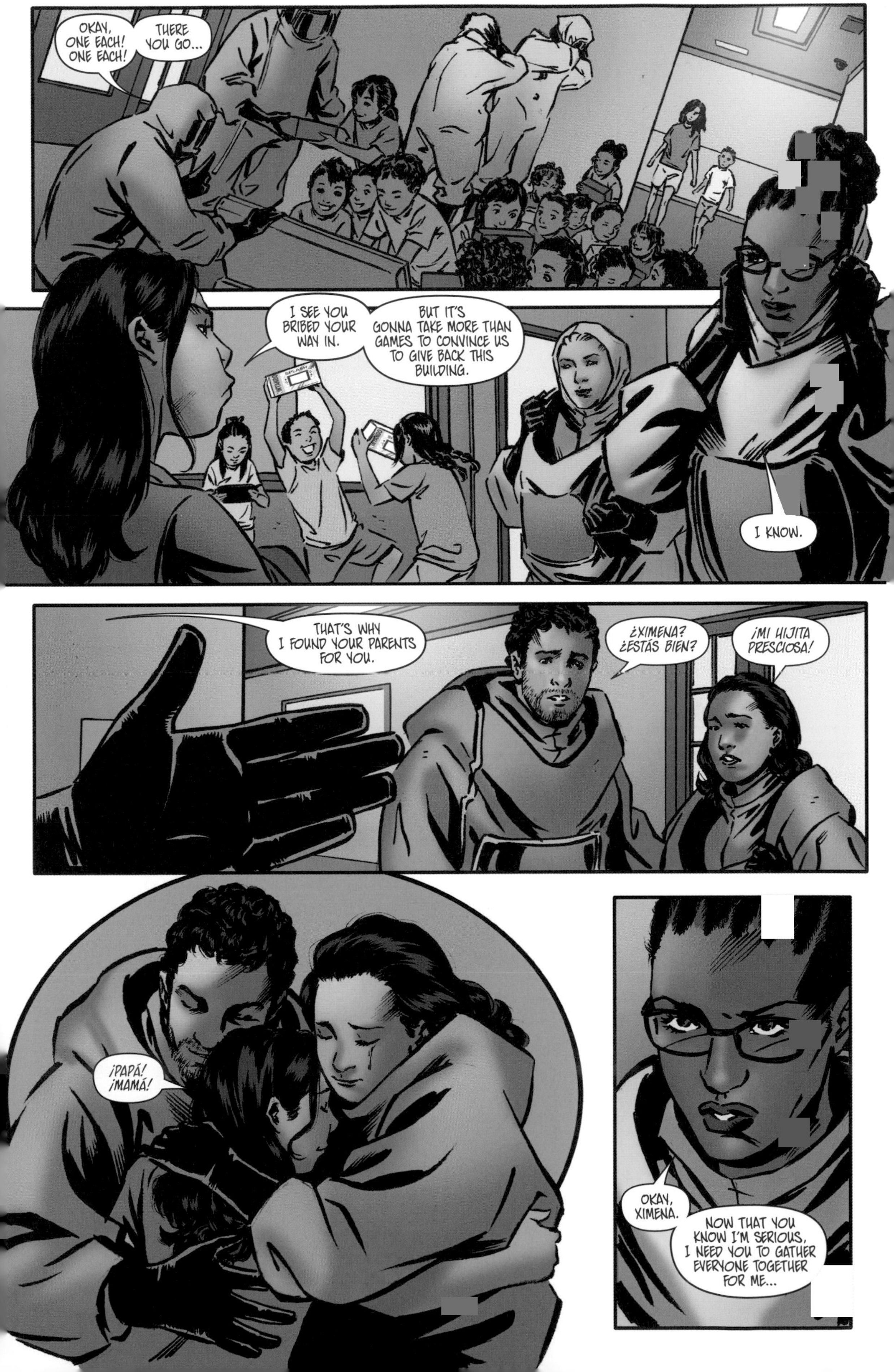
OKAY, ONE EACH! ONE EACH!
THERE YOU GO...
SPLASH
I SEE YOU BRIBED YOUR WAY IN.
BUT IT'S GONNA TAKE MORE THAN GAMES TO CONVINCE US TO GIVE BACK THIS BUILDING.
I KNOW.
THAT'S WHY I FOUND YOUR PARENTS FOR YOU.
¿XIMENA? ¿ESTÁS BIEN?
¡MI HIJITA PRESCIOSA!
¡PAPÁ! ¡MAMÁ!
OKAY, XIMENA.
NOW THAT YOU KNOW I'M SERIOUS, I NEED YOU TO GATHER EVERYONE TOGETHER FOR ME...

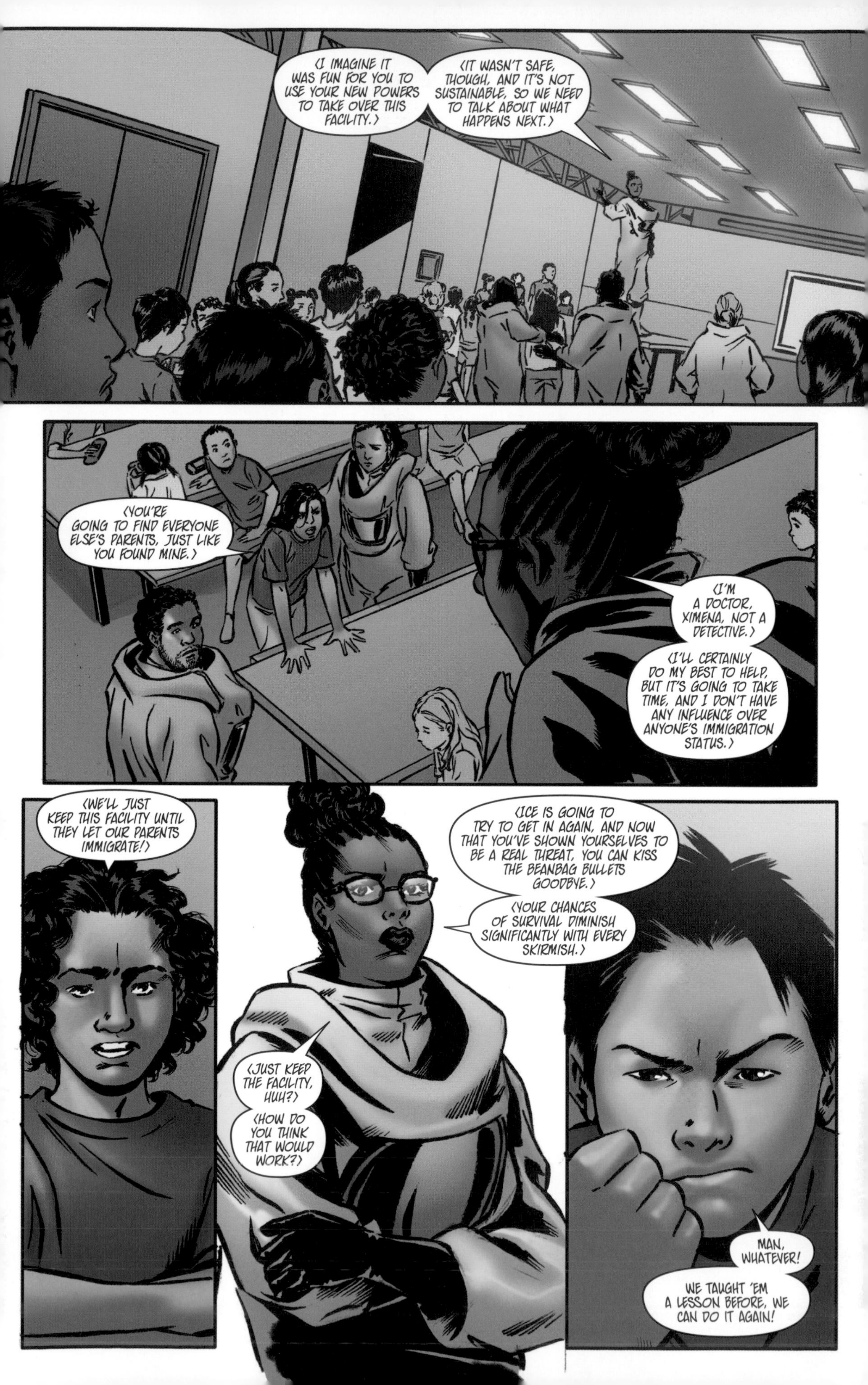

‹I IMAGINE IT WAS FUN FOR YOU TO USE YOUR NEW POWERS TO TAKE OVER THIS FACILITY.›
‹IT WASN'T SAFE, THOUGH, AND IT'S NOT SUSTAINABLE, SO WE NEED TO TALK ABOUT WHAT HAPPENS NEXT.›
‹YOU'RE GOING TO FIND EVERYONE ELSE'S PARENTS, JUST LIKE YOU FOUND MINE.›
‹I'M A DOCTOR, XIMENA, NOT A DETECTIVE.›
‹I'LL CERTAINLY DO MY BEST TO HELP, BUT IT'S GOING TO TAKE TIME, AND I DON'T HAVE ANY INFLUENCE OVER ANYONE'S IMMIGRATION STATUS.›
‹WE'LL JUST KEEP THIS FACILITY UNTIL THEY LET OUR PARENTS IMMIGRATE!›
‹ICE IS GOING TO TRY TO GET IN AGAIN, AND NOW THAT YOU'VE SHOWN YOURSELVES TO BE A REAL THREAT, YOU CAN KISS THE BEANBAG BULLETS GOODBYE.›
‹YOUR CHANCES OF SURVIVAL DIMINISH SIGNIFICANTLY WITH EVERY SKIRMISH.›
‹JUST KEEP THE FACILITY, HUH?›
‹HOW DO YOU THINK THAT WOULD WORK?›
MAN, WHATEVER!
WE TAUGHT 'EM A LESSON BEFORE, WE CAN DO IT AGAIN!

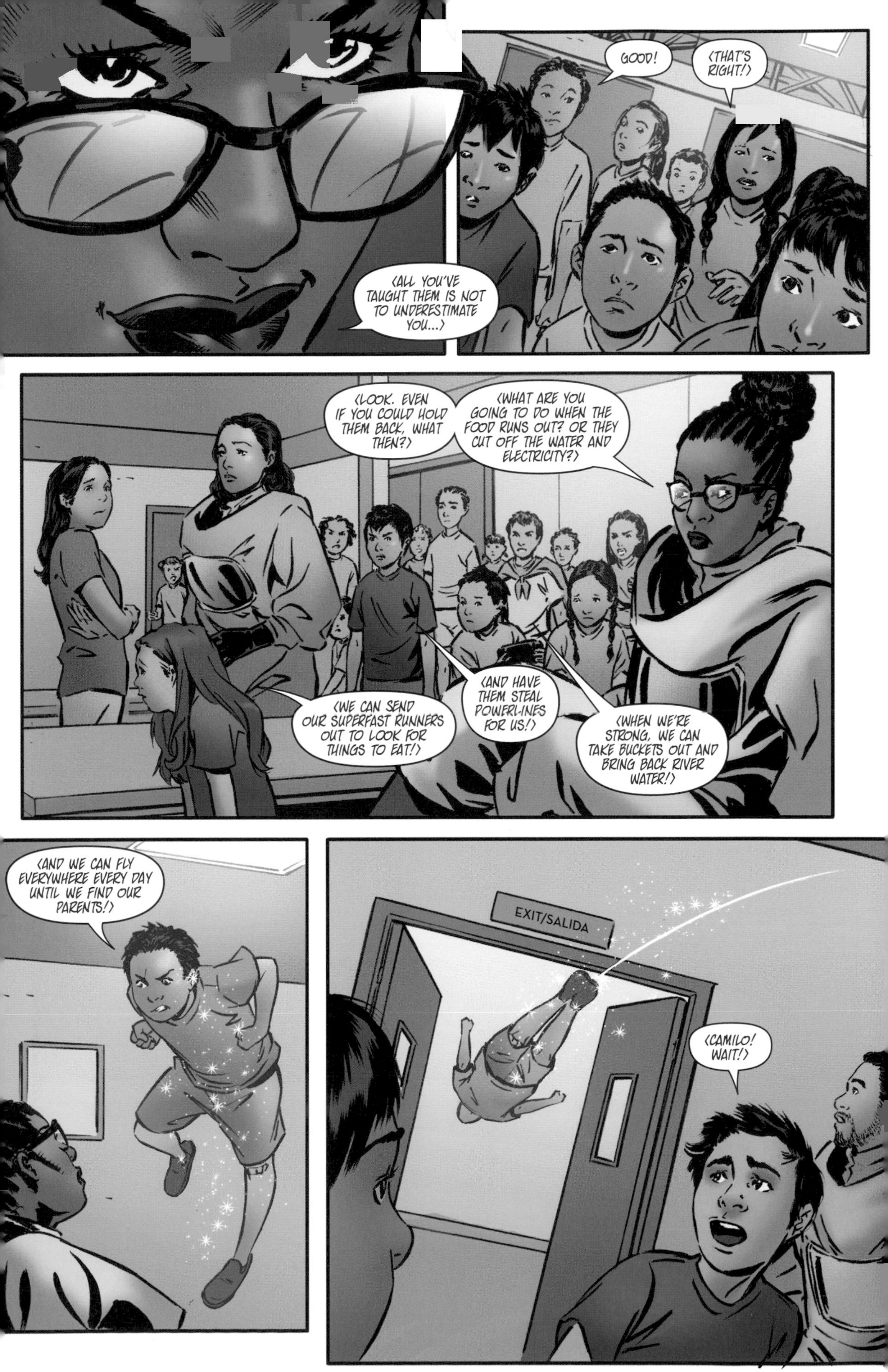

GOOD!
‹THAT'S RIGHT!›
‹ALL YOU'VE TAUGHT THEM IS NOT TO UNDERESTIMATE YOU...›
‹LOOK. EVEN IF YOU COULD HOLD THEM BACK, WHAT THEN?›
‹WHAT ARE YOU GOING TO DO WHEN THE FOOD RUNS OUT? OR THEY CUT OFF THE WATER AND ELECTRICITY?›
‹WE CAN SEND OUR SUPERFAST RUNNERS OUT TO LOOK FOR THINGS TO EAT!›
‹AND HAVE THEM STEAL POWERLINES FOR US!›
‹WHEN WE'RE STRONG, WE CAN TAKE BUCKETS OUT AND BRING BACK RIVER WATER!›
‹AND WE CAN FLY EVERYWHERE EVERY DAY UNTIL WE FIND OUR PARENTS!›
EXIT/SALIDA
‹CAMILO! WAIT!›

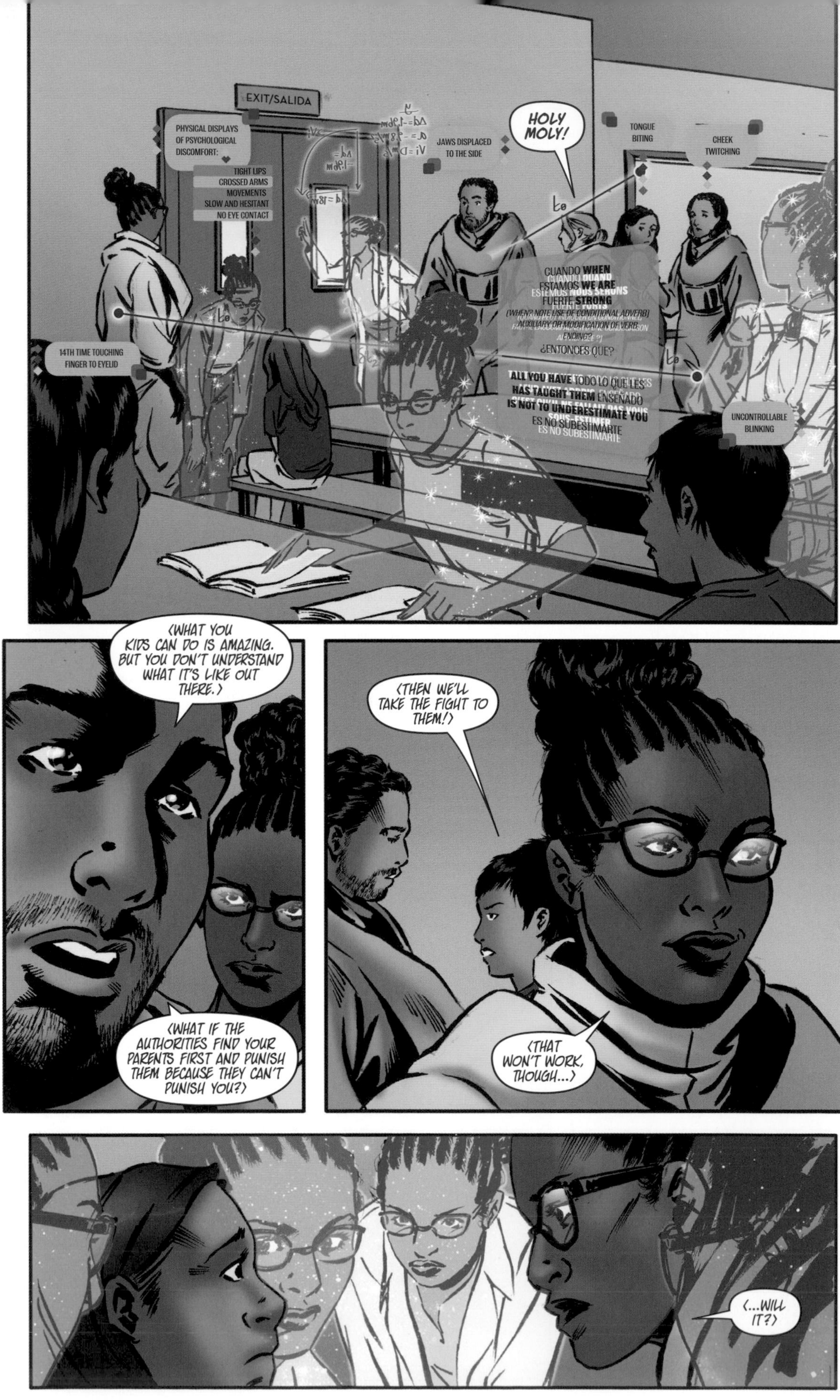
EXIT/SALIDA
PHYSICAL DISPLAYS OF PSYCHOLOGICAL DISCOMFORT:
TIGHT LIPS
CROSSED ARMS
MOVEMENTS SLOW AND HESITANT
NO EYE CONTACT
JAWS DISPLACED TO THE SIDE
HOLY MOLY!
TONGUE BITING
CHEEK TWITCHING
CUANDO WHEN
ESTAMOS WE ARE
FUERTE STRONG
(WHEN? NOTE USE OF CONDITIONAL ADVERB) AUXILIARY OR MODIFICATION OF VERB ENDING?
¿ENTONCES QUE?
ALL YOU HAVE TODO LO QUE LES
HAS TAUGHT THEM ENSEÑADO
IS NOT TO UNDERESTIMATE YOU
ES NO SUBESTIMARTE
14TH TIME TOUCHING FINGER TO EYELID
UNCONTROLLABLE BLINKING
‹WHAT YOU KIDS CAN DO IS AMAZING. BUT YOU DON'T UNDERSTAND WHAT IT'S LIKE OUT THERE.›
‹WHAT IF THE AUTHORITIES FIND YOUR PARENTS FIRST AND PUNISH THEM BECAUSE THEY CAN'T PUNISH YOU?›
‹THEN WE'LL TAKE THE FIGHT TO THEM!›
‹THAT WON'T WORK, THOUGH...›
‹...WILL IT?›

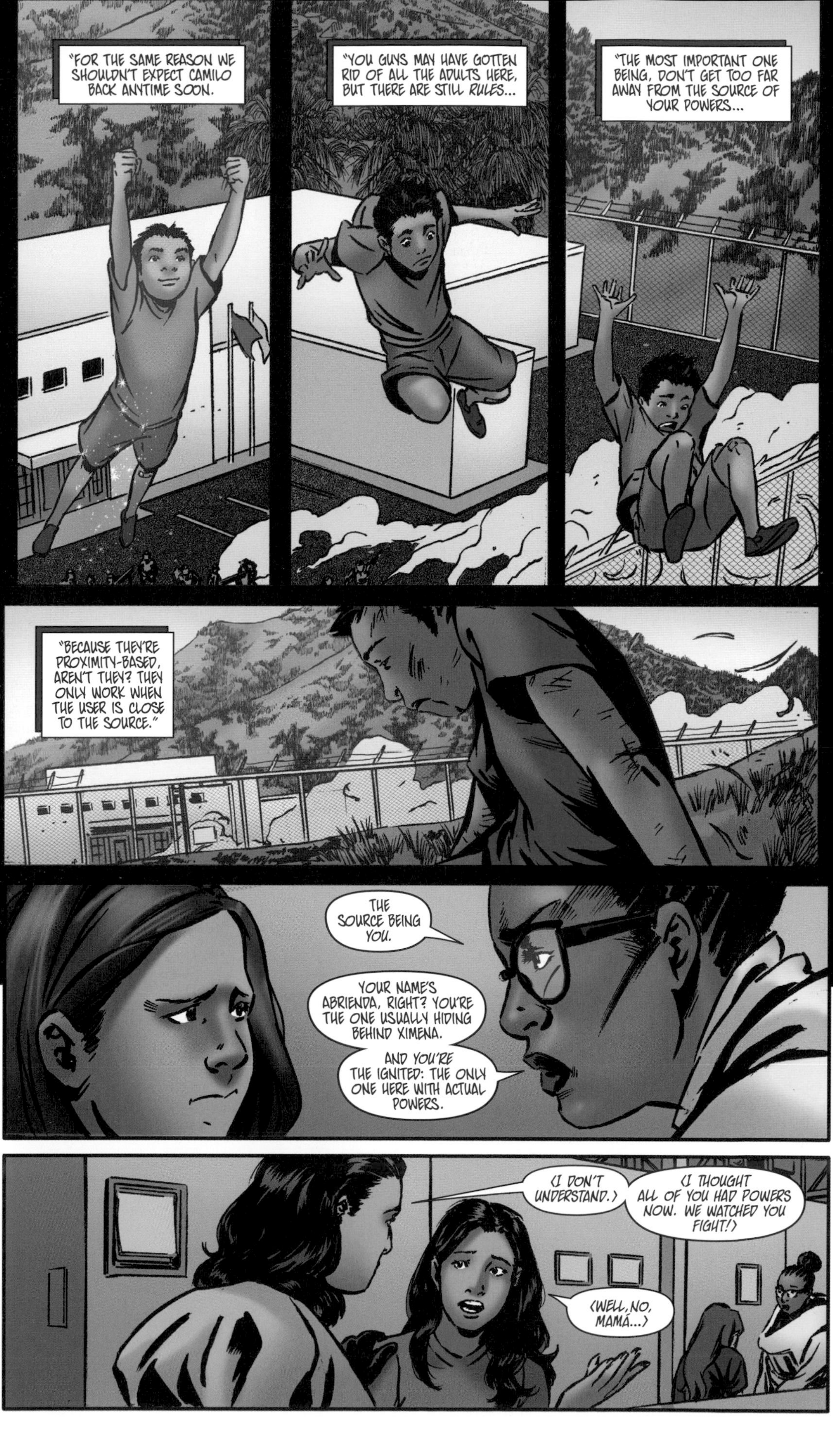
"FOR THE SAME REASON WE SHOULDN'T EXPECT CAMILO BACK ANYTIME SOON.
"YOU GUYS MAY HAVE GOTTEN RID OF ALL THE ADULTS HERE, BUT THERE ARE STILL *RULES*...
"THE MOST IMPORTANT ONE BEING, DON'T GET TOO FAR AWAY FROM THE SOURCE OF YOUR POWERS...
"BECAUSE THEY'RE PROXIMITY-BASED, AREN'T THEY? THEY ONLY WORK WHEN THE USER IS CLOSE TO THE SOURCE."
THE SOURCE BEING YOU.
YOUR NAME'S ABRIENDA, RIGHT? YOU'RE THE ONE USUALLY HIDING BEHIND XIMENA.
AND YOU'RE THE IGNITED: THE ONLY ONE HERE WITH ACTUAL POWERS.
‹I DON'T UNDERSTAND.›
‹I THOUGHT ALL OF YOU HAD POWERS NOW. WE WATCHED YOU FIGHT!›
‹WELL, NO, MAMÁ...›

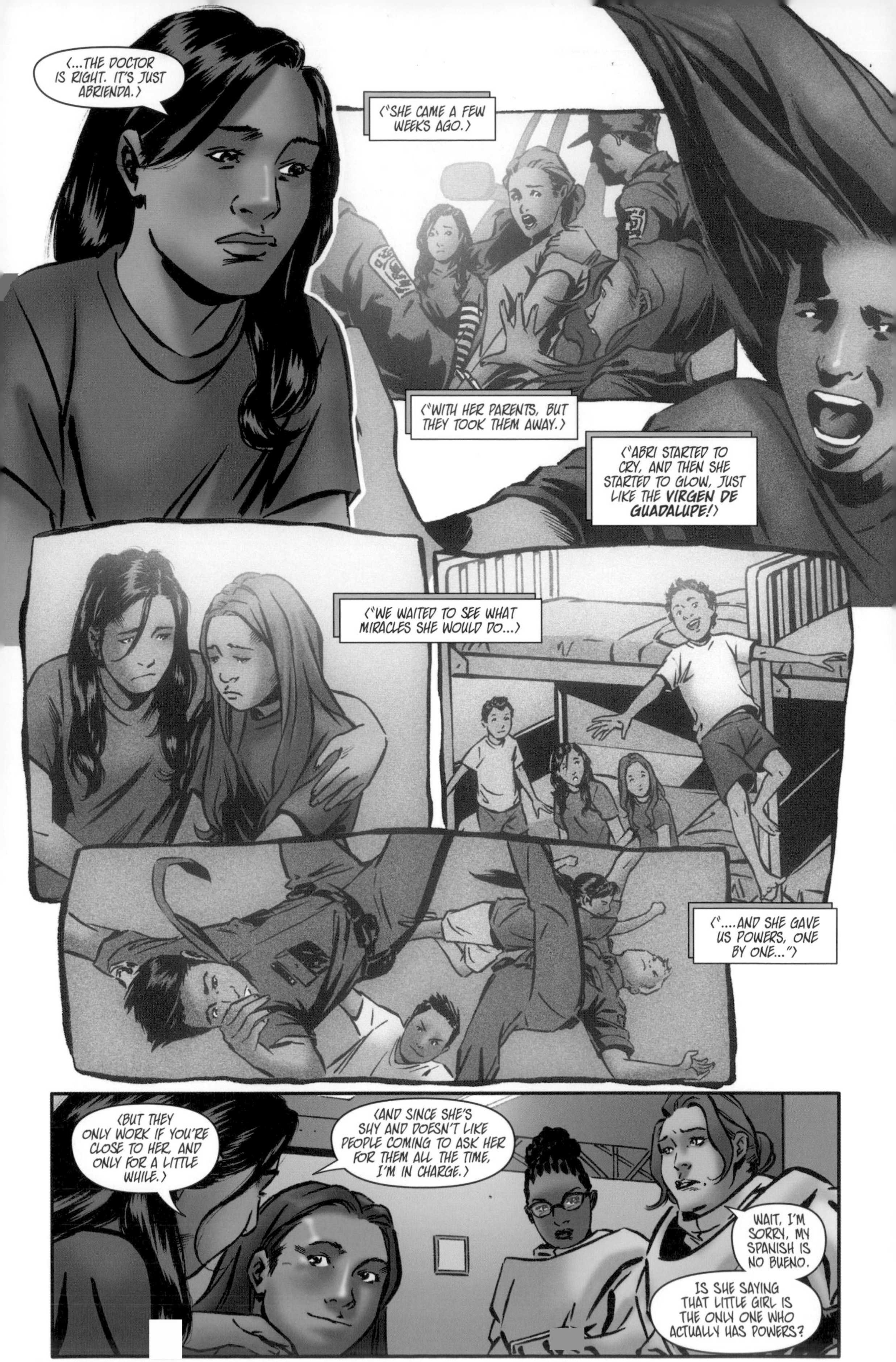
‹...THE DOCTOR IS RIGHT. IT'S JUST ABRIENDA.›
‹"SHE CAME A FEW WEEKS AGO.›
‹"WITH HER PARENTS, BUT THEY TOOK THEM AWAY.›
‹"ABRI STARTED TO CRY, AND THEN SHE STARTED TO GLOW, JUST LIKE THE **VIRGEN DE GUADALUPE!**›
‹"WE WAITED TO SEE WHAT MIRACLES SHE WOULD DO...›
‹"....AND SHE GAVE US POWERS, ONE BY ONE..."›
‹BUT THEY ONLY WORK IF YOU'RE CLOSE TO HER, AND ONLY FOR A LITTLE WHILE.›
‹AND SINCE SHE'S SHY AND DOESN'T LIKE PEOPLE COMING TO ASK HER FOR THEM ALL THE TIME, I'M IN CHARGE.›
WAIT, I'M SORRY, MY SPANISH IS NO BUENO.
IS SHE SAYING THAT LITTLE GIRL IS THE ONLY ONE WHO ACTUALLY HAS POWERS?

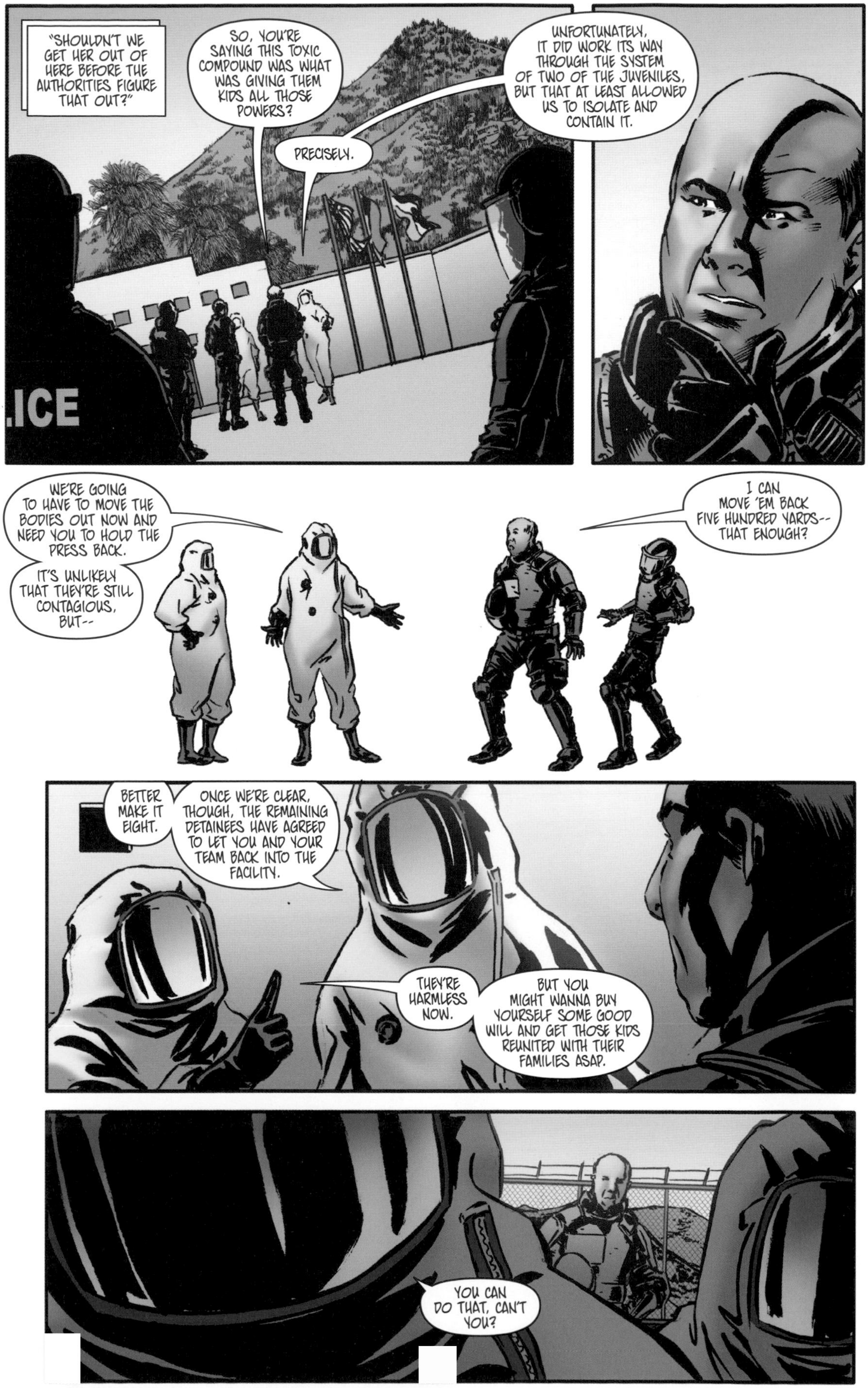
"SHOULDN'T WE GET HER OUT OF HERE BEFORE THE AUTHORITIES FIGURE THAT OUT?"
SO, YOU'RE SAYING THIS TOXIC COMPOUND WAS WHAT WAS GIVING THEM KIDS ALL THOSE POWERS?
PRECISELY.
UNFORTUNATELY, IT DID WORK ITS WAY THROUGH THE SYSTEM OF TWO OF THE JUVENILES, BUT THAT AT LEAST ALLOWED US TO ISOLATE AND CONTAIN IT.
.ICE
WE'RE GOING TO HAVE TO MOVE THE BODIES OUT NOW AND NEED YOU TO HOLD THE PRESS BACK.
IT'S UNLIKELY THAT THEY'RE STILL CONTAGIOUS, BUT--
I CAN MOVE 'EM BACK FIVE HUNDRED YARDS--THAT ENOUGH?
BETTER MAKE IT EIGHT.
ONCE WE'RE CLEAR, THOUGH, THE REMAINING DETAINEES HAVE AGREED TO LET YOU AND YOUR TEAM BACK INTO THE FACILITY.
THEY'RE HARMLESS NOW.
BUT YOU MIGHT WANNA BUY YOURSELF SOME GOOD WILL AND GET THOSE KIDS REUNITED WITH THEIR FAMILIES ASAP.
YOU CAN DO THAT, CAN'T YOU?

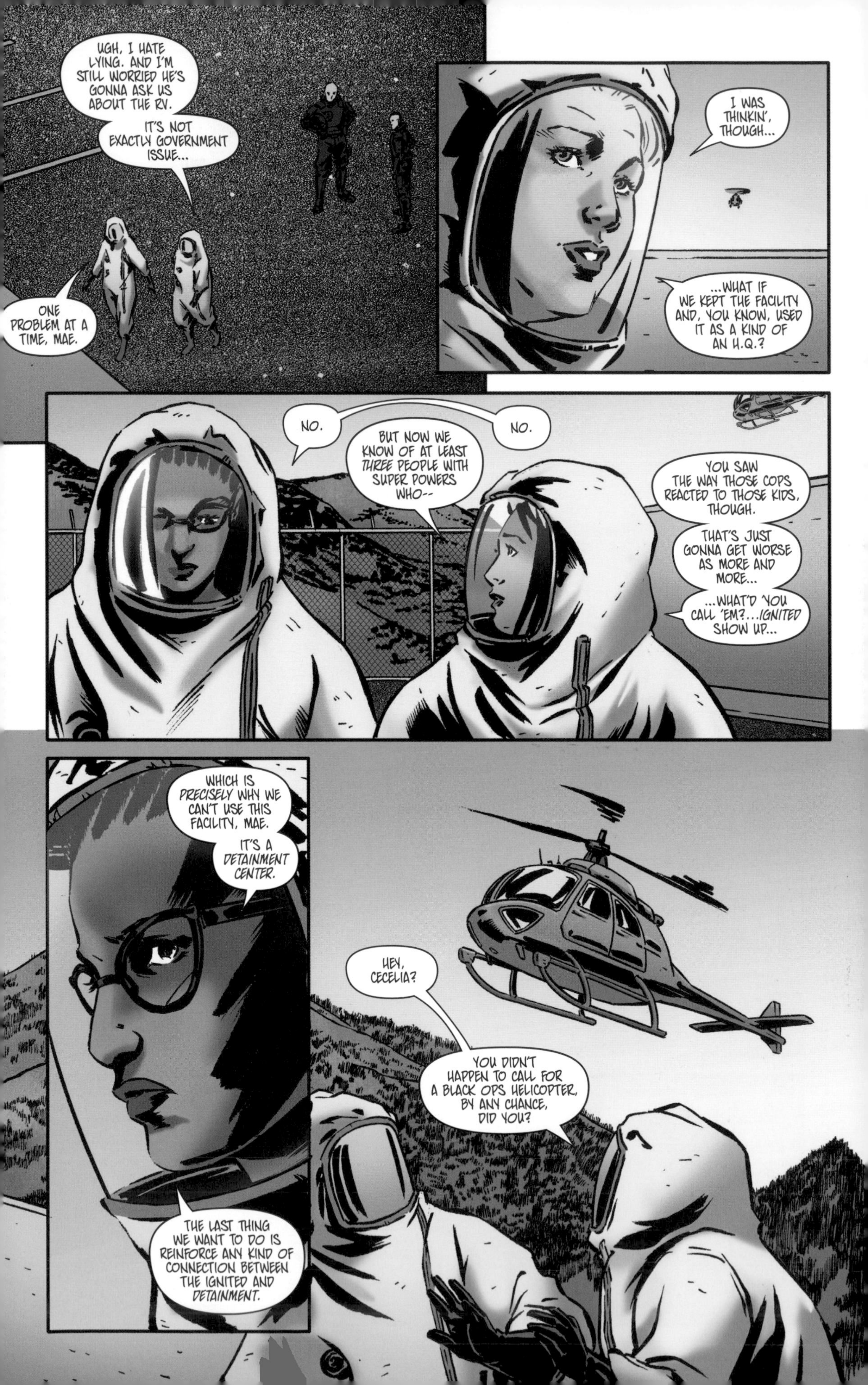
UGH, I HATE LYING. AND I'M STILL WORRIED HE'S GONNA ASK US ABOUT THE RV.
IT'S NOT EXACTLY GOVERNMENT ISSUE...
ONE PROBLEM AT A TIME, MAE.
I WAS THINKIN', THOUGH...
...WHAT IF WE KEPT THE FACILITY AND, YOU KNOW, USED IT AS A KIND OF AN H.Q.?
NO.
NO.
BUT NOW WE KNOW OF AT LEAST THREE PEOPLE WITH SUPER POWERS WHO--
YOU SAW THE WAY THOSE COPS REACTED TO THOSE KIDS, THOUGH.
THAT'S JUST GONNA GET WORSE AS MORE AND MORE...
...WHAT'D 'YOU CALL 'EM?...IGNITED SHOW UP...
WHICH IS PRECISELY WHY WE CAN'T USE THIS FACILITY, MAE.
IT'S A DETAINMENT CENTER.
THE LAST THING WE WANT TO DO IS REINFORCE ANY KIND OF CONNECTION BETWEEN THE IGNITED AND DETAINMENT.
HEY, CECELIA?
YOU DIDN'T HAPPEN TO CALL FOR A BLACK OPS HELICOPTER, BY ANY CHANCE, DID YOU?

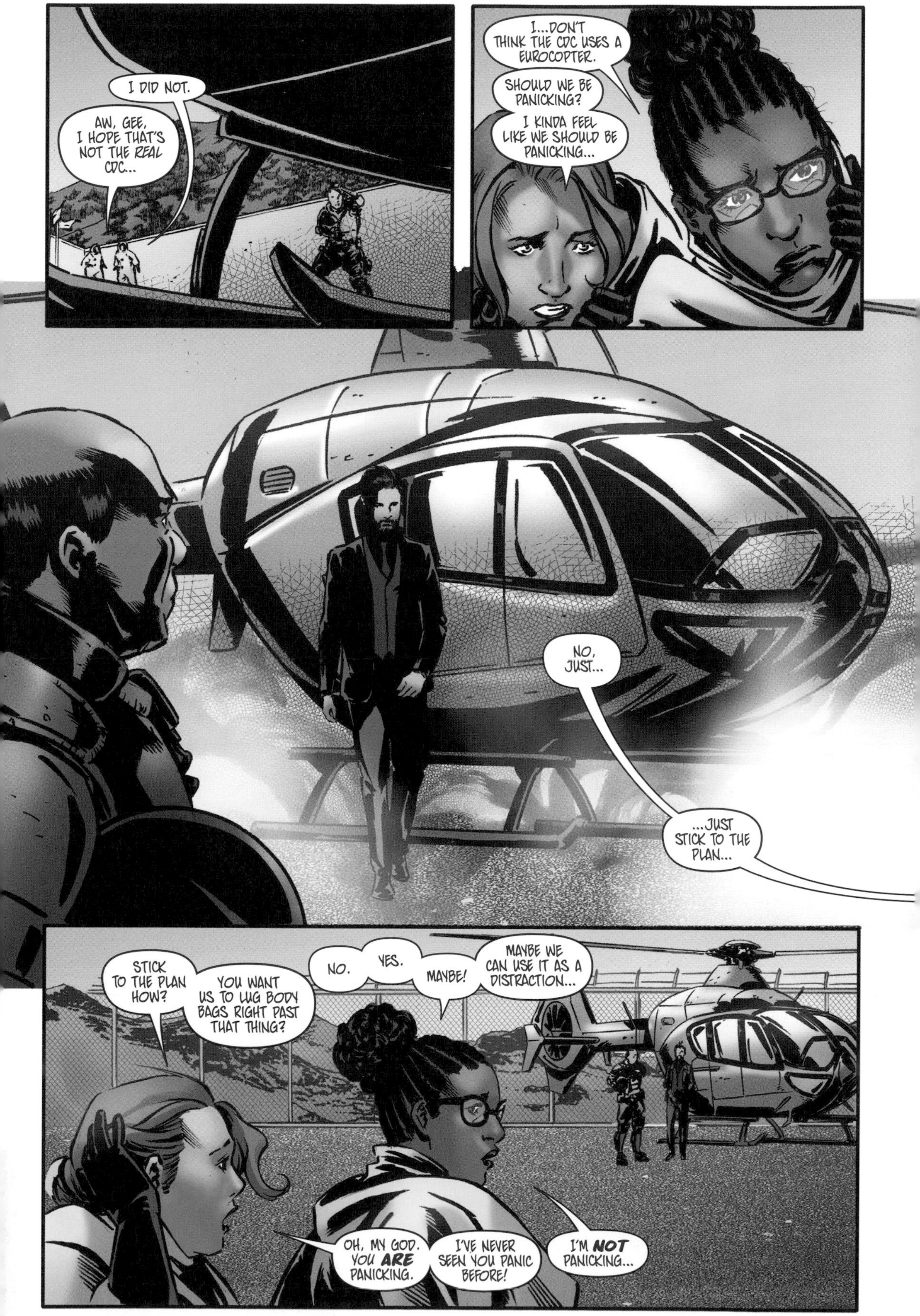

I DID NOT.
AW, GEE, I HOPE THAT'S NOT THE REAL CDC...
I...DON'T THINK THE CDC USES A EUROCOPTER.
SHOULD WE BE PANICKING?
I KINDA FEEL LIKE WE SHOULD BE PANICKING...
NO, JUST...
...JUST STICK TO THE PLAN...
STICK TO THE PLAN HOW?
YOU WANT US TO LUG BODY BAGS RIGHT PAST THAT THING?
NO.
YES.
MAYBE!
MAYBE WE CAN USE IT AS A DISTRACTION...
OH, MY GOD. YOU **ARE** PANICKING.
I'VE NEVER SEEN YOU PANIC BEFORE!
I'M **NOT** PANICKING...

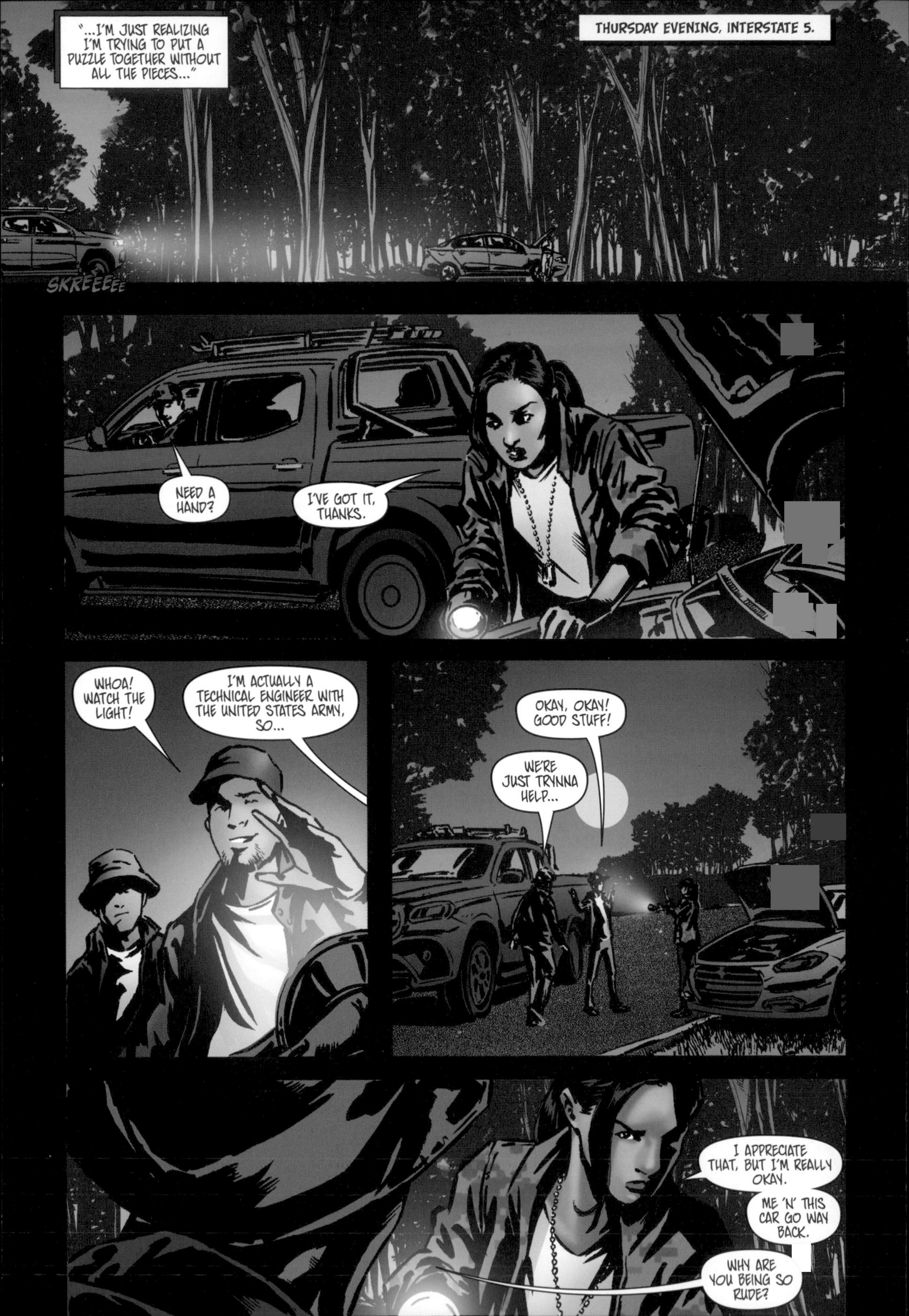
"...I'M JUST REALIZING I'M TRYING TO PUT A PUZZLE TOGETHER WITHOUT ALL THE PIECES..."
THURSDAY EVENING, INTERSTATE 5.
SKREEEEee
NEED A HAND?
I'VE GOT IT, THANKS.
WHOA! WATCH THE LIGHT!
I'M ACTUALLY A TECHNICAL ENGINEER WITH THE UNITED STATES ARMY, SO...
OKAY, OKAY! GOOD STUFF!
WE'RE JUST TRYNNA HELP...
I APPRECIATE THAT, BUT I'M REALLY OKAY.
ME 'N' THIS CAR GO WAY BACK.
WHY ARE YOU BEING SO RUDE?

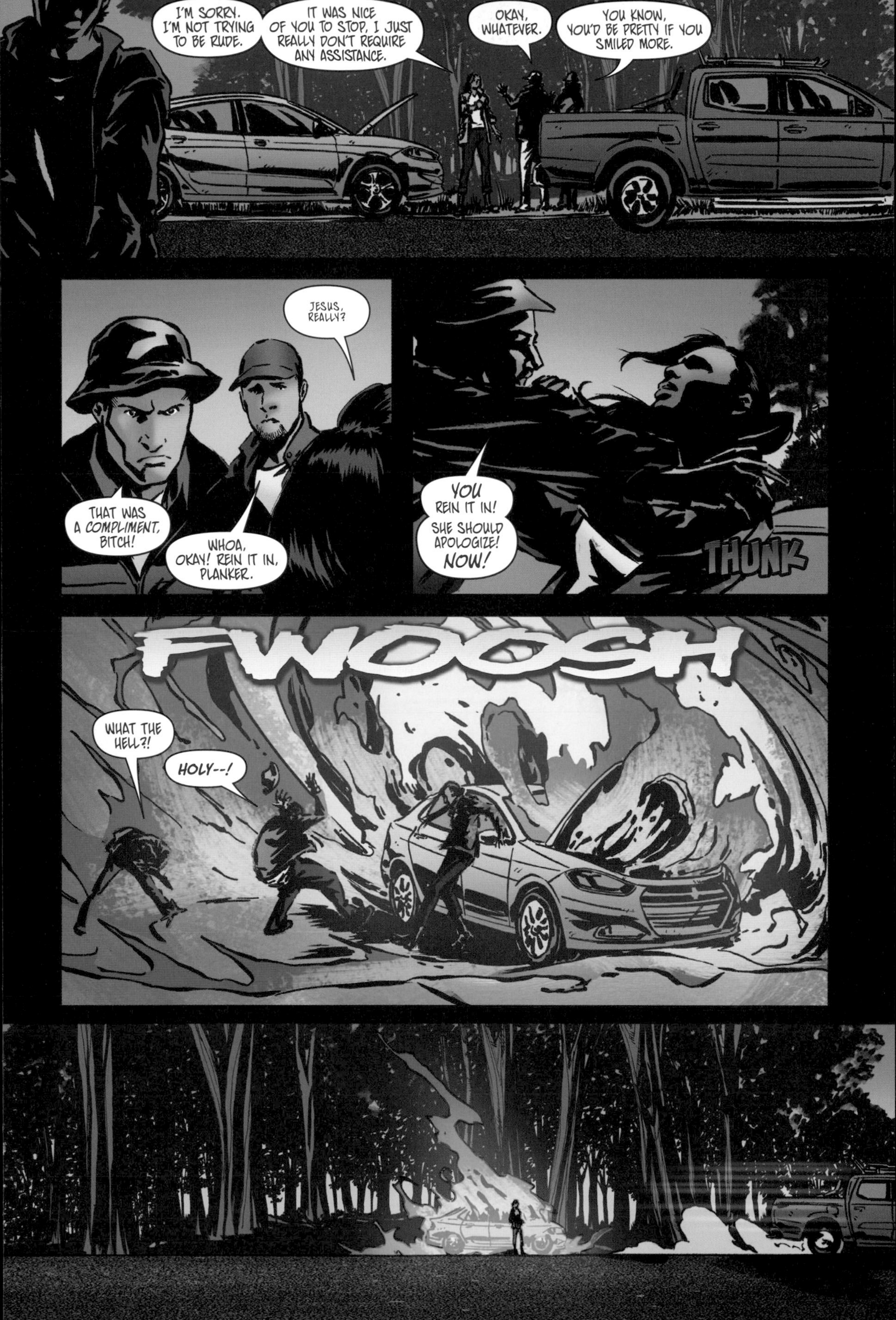
I'M SORRY. I'M NOT TRYING TO BE RUDE.
IT WAS NICE OF YOU TO STOP, I JUST REALLY DON'T REQUIRE ANY ASSISTANCE.
OKAY, WHATEVER.
YOU KNOW, YOU'D BE PRETTY IF YOU SMILED MORE.
JESUS, REALLY?
THAT WAS A COMPLIMENT, BITCH!
WHOA, OKAY! REIN IT IN, PLANKER.
YOU REIN IT IN! SHE SHOULD APOLOGIZE! NOW!
THUNK
FWOOSH
WHAT THE HELL?!
HOLY--!

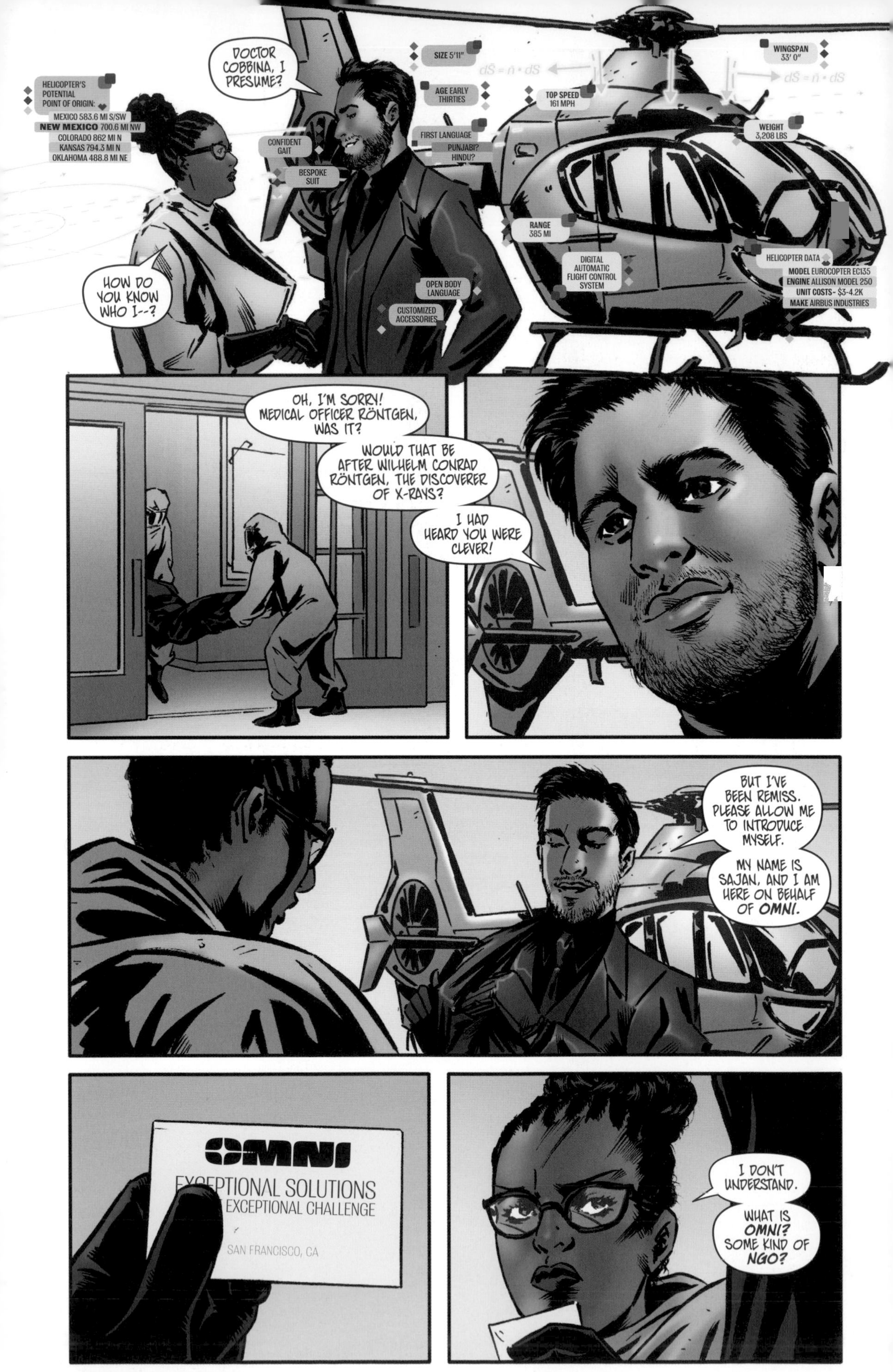
DOCTOR COBBINA, I PRESUME?
HELICOPTER'S POTENTIAL POINT OF ORIGIN:
MEXICO 583.6 MI S/SW
NEW MEXICO 700.6 MI NW
COLORADO 862 MI N
KANSAS 794.3 MI N
OKLAHOMA 488.8 MI NE
SIZE 5'11"
AGE EARLY THIRTIES
FIRST LANGUAGE PUNJABI? HINDU?
CONFIDENT GAIT
BESPOKE SUIT
OPEN BODY LANGUAGE
CUSTOMIZED ACCESSORIES
TOP SPEED 161 MPH
WINGSPAN 33' 0"
WEIGHT 3,208 LBS
RANGE 385 MI
DIGITAL AUTOMATIC FLIGHT CONTROL SYSTEM
HELICOPTER DATA
MODEL EUROCOPTER EC135
ENGINE ALLISON MODEL 250
UNIT COSTS- $3-4.2K
MAKE AIRBUS INDUSTRIES
HOW DO YOU KNOW WHO I--?
OH, I'M SORRY! MEDICAL OFFICER RÖNTGEN, WAS IT?
WOULD THAT BE AFTER WILHELM CONRAD RÖNTGEN, THE DISCOVERER OF X-RAYS?
I HAD HEARD YOU WERE CLEVER!
BUT I'VE BEEN REMISS. PLEASE ALLOW ME TO INTRODUCE MYSELF.
MY NAME IS SAJAN, AND I AM HERE ON BEHALF OF *OMNI*.
OMNI
EXCEPTIONAL SOLUTIONS
EXCEPTIONAL CHALLENGE
SAN FRANCISCO, CA
I DON'T UNDERSTAND.
WHAT IS *OMNI?* SOME KIND OF *NGO?*

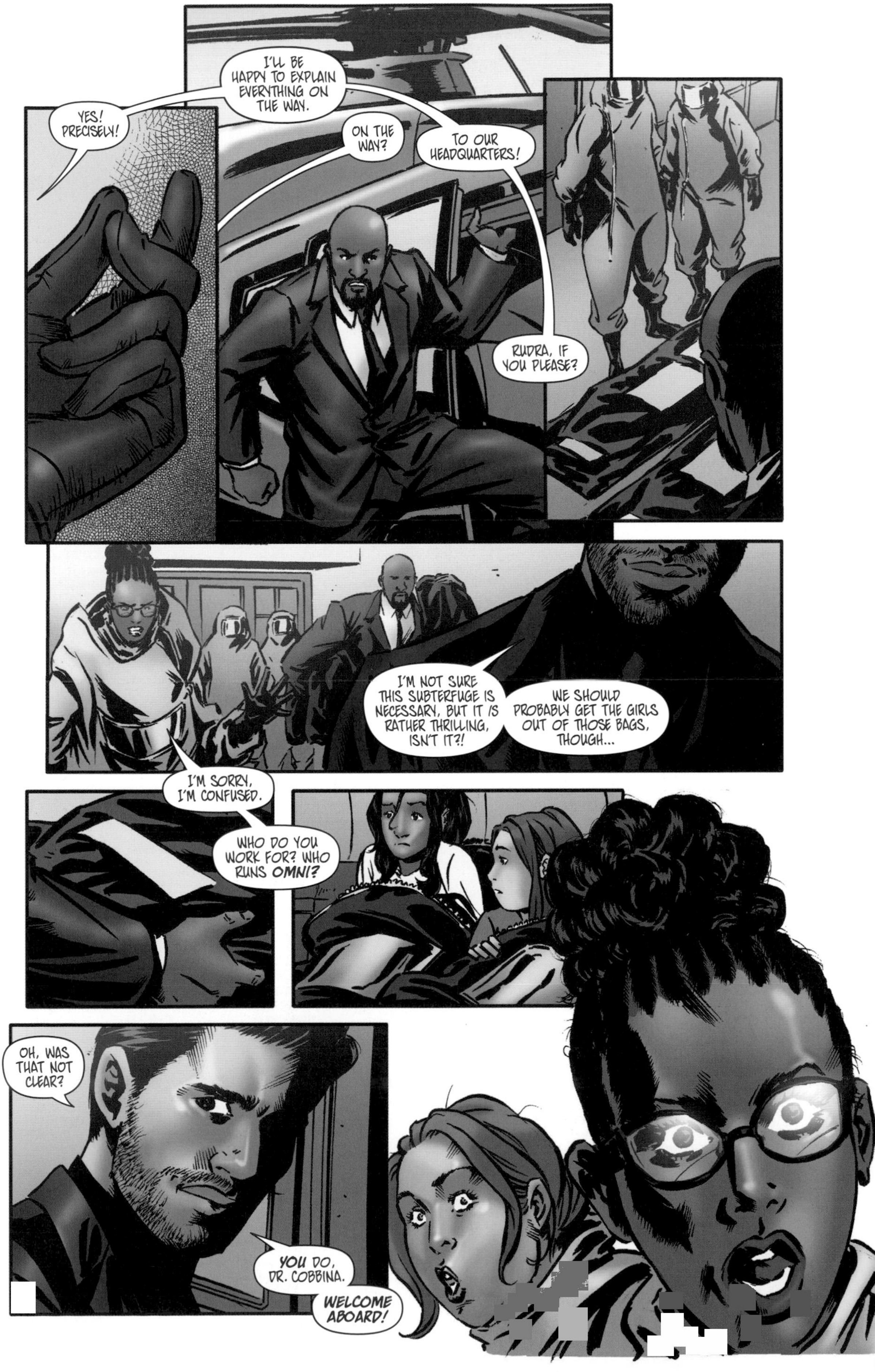
YES! PRECISELY!
I'LL BE HAPPY TO EXPLAIN EVERYTHING ON THE WAY.
ON THE WAY?
TO OUR HEADQUARTERS!
RUDRA, IF YOU PLEASE?
I'M NOT SURE THIS SUBTERFUGE IS NECESSARY, BUT IT IS RATHER THRILLING, ISN'T IT?!
WE SHOULD PROBABLY GET THE GIRLS OUT OF THOSE BAGS, THOUGH...
I'M SORRY, I'M CONFUSED.
WHO DO YOU WORK FOR? WHO RUNS OMNI?
OH, WAS THAT NOT CLEAR?
YOU DO, DR. COBBINA.
WELCOME ABOARD!

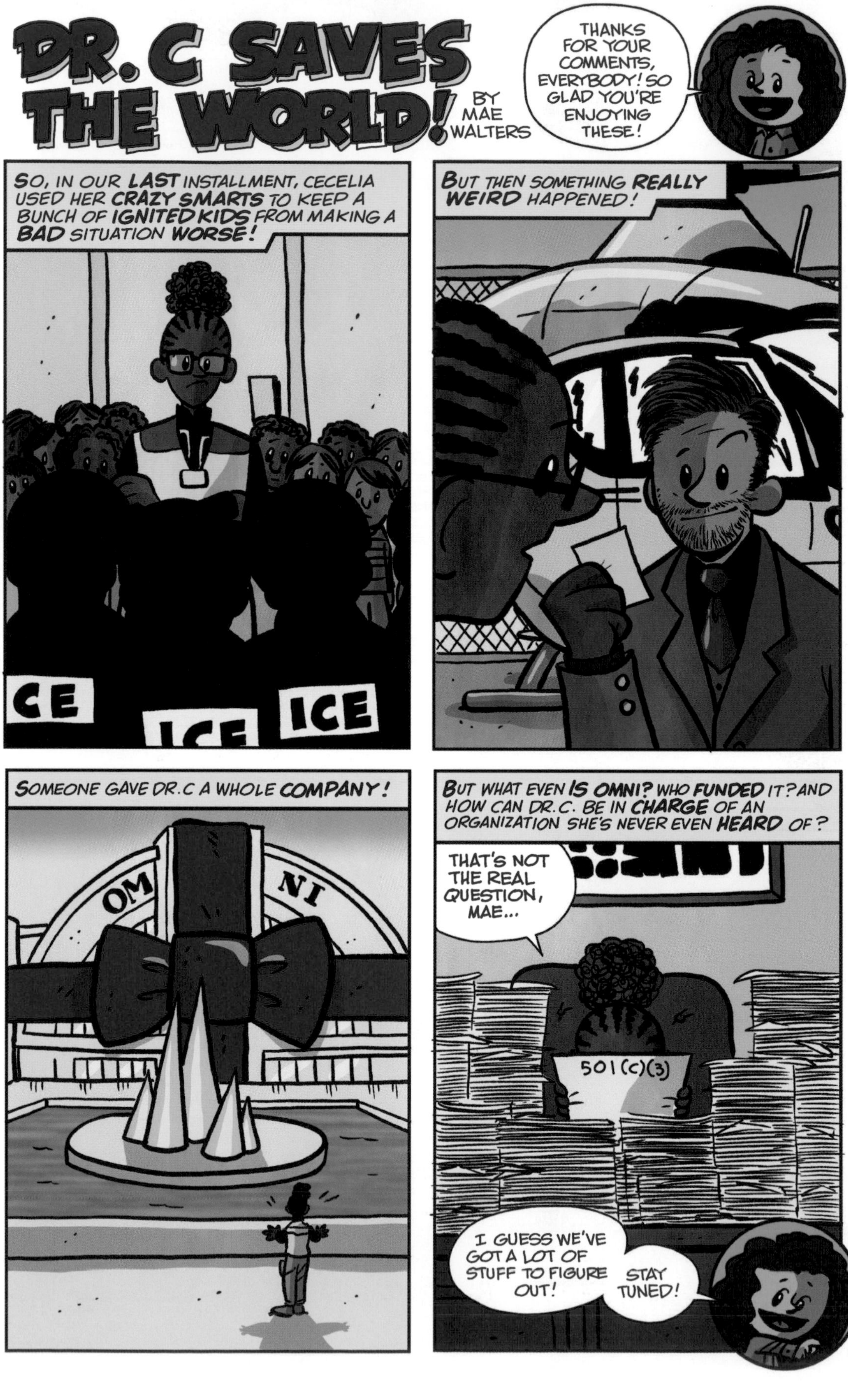
DR. C SAVES THE WORLD!
BY MAE WALTERS
THANKS FOR YOUR COMMENTS, EVERYBODY! SO GLAD YOU'RE ENJOYING THESE!
SO, IN OUR LAST INSTALLMENT, CECELIA USED HER CRAZY SMARTS TO KEEP A BUNCH OF IGNITED KIDS FROM MAKING A BAD SITUATION WORSE!
CE
ICE
BUT THEN SOMETHING REALLY WEIRD HAPPENED!
SOMEONE GAVE DR. C A WHOLE COMPANY!
OM
NI
BUT WHAT EVEN IS OMNI? WHO FUNDED IT? AND HOW CAN DR. C. BE IN CHARGE OF AN ORGANIZATION SHE'S NEVER EVEN HEARD OF?
THAT'S NOT THE REAL QUESTION, MAE...
501(C)(3)
I GUESS WE'VE GOT A LOT OF STUFF TO FIGURE OUT!
STAY TUNED!

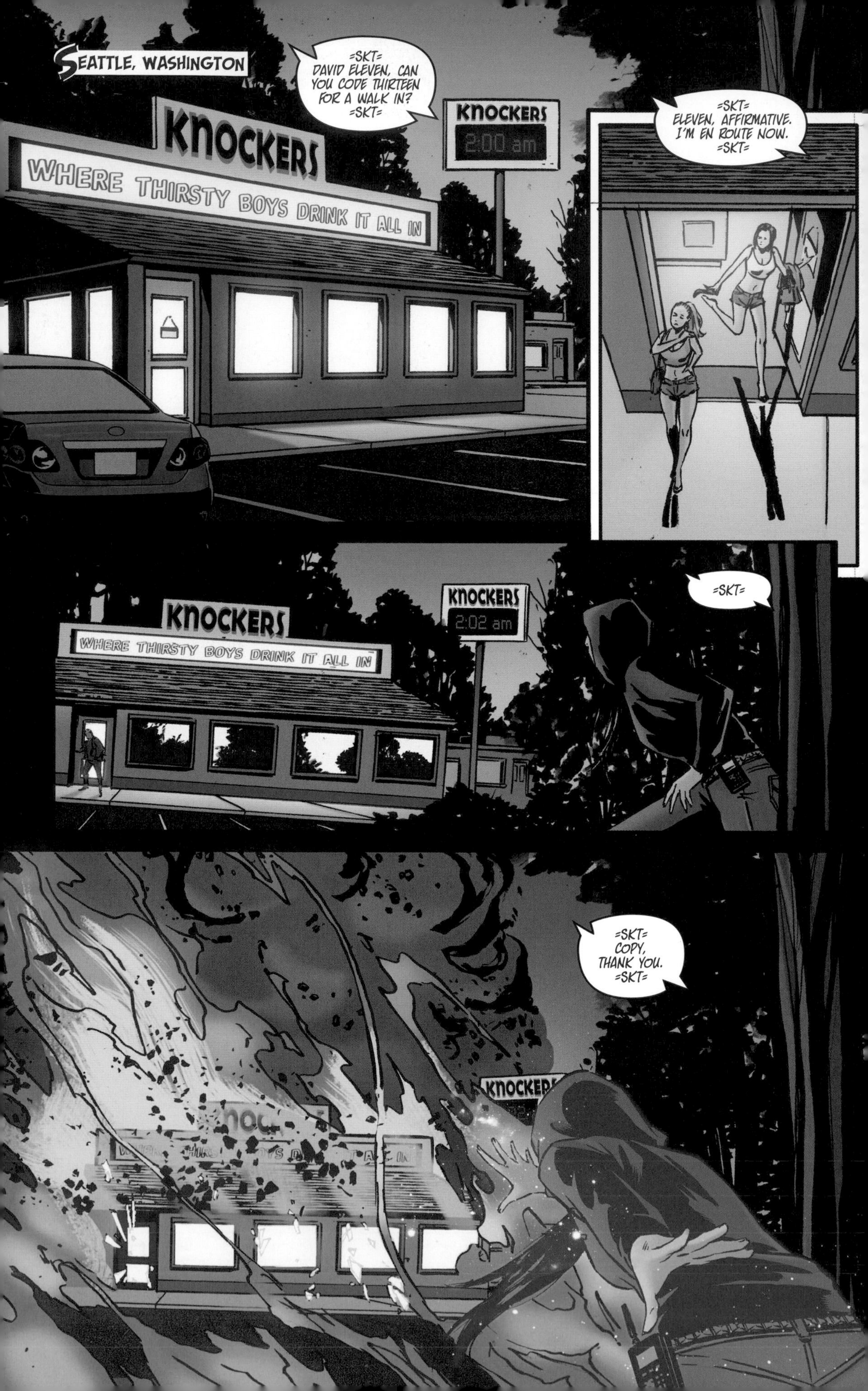
SEATTLE, WASHINGTON
=SKT= DAVID ELEVEN, CAN YOU CODE THIRTEEN FOR A WALK IN? =SKT=
KNOCKERS
WHERE THIRSTY BOYS DRINK IT ALL IN
KNOCKERS
2:00 am
=SKT= ELEVEN, AFFIRMATIVE. I'M EN ROUTE NOW. =SKT=
KNOCKERS
WHERE THIRSTY BOYS DRINK IT ALL IN
KNOCKERS
2:02 am
=SKT=
=SKT= COPY, THANK YOU. =SKT=
KNOCKERS

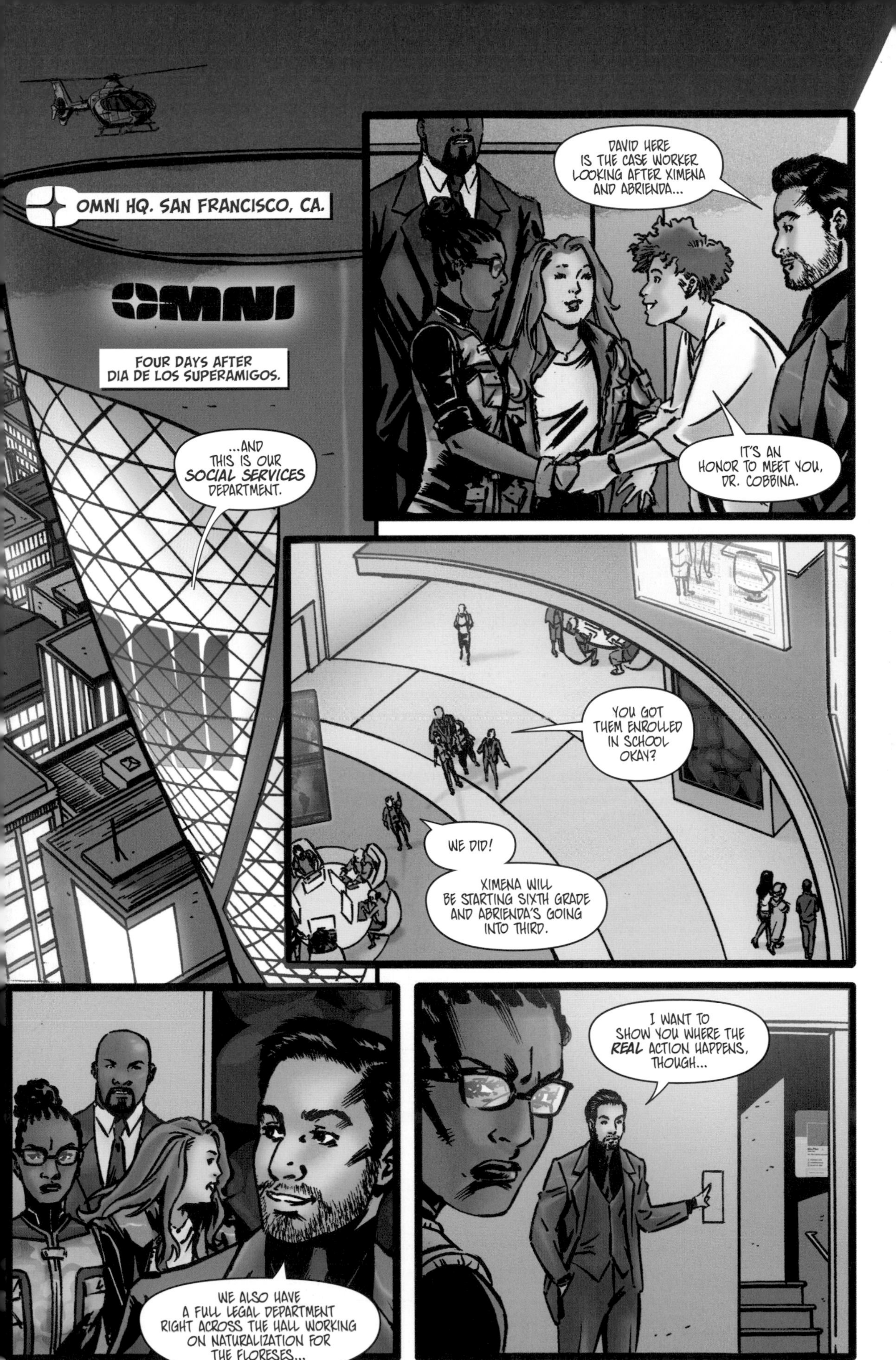
OMNI HQ. SAN FRANCISCO, CA.
OMNI
FOUR DAYS AFTER DIA DE LOS SUPERAMIGOS.
...AND THIS IS OUR *SOCIAL SERVICES* DEPARTMENT.
DAVID HERE IS THE CASE WORKER LOOKING AFTER XIMENA AND ABRIENDA...
IT'S AN HONOR TO MEET YOU, DR. COBBINA.
YOU GOT THEM ENROLLED IN SCHOOL OKAY?
WE DID!
XIMENA WILL BE STARTING SIXTH GRADE AND ABRIENDA'S GOING INTO THIRD.
WE ALSO HAVE A FULL LEGAL DEPARTMENT RIGHT ACROSS THE HALL WORKING ON NATURALIZATION FOR THE FLORESES...
I WANT TO SHOW YOU WHERE THE ***REAL*** ACTION HAPPENS, THOUGH...

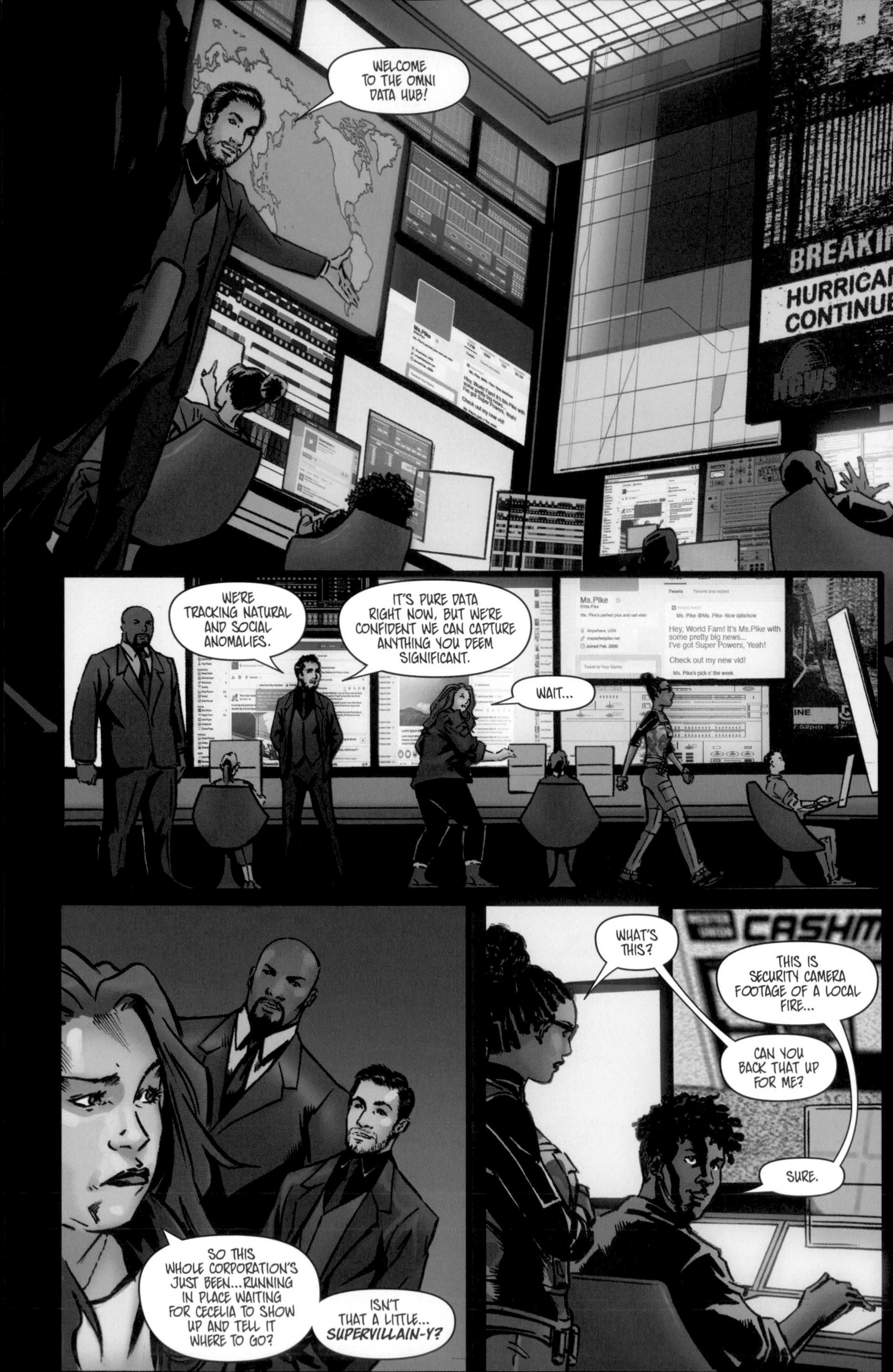

WELCOME TO THE OMNI DATA HUB!
BREAKING
HURRICAN
CONTINUE
NEWS
Ms.Pike
Hey, World Fam! It's Ms.Pike with some pretty big news... I've got Super Powers, Yeah!
Check out my new vid!
WE'RE TRACKING NATURAL AND SOCIAL ANOMALIES.
IT'S PURE DATA RIGHT NOW, BUT WE'RE CONFIDENT WE CAN CAPTURE ANYTHING YOU DEEM SIGNIFICANT.
WAIT...
Ms.Pike
@Ms.Pike
Ms. Pike's perfect pics and rad vids!
Anywhere, USA
Joined Feb. 2000
Tweets
Tweets and replies
Ms. Pike @Ms. Pike- Now date/now
Hey, World Fam! It's Ms.Pike with some pretty big news... I've got Super Powers, Yeah!
Check out my new vid!
Ms. Pike's pick o' the week.
SO THIS WHOLE CORPORATION'S JUST BEEN...RUNNING IN PLACE WAITING FOR CECELIA TO SHOW UP AND TELL IT WHERE TO GO?
ISN'T THAT A LITTLE... *SUPERVILLAIN-Y?*
CASHM
WHAT'S THIS?
THIS IS SECURITY CAMERA FOOTAGE OF A LOCAL FIRE...
CAN YOU BACK THAT UP FOR ME?
SURE.

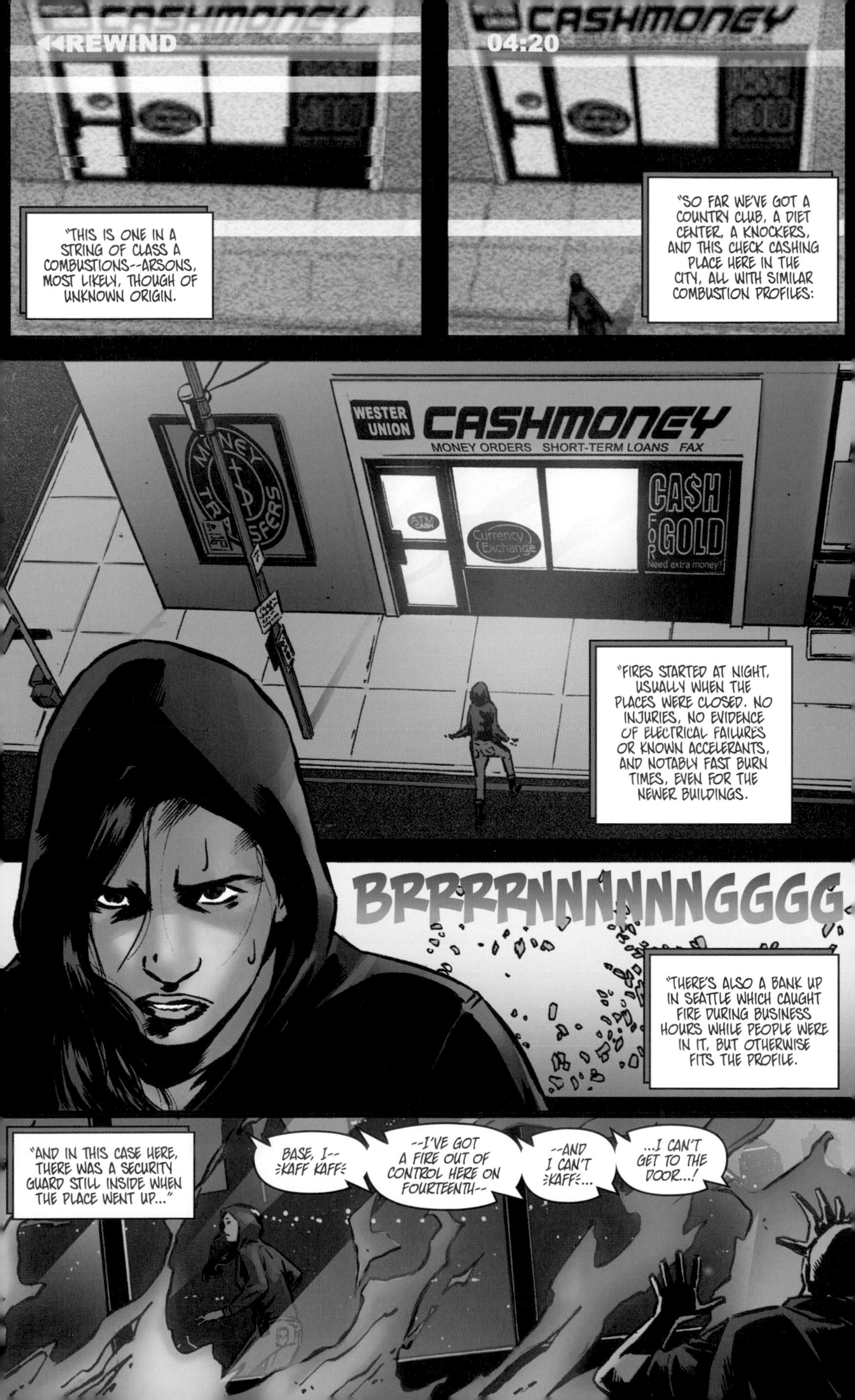
CASHMONEY
◀◀REWIND
"THIS IS ONE IN A STRING OF CLASS A COMBUSTIONS--ARSONS, MOST LIKELY, THOUGH OF UNKNOWN ORIGIN.
CASHMONEY
04:20
"SO FAR WE'VE GOT A COUNTRY CLUB, A DIET CENTER, A KNOCKERS, AND THIS CHECK CASHING PLACE HERE IN THE CITY, ALL WITH SIMILAR COMBUSTION PROFILES:
WESTER UNION
CASHMONEY
MONEY ORDERS SHORT-TERM LOANS FAX
MONEY TRANSFERS
ATM CASH
Currency Exchange
CA$H FOR GOLD
Need extra money?
"FIRES STARTED AT NIGHT, USUALLY WHEN THE PLACES WERE CLOSED. NO INJURIES, NO EVIDENCE OF ELECTRICAL FAILURES OR KNOWN ACCELERANTS, AND NOTABLY FAST BURN TIMES, EVEN FOR THE NEWER BUILDINGS.
BRRRRNNNNNNGGGG
"THERE'S ALSO A BANK UP IN SEATTLE WHICH CAUGHT FIRE DURING BUSINESS HOURS WHILE PEOPLE WERE IN IT, BUT OTHERWISE FITS THE PROFILE.
"AND IN THIS CASE HERE, THERE WAS A SECURITY GUARD STILL INSIDE WHEN THE PLACE WENT UP..."
BASE, I-- KAFF KAFF
--I'VE GOT A FIRE OUT OF CONTROL HERE ON FOURTEENTH--
--AND I CAN'T KAFF...
...I CAN'T GET TO THE DOOR...!

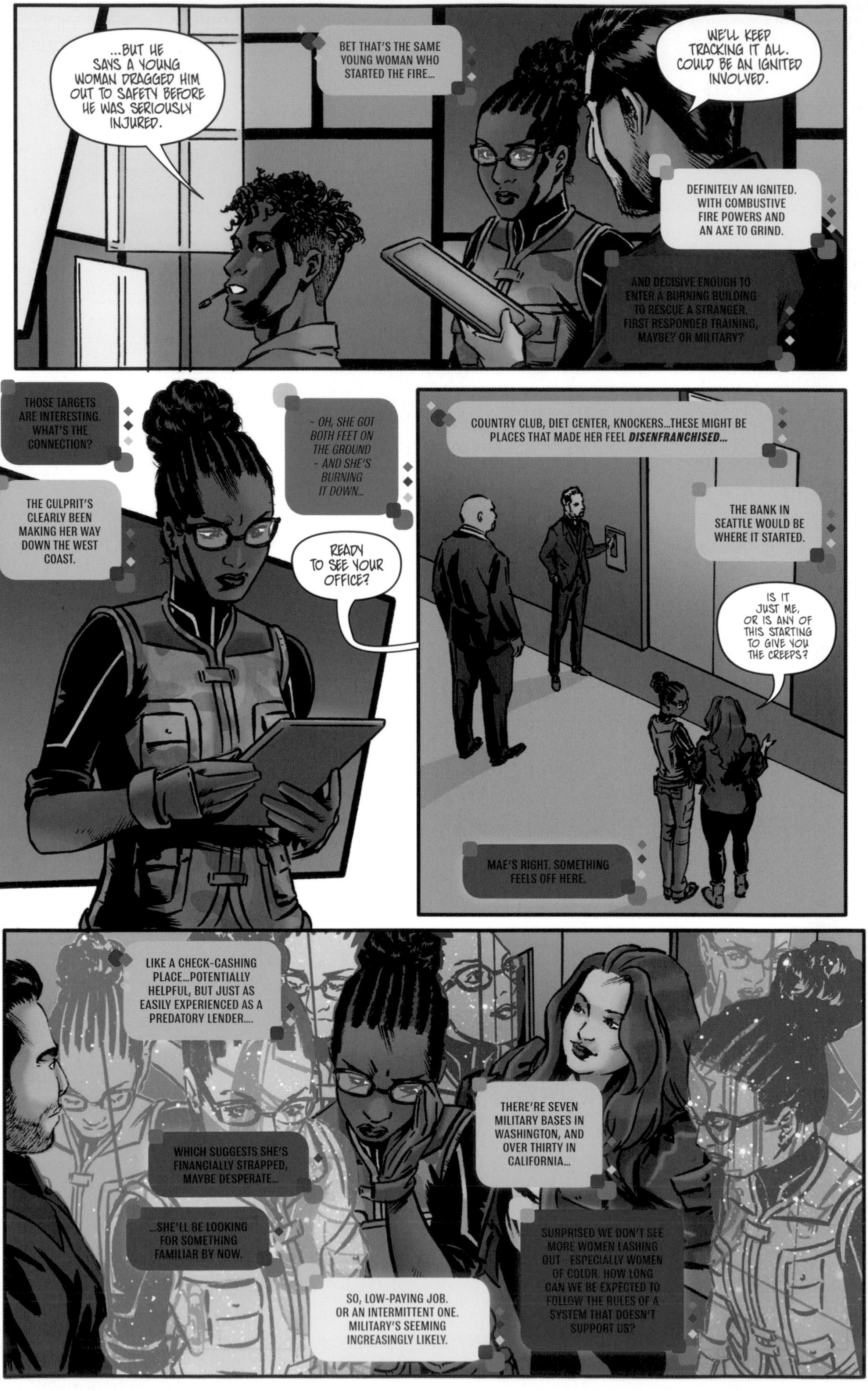
...BUT HE SAYS A YOUNG WOMAN DRAGGED HIM OUT TO SAFETY BEFORE HE WAS SERIOUSLY INJURED.
BET THAT'S THE SAME YOUNG WOMAN WHO STARTED THE FIRE...
WE'LL KEEP TRACKING IT ALL. COULD BE AN IGNITED INVOLVED.
DEFINITELY AN IGNITED. WITH COMBUSTIVE FIRE POWERS AND AN AXE TO GRIND.
AND DECISIVE ENOUGH TO ENTER A BURNING BUILDING TO RESCUE A STRANGER. FIRST RESPONDER TRAINING, MAYBE? OR MILITARY?
THOSE TARGETS ARE INTERESTING. WHAT'S THE CONNECTION?
THE CULPRIT'S CLEARLY BEEN MAKING HER WAY DOWN THE WEST COAST.
~ OH, SHE GOT BOTH FEET ON THE GROUND ~ AND SHE'S BURNING IT DOWN...
READY TO SEE YOUR OFFICE?
COUNTRY CLUB, DIET CENTER, KNOCKERS...THESE MIGHT BE PLACES THAT MADE HER FEEL *DISENFRANCHISED...*
THE BANK IN SEATTLE WOULD BE WHERE IT STARTED.
IS IT JUST ME, OR IS ANY OF THIS STARTING TO GIVE YOU THE CREEPS?
MAE'S RIGHT. SOMETHING FEELS OFF HERE.
LIKE A CHECK-CASHING PLACE...POTENTIALLY HELPFUL, BUT JUST AS EASILY EXPERIENCED AS A PREDATORY LENDER....
WHICH SUGGESTS SHE'S FINANCIALLY STRAPPED, MAYBE DESPERATE...
...SHE'LL BE LOOKING FOR SOMETHING FAMILIAR BY NOW.
SO, LOW-PAYING JOB. OR AN INTERMITTENT ONE. MILITARY'S SEEMING INCREASINGLY LIKELY.
THERE'RE SEVEN MILITARY BASES IN WASHINGTON, AND OVER THIRTY IN CALIFORNIA...
SURPRISED WE DON'T SEE MORE WOMEN LASHING OUT - ESPECIALLY WOMEN OF COLOR. HOW LONG CAN WE BE EXPECTED TO FOLLOW THE RULES OF A SYSTEM THAT DOESN'T SUPPORT US?

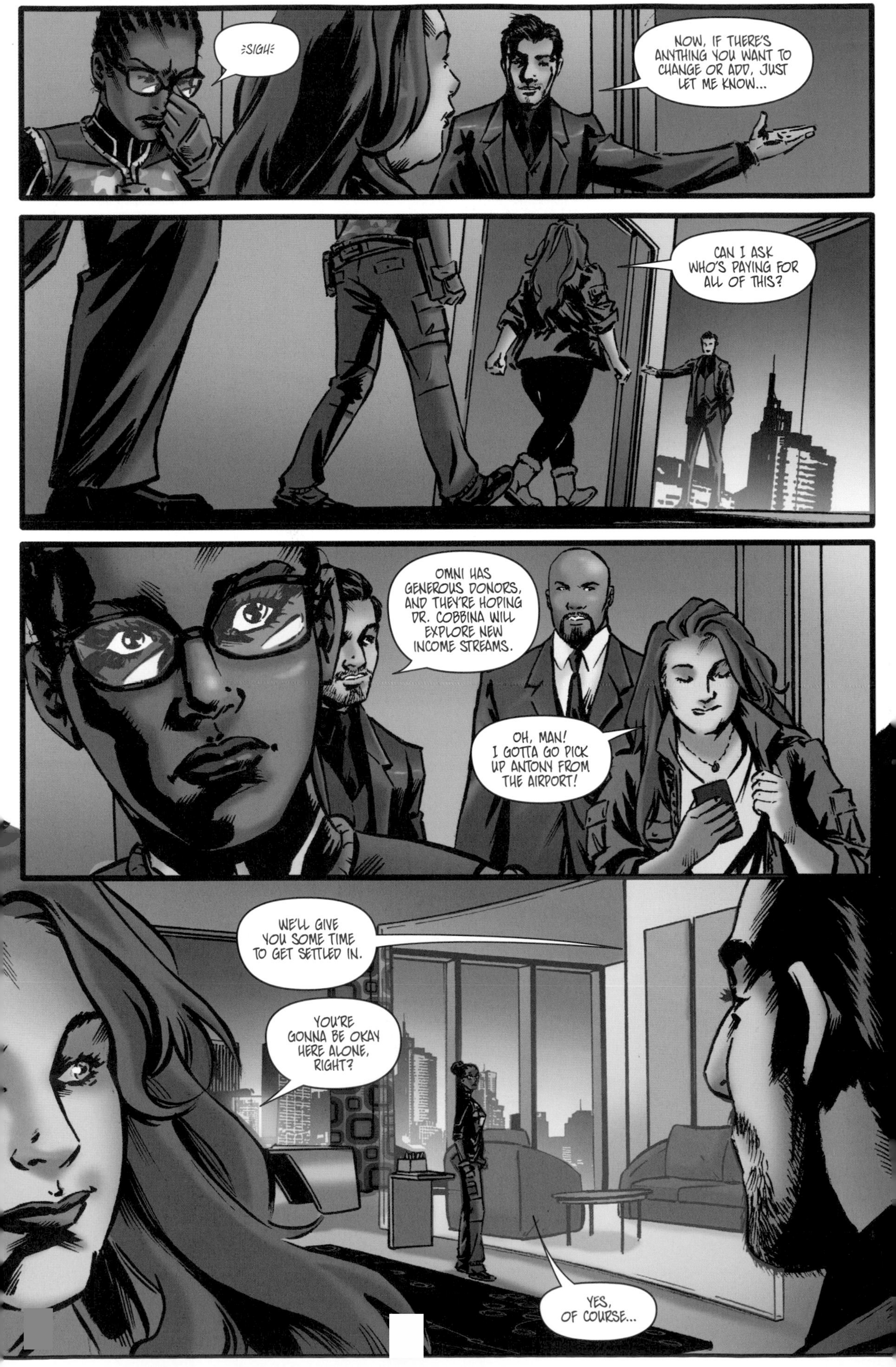
NOW, IF THERE'S ANYTHING YOU WANT TO CHANGE OR ADD, JUST LET ME KNOW...
≈SIGH≈
CAN I ASK WHO'S PAYING FOR ALL OF THIS?
OMNI HAS GENEROUS DONORS, AND THEY'RE HOPING DR. COBBINA WILL EXPLORE NEW INCOME STREAMS.
OH, MAN! I GOTTA GO PICK UP ANTONY FROM THE AIRPORT!
WE'LL GIVE YOU SOME TIME TO GET SETTLED IN.
YOU'RE GONNA BE OKAY HERE ALONE, RIGHT?
YES, OF COURSE...

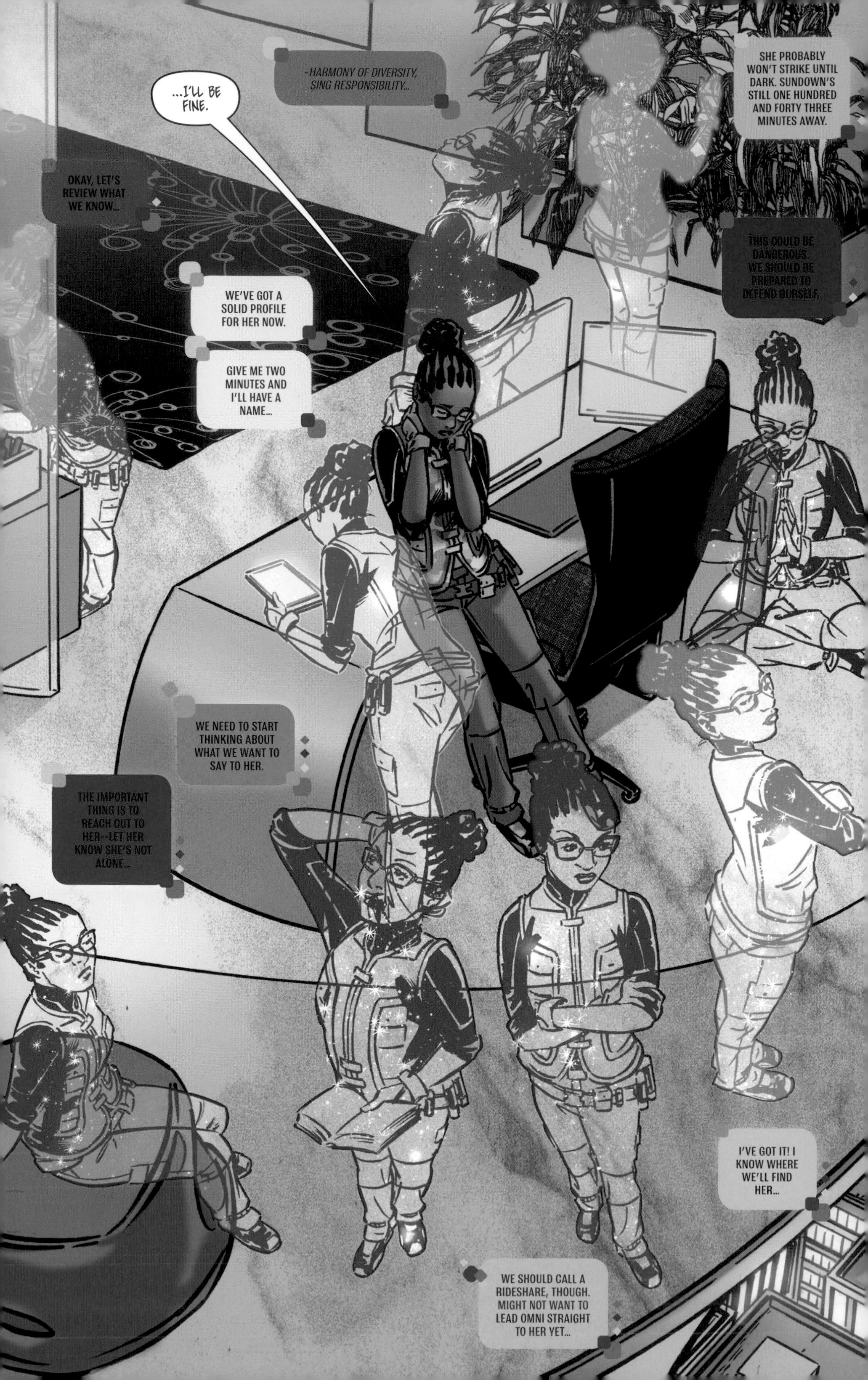
…I'LL BE FINE.
~HARMONY OF DIVERSITY, SING RESPONSIBILITY…
SHE PROBABLY WON'T STRIKE UNTIL DARK. SUNDOWN'S STILL ONE HUNDRED AND FORTY THREE MINUTES AWAY.
OKAY, LET'S REVIEW WHAT WE KNOW…
THIS COULD BE DANGEROUS. WE SHOULD BE PREPARED TO DEFEND OURSELF.
WE'VE GOT A SOLID PROFILE FOR HER NOW.
GIVE ME TWO MINUTES AND I'LL HAVE A NAME…
WE NEED TO START THINKING ABOUT WHAT WE WANT TO SAY TO HER.
THE IMPORTANT THING IS TO REACH OUT TO HER--LET HER KNOW SHE'S NOT ALONE…
I'VE GOT IT! I KNOW WHERE WE'LL FIND HER…
WE SHOULD CALL A RIDESHARE, THOUGH. MIGHT NOT WANT TO LEAD OMNI STRAIGHT TO HER YET…

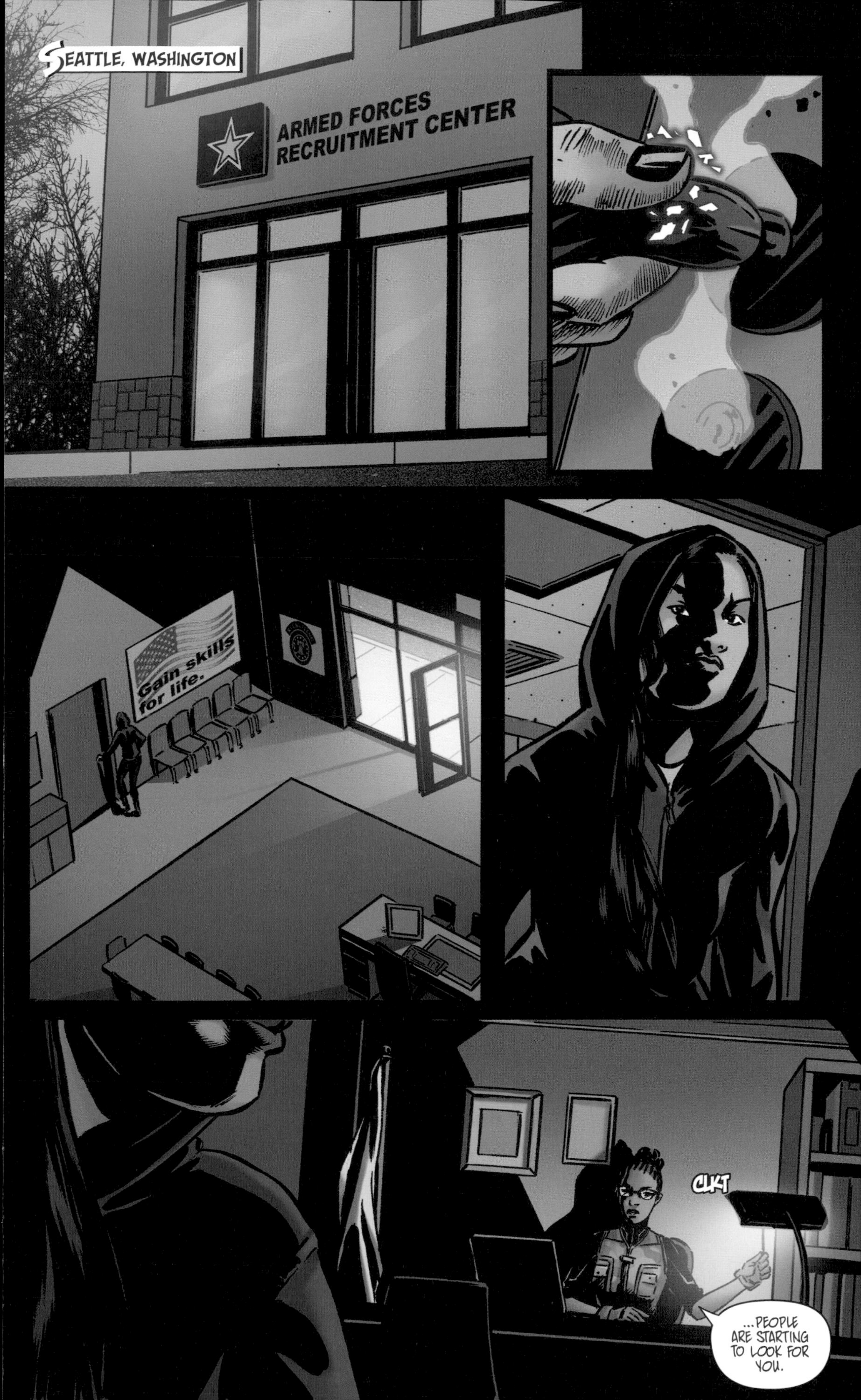
SEATTLE, WASHINGTON
ARMED FORCES
RECRUITMENT CENTER
Gain skills
for life.
CLKT
...PEOPLE
ARE STARTING
TO LOOK FOR
YOU.

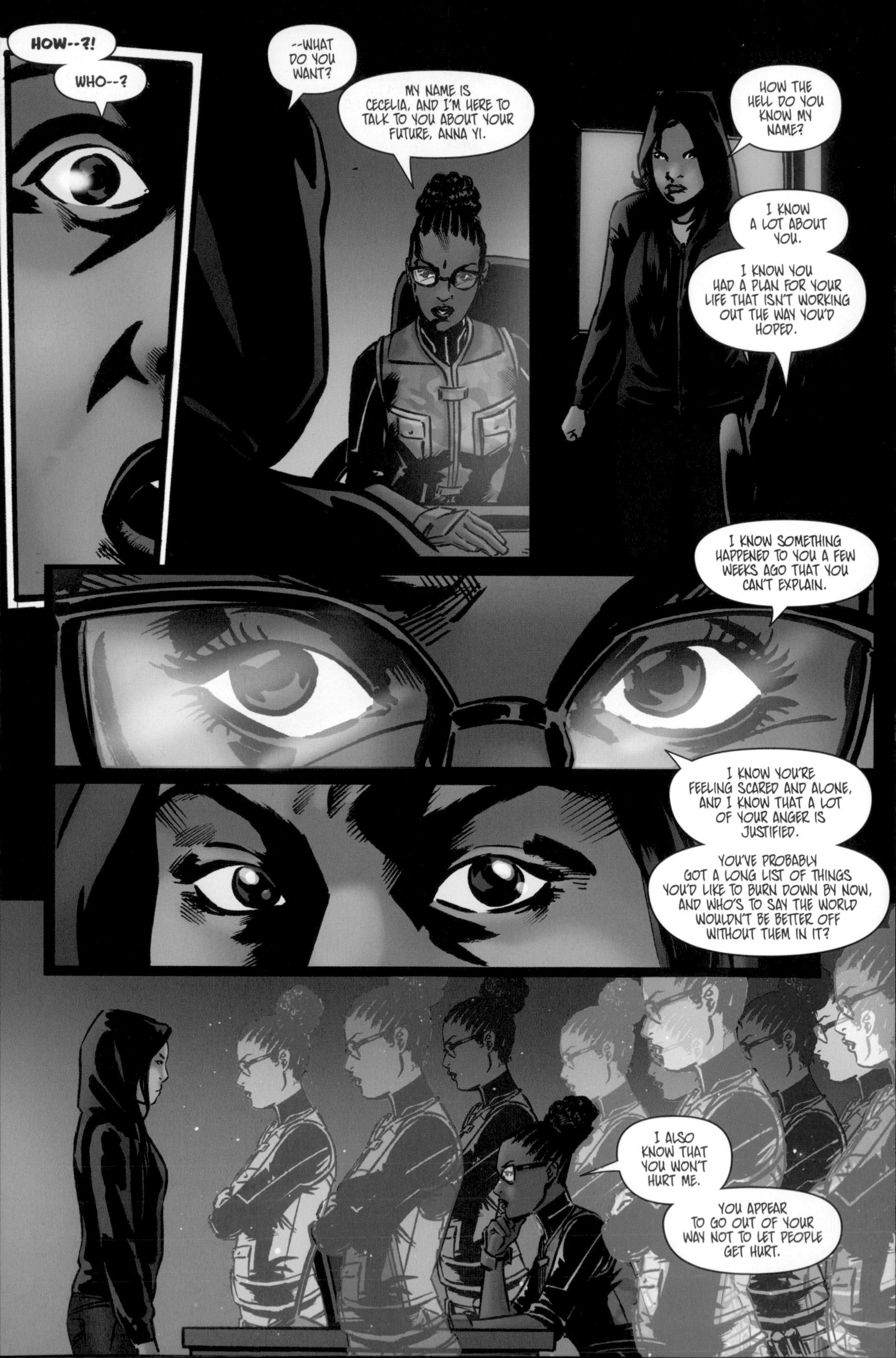
HOW--?!
WHO--?
--WHAT DO YOU WANT?
MY NAME IS CECELIA, AND I'M HERE TO TALK TO YOU ABOUT YOUR FUTURE, ANNA YI.
HOW THE HELL DO YOU KNOW MY NAME?
I KNOW A LOT ABOUT YOU.
I KNOW YOU HAD A PLAN FOR YOUR LIFE THAT ISN'T WORKING OUT THE WAY YOU'D HOPED.
I KNOW SOMETHING HAPPENED TO YOU A FEW WEEKS AGO THAT YOU CAN'T EXPLAIN.
I KNOW YOU'RE FEELING SCARED AND ALONE, AND I KNOW THAT A LOT OF YOUR ANGER IS JUSTIFIED.
YOU'VE PROBABLY GOT A LONG LIST OF THINGS YOU'D LIKE TO BURN DOWN BY NOW, AND WHO'S TO SAY THE WORLD WOULDN'T BE BETTER OFF WITHOUT THEM IN IT?
I ALSO KNOW THAT YOU WON'T HURT ME.
YOU APPEAR TO GO OUT OF YOUR WAY NOT TO LET PEOPLE GET HURT.

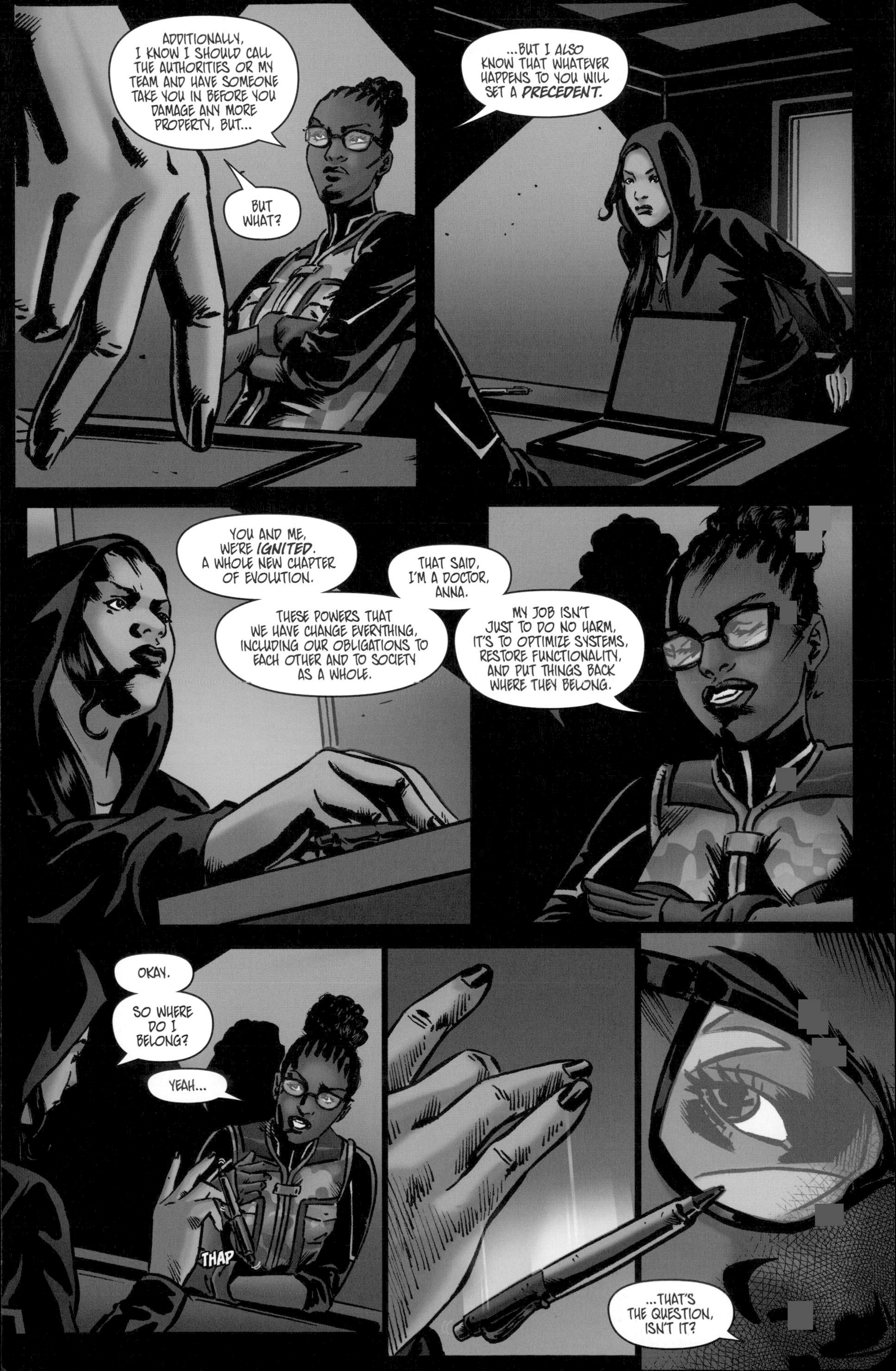
ADDITIONALLY, I KNOW I SHOULD CALL THE AUTHORITIES OR MY TEAM AND HAVE SOMEONE TAKE YOU IN BEFORE YOU DAMAGE ANY MORE PROPERTY, BUT...
BUT WHAT?
...BUT I ALSO KNOW THAT WHATEVER HAPPENS TO YOU WILL SET A PRECEDENT.
YOU AND ME, WE'RE IGNITED. A WHOLE NEW CHAPTER OF EVOLUTION.
THESE POWERS THAT WE HAVE CHANGE EVERYTHING, INCLUDING OUR OBLIGATIONS TO EACH OTHER AND TO SOCIETY AS A WHOLE.
THAT SAID, I'M A DOCTOR, ANNA.
MY JOB ISN'T JUST TO DO NO HARM, IT'S TO OPTIMIZE SYSTEMS, RESTORE FUNCTIONALITY, AND PUT THINGS BACK WHERE THEY BELONG.
OKAY.
SO WHERE DO I BELONG?
YEAH...
THAP
...THAT'S THE QUESTION, ISN'T IT?

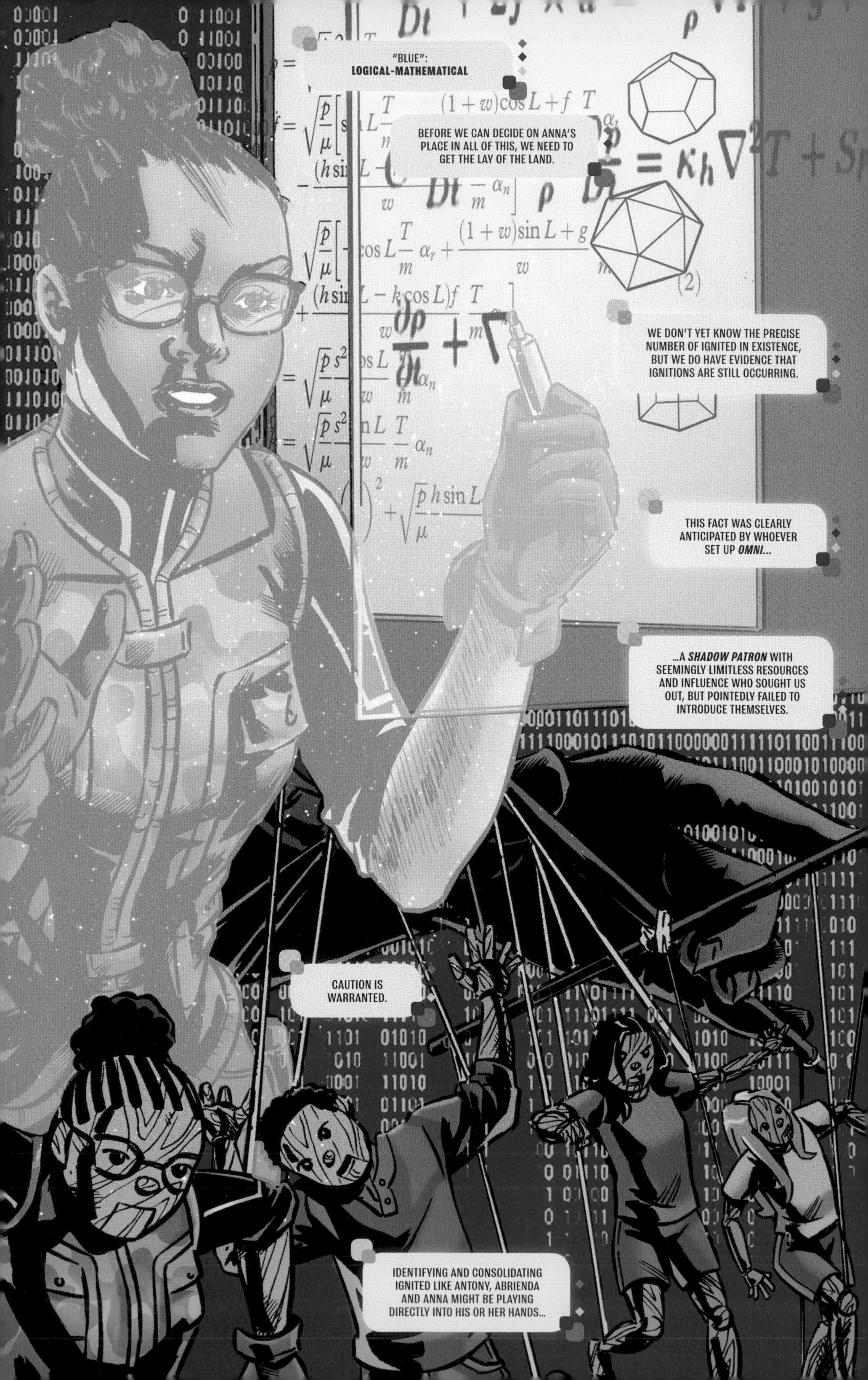
"BLUE":
LOGICAL-MATHEMATICAL
BEFORE WE CAN DECIDE ON ANNA'S PLACE IN ALL OF THIS, WE NEED TO GET THE LAY OF THE LAND.
WE DON'T YET KNOW THE PRECISE NUMBER OF IGNITED IN EXISTENCE, BUT WE DO HAVE EVIDENCE THAT IGNITIONS ARE STILL OCCURRING.
THIS FACT WAS CLEARLY ANTICIPATED BY WHOEVER SET UP *OMNI*...
...A *SHADOW PATRON* WITH SEEMINGLY LIMITLESS RESOURCES AND INFLUENCE WHO SOUGHT US OUT, BUT POINTEDLY FAILED TO INTRODUCE THEMSELVES.
CAUTION IS WARRANTED.
IDENTIFYING AND CONSOLIDATING IGNITED LIKE ANTONY, ABRIENDA AND ANNA MIGHT BE PLAYING DIRECTLY INTO HIS OR HER HANDS...

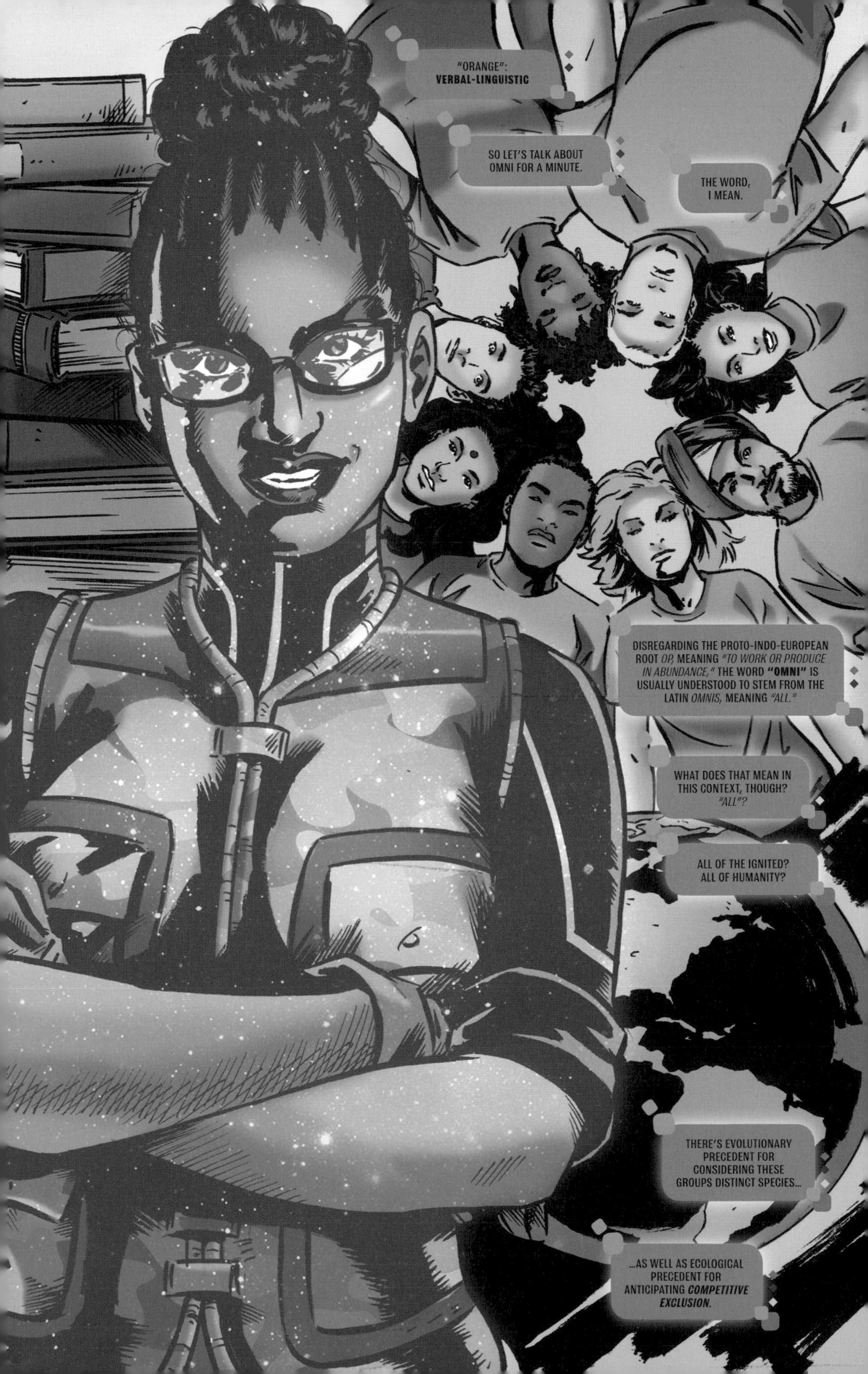

"ORANGE": **VERBAL-LINGUISTIC**
SO LET'S TALK ABOUT OMNI FOR A MINUTE.
THE WORD, I MEAN.
DISREGARDING THE PROTO-INDO-EUROPEAN ROOT *OP,* MEANING *"TO WORK OR PRODUCE IN ABUNDANCE,"* THE WORD **"OMNI"** IS USUALLY UNDERSTOOD TO STEM FROM THE LATIN *OMNIS,* MEANING *"ALL."*
WHAT DOES THAT MEAN IN THIS CONTEXT, THOUGH? *"ALL"*?
ALL OF THE IGNITED? ALL OF HUMANITY?
THERE'S EVOLUTIONARY PRECEDENT FOR CONSIDERING THESE GROUPS DISTINCT SPECIES...
...AS WELL AS ECOLOGICAL PRECEDENT FOR ANTICIPATING ***COMPETITIVE EXCLUSION.***

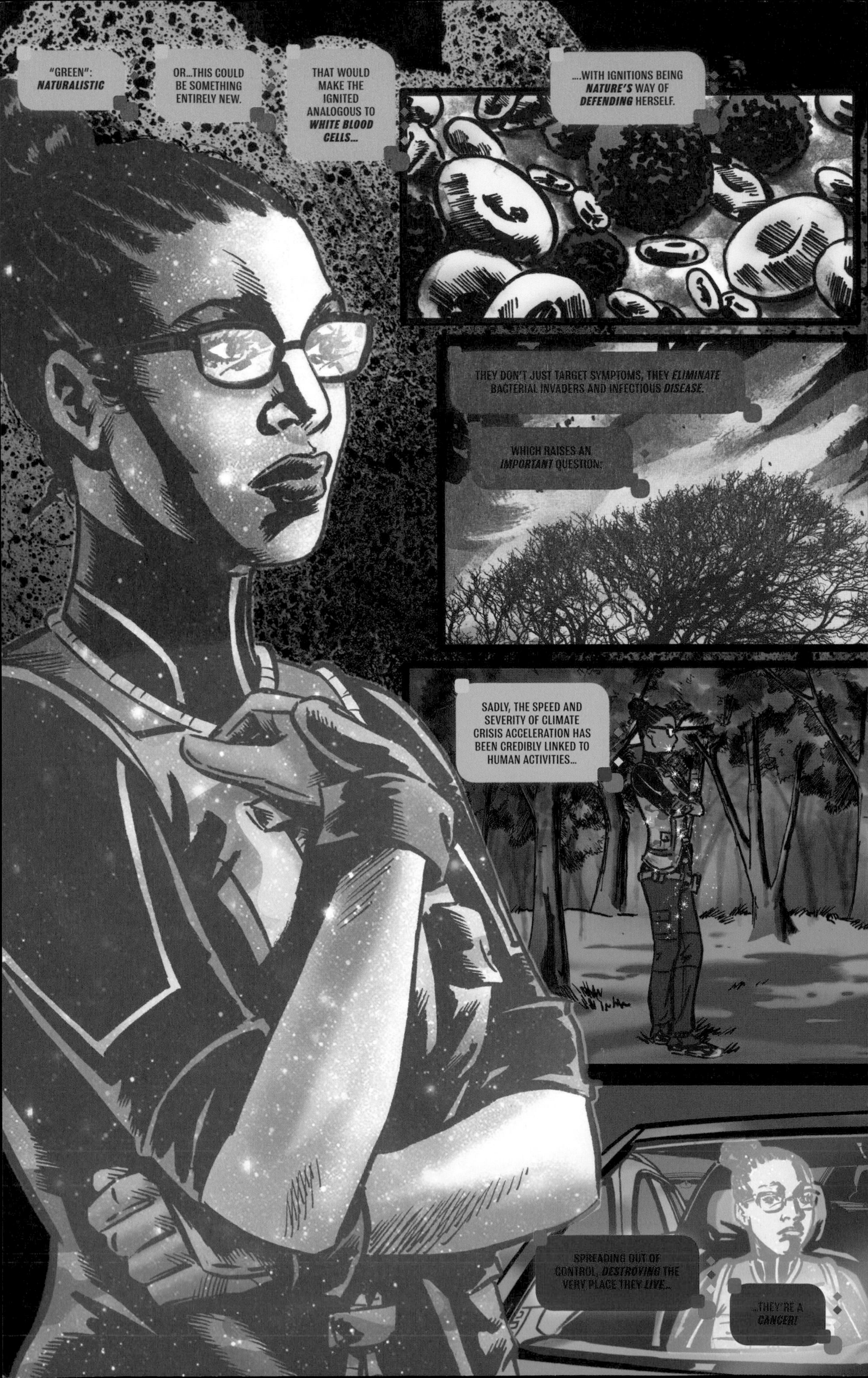
"GREEN": NATURALISTIC
OR...THIS COULD BE SOMETHING ENTIRELY NEW.
THAT WOULD MAKE THE IGNITED ANALOGOUS TO WHITE BLOOD CELLS...
...WITH IGNITIONS BEING NATURE'S WAY OF DEFENDING HERSELF.
THEY DON'T JUST TARGET SYMPTOMS, THEY ELIMINATE BACTERIAL INVADERS AND INFECTIOUS DISEASE.
WHICH RAISES AN IMPORTANT QUESTION:
SADLY, THE SPEED AND SEVERITY OF CLIMATE CRISIS ACCELERATION HAS BEEN CREDIBLY LINKED TO HUMAN ACTIVITIES...
SPREADING OUT OF CONTROL, DESTROYING THE VERY PLACE THEY LIVE...
...THEY'RE A CANCER!

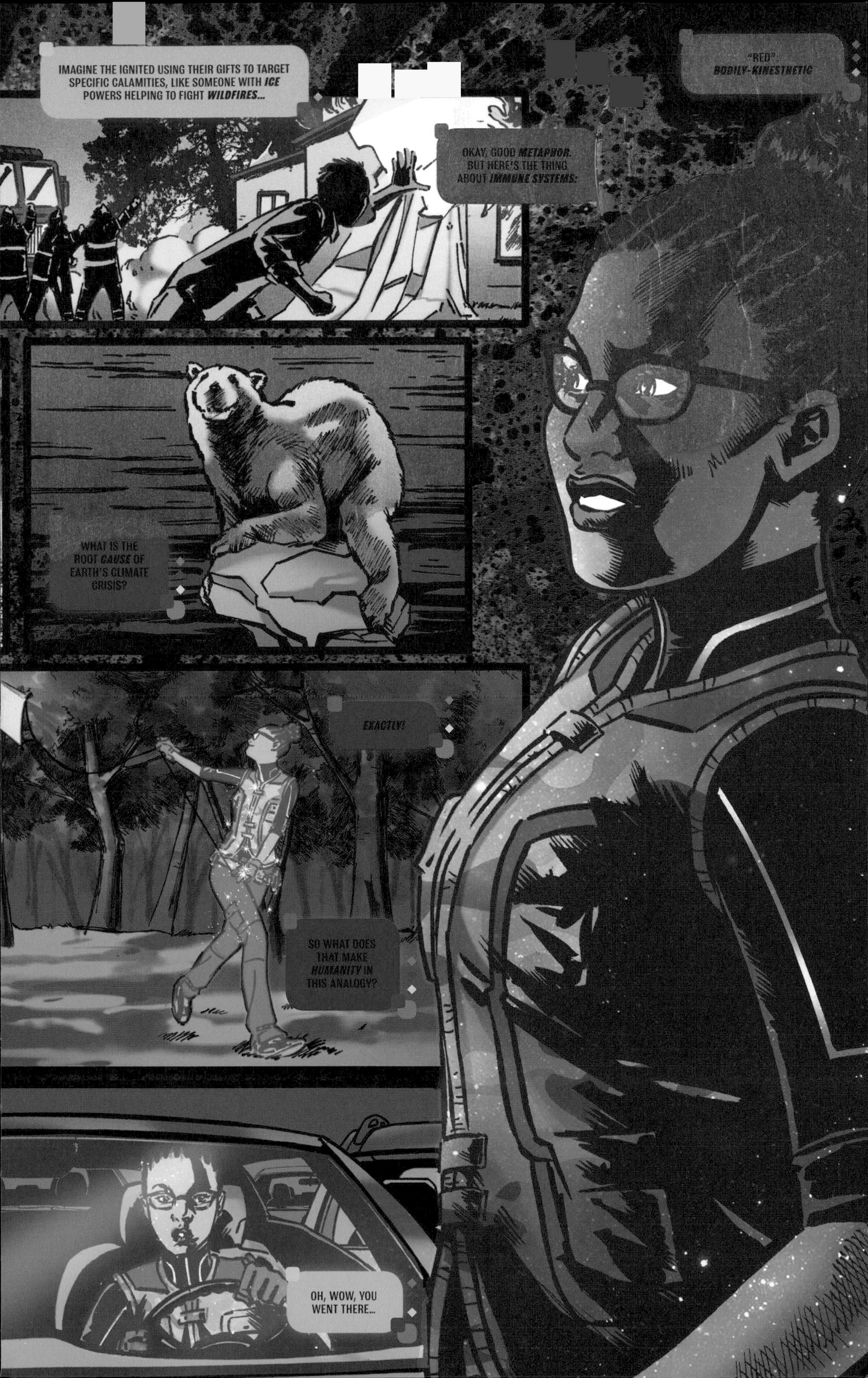
IMAGINE THE IGNITED USING THEIR GIFTS TO TARGET SPECIFIC CALAMITIES, LIKE SOMEONE WITH *ICE* POWERS HELPING TO FIGHT *WILDFIRES...*
"RED"
BODILY-KINESTHETIC
OKAY, GOOD *METAPHOR.* BUT HERE'S THE THING ABOUT *IMMUNE SYSTEMS:*
WHAT IS THE ROOT *CAUSE* OF EARTH'S CLIMATE CRISIS?
EXACTLY!
SO WHAT DOES THAT MAKE *HUMANITY* IN THIS ANALOGY?
OH, WOW, YOU WENT THERE...

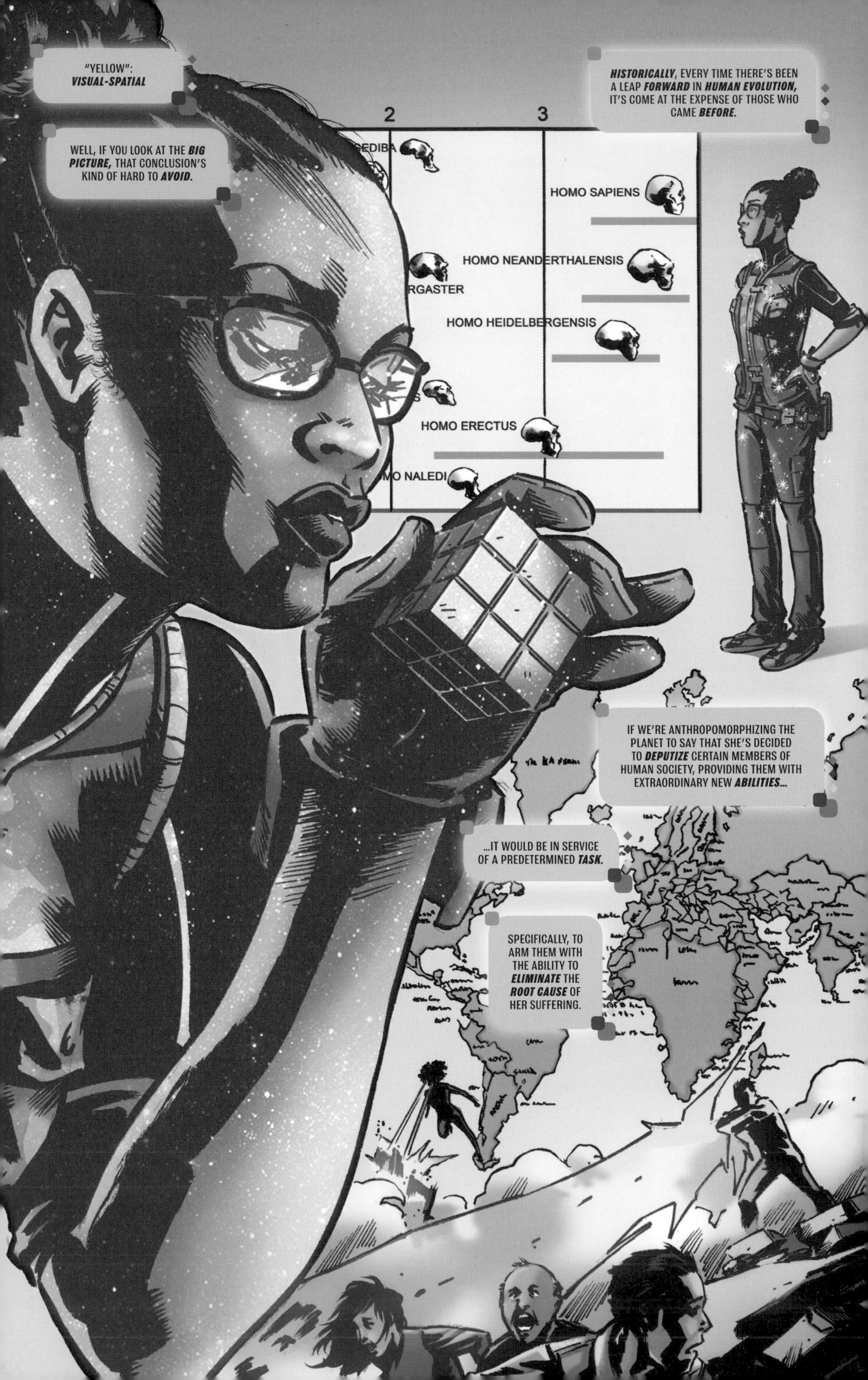

"YELLOW": VISUAL-SPATIAL
WELL, IF YOU LOOK AT THE BIG PICTURE, THAT CONCLUSION'S KIND OF HARD TO AVOID.
HISTORICALLY, EVERY TIME THERE'S BEEN A LEAP FORWARD IN HUMAN EVOLUTION, IT'S COME AT THE EXPENSE OF THOSE WHO CAME BEFORE.
2
3
SEDIBA
HOMO SAPIENS
HOMO NEANDERTHALENSIS
RGASTER
HOMO HEIDELBERGENSIS
HOMO ERECTUS
MO NALEDI
IF WE'RE ANTHROPOMORPHIZING THE PLANET TO SAY THAT SHE'S DECIDED TO DEPUTIZE CERTAIN MEMBERS OF HUMAN SOCIETY, PROVIDING THEM WITH EXTRAORDINARY NEW ABILITIES...
...IT WOULD BE IN SERVICE OF A PREDETERMINED TASK.
SPECIFICALLY, TO ARM THEM WITH THE ABILITY TO ELIMINATE THE ROOT CAUSE OF HER SUFFERING.

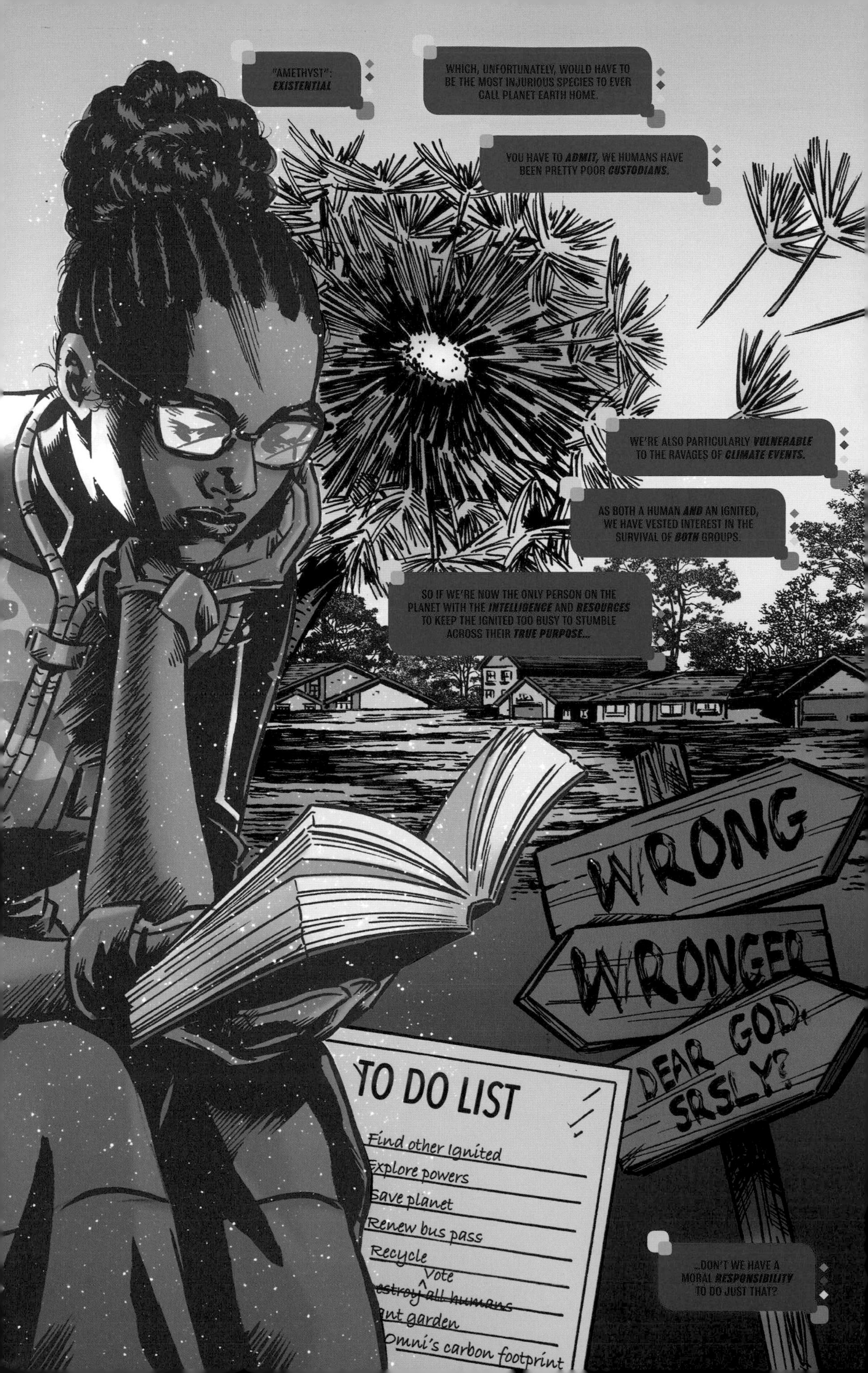
"AMETHYST": EXISTENTIAL
WHICH, UNFORTUNATELY, WOULD HAVE TO BE THE MOST INJURIOUS SPECIES TO EVER CALL PLANET EARTH HOME.
YOU HAVE TO ADMIT, WE HUMANS HAVE BEEN PRETTY POOR CUSTODIANS.
WE'RE ALSO PARTICULARLY VULNERABLE TO THE RAVAGES OF CLIMATE EVENTS.
AS BOTH A HUMAN AND AN IGNITED, WE HAVE VESTED INTEREST IN THE SURVIVAL OF BOTH GROUPS.
SO IF WE'RE NOW THE ONLY PERSON ON THE PLANET WITH THE INTELLIGENCE AND RESOURCES TO KEEP THE IGNITED TOO BUSY TO STUMBLE ACROSS THEIR TRUE PURPOSE...
WRONG
WRONGER
DEAR GOD, SRSLY?
TO DO LIST
Find other Ignited
Explore powers
Save planet
Renew bus pass
Recycle
Vote
estroy all humans
ant garden
Omni's carbon footprint
...DON'T WE HAVE A MORAL RESPONSIBILITY TO DO JUST THAT?

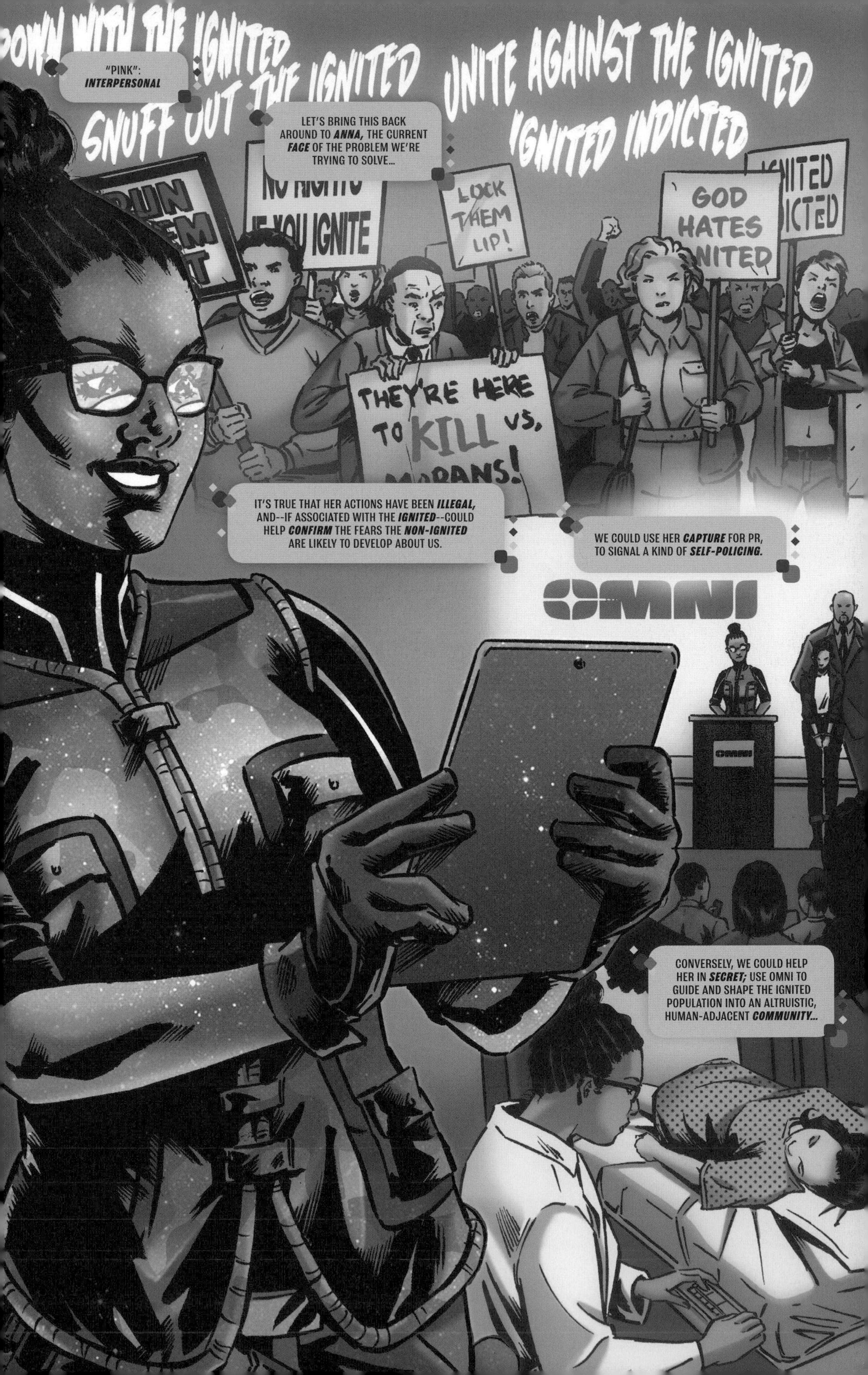

DOWN WITH THE IGNITED
SNUFF OUT THE IGNITED
UNITE AGAINST THE IGNITED
IGNITED INDICTED
"PINK": INTERPERSONAL
LET'S BRING THIS BACK AROUND TO ANNA, THE CURRENT FACE OF THE PROBLEM WE'RE TRYING TO SOLVE...
NO RIGHTS IF YOU IGNITE
LOCK THEM UP!
GOD HATES IGNITED
IGNITED INDICTED
THEY'RE HERE TO KILL US,
IT'S TRUE THAT HER ACTIONS HAVE BEEN ILLEGAL, AND--IF ASSOCIATED WITH THE IGNITED--COULD HELP CONFIRM THE FEARS THE NON-IGNITED ARE LIKELY TO DEVELOP ABOUT US.
WE COULD USE HER CAPTURE FOR PR, TO SIGNAL A KIND OF SELF-POLICING.
OMNI
CONVERSELY, WE COULD HELP HER IN SECRET; USE OMNI TO GUIDE AND SHAPE THE IGNITED POPULATION INTO AN ALTRUISTIC, HUMAN-ADJACENT COMMUNITY...

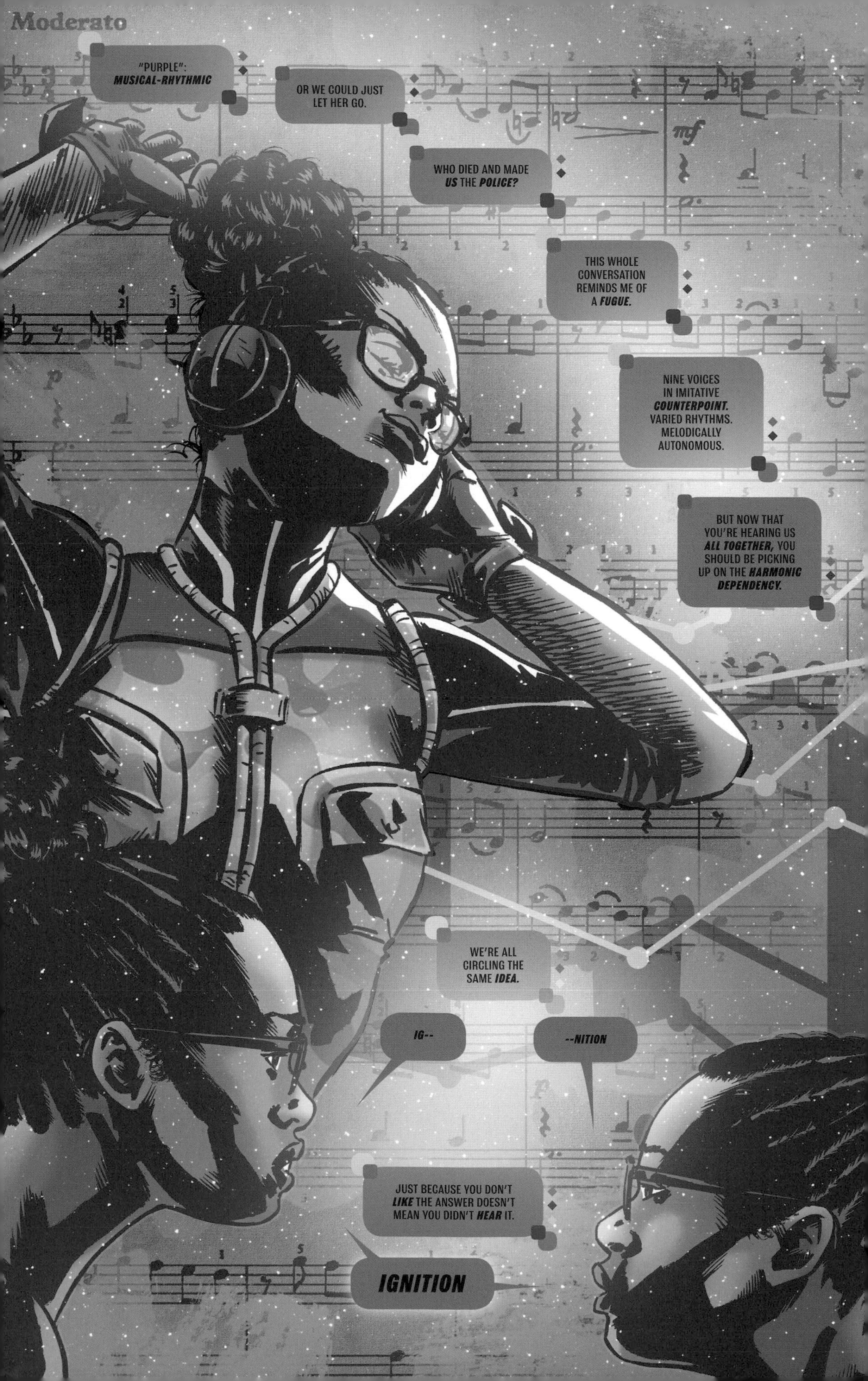
Moderato
"PURPLE": MUSICAL-RHYTHMIC
OR WE COULD JUST LET HER GO.
WHO DIED AND MADE US THE POLICE?
THIS WHOLE CONVERSATION REMINDS ME OF A FUGUE.
NINE VOICES IN IMITATIVE COUNTERPOINT. VARIED RHYTHMS. MELODICALLY AUTONOMOUS.
BUT NOW THAT YOU'RE HEARING US ALL TOGETHER, YOU SHOULD BE PICKING UP ON THE HARMONIC DEPENDENCY.
WE'RE ALL CIRCLING THE SAME IDEA.
IG--
--NITION
JUST BECAUSE YOU DON'T LIKE THE ANSWER DOESN'T MEAN YOU DIDN'T HEAR IT.
IGNITION

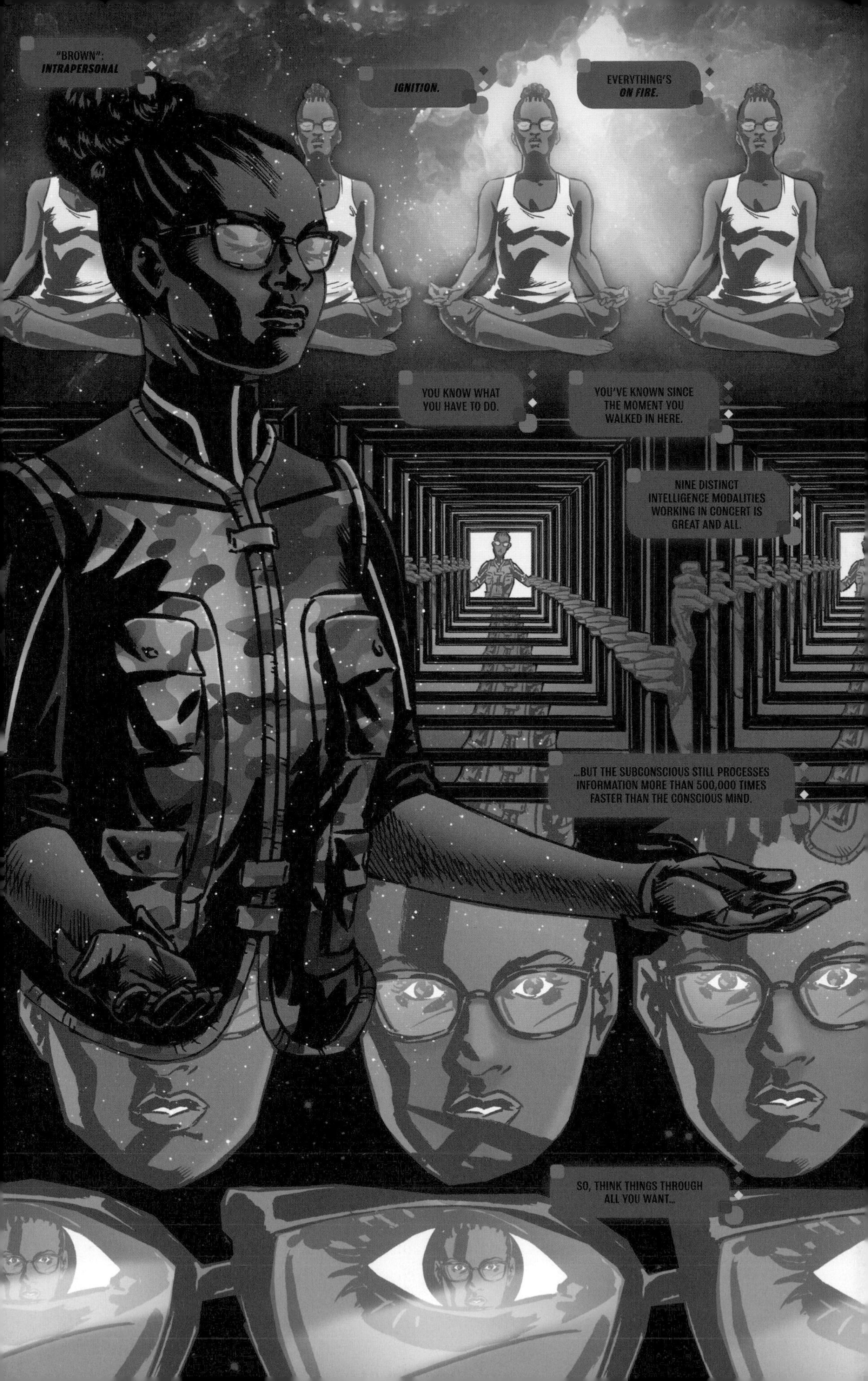
"BROWN": *INTRAPERSONAL*
IGNITION.
EVERYTHING'S *ON FIRE.*
YOU KNOW WHAT YOU HAVE TO DO.
YOU'VE KNOWN SINCE THE MOMENT YOU WALKED IN HERE.
NINE DISTINCT INTELLIGENCE MODALITIES WORKING IN CONCERT IS GREAT AND ALL.
...BUT THE SUBCONSCIOUS STILL PROCESSES INFORMATION MORE THAN 500,000 TIMES FASTER THAN THE CONSCIOUS MIND.
SO, THINK THINGS THROUGH ALL YOU WANT...

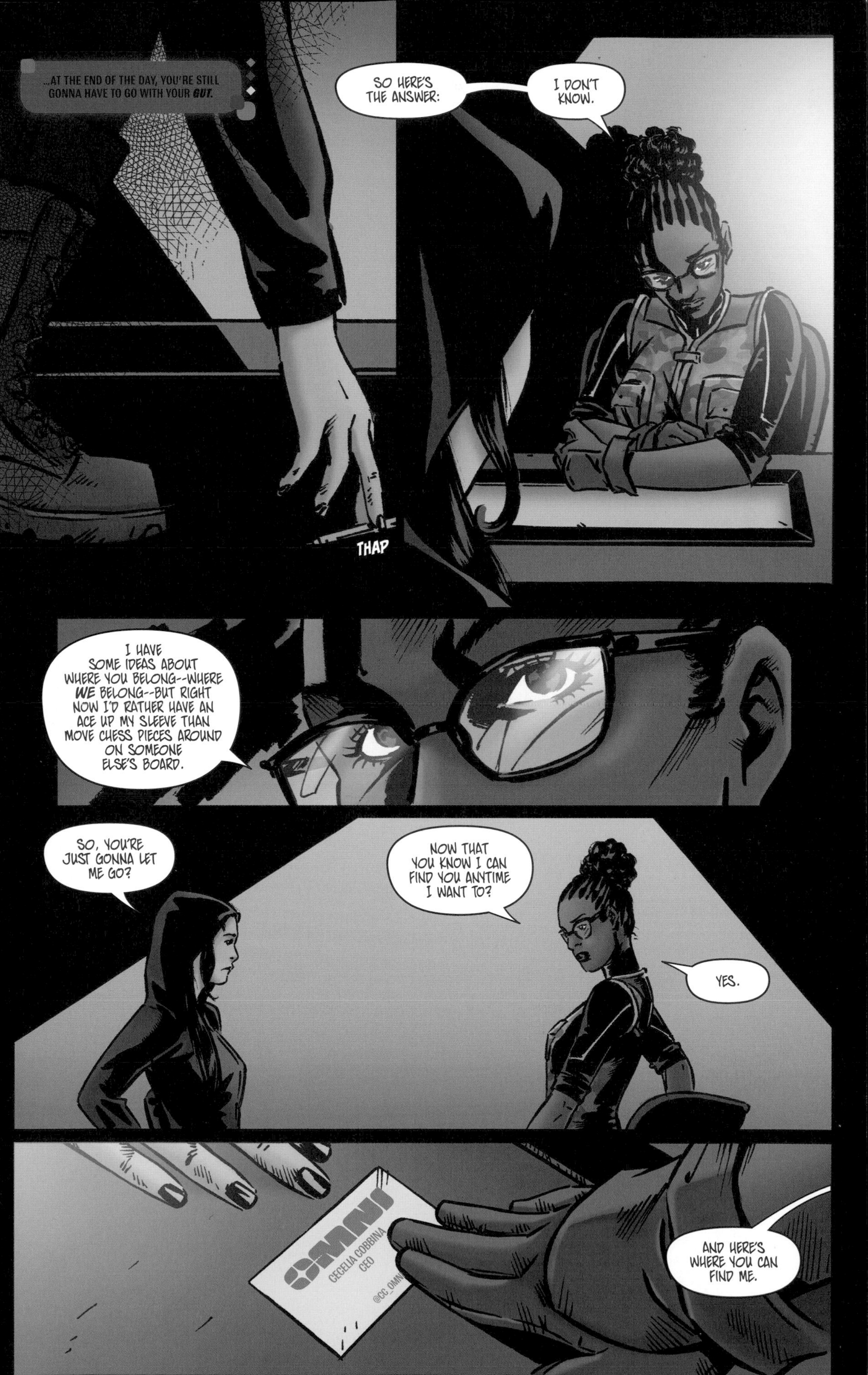
...AT THE END OF THE DAY, YOU'RE STILL GONNA HAVE TO GO WITH YOUR GUT.
SO HERE'S THE ANSWER:
I DON'T KNOW.
THAP
I HAVE SOME IDEAS ABOUT WHERE YOU BELONG--WHERE WE BELONG--BUT RIGHT NOW I'D RATHER HAVE AN ACE UP MY SLEEVE THAN MOVE CHESS PIECES AROUND ON SOMEONE ELSE'S BOARD.
SO, YOU'RE JUST GONNA LET ME GO?
NOW THAT YOU KNOW I CAN FIND YOU ANYTIME I WANT TO?
YES.
OMNI
CECELIA COBBINA
CEO
AND HERE'S WHERE YOU CAN FIND ME.

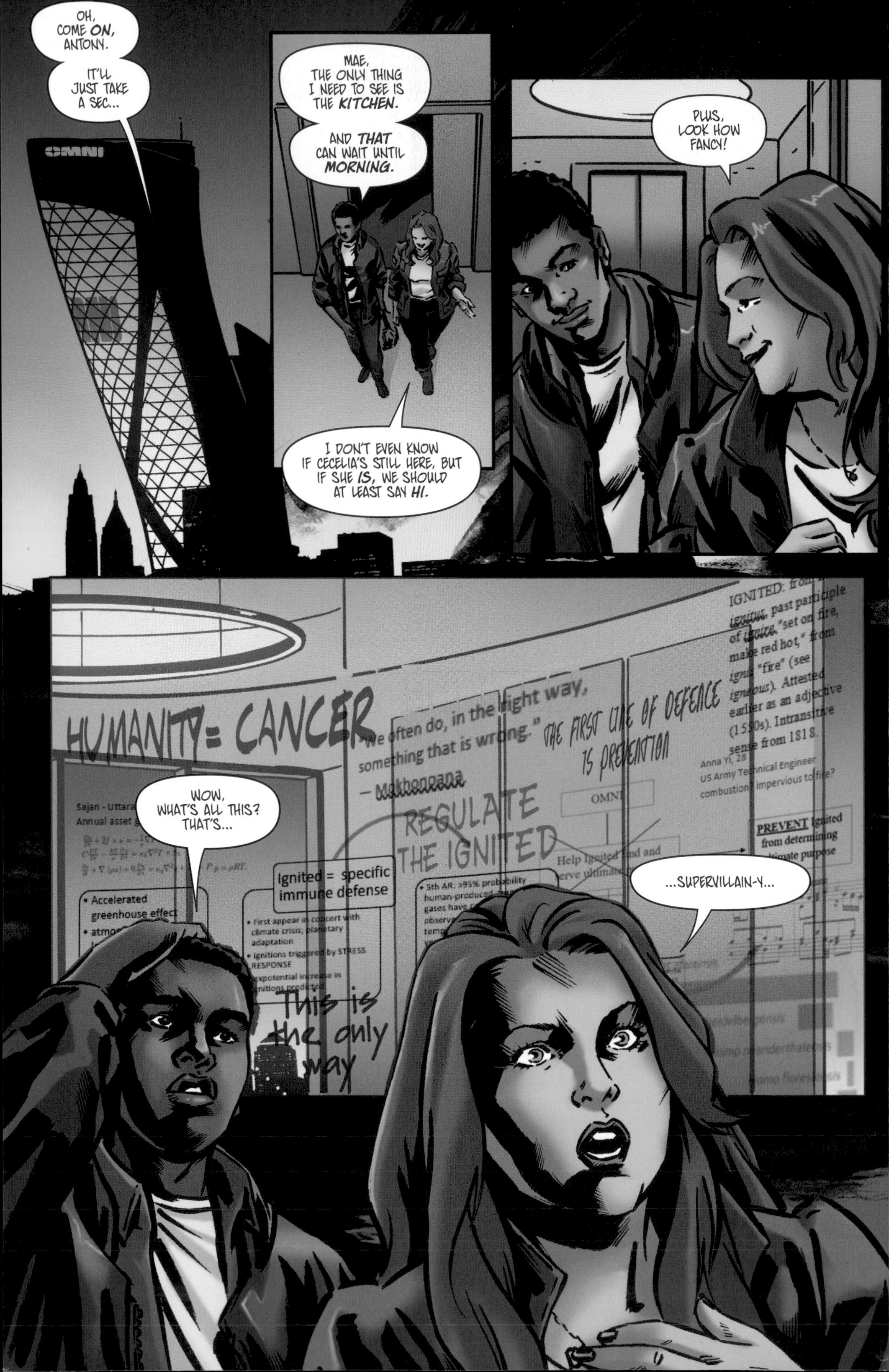
OMNI
OH, COME ON, ANTONY.
IT'LL JUST TAKE A SEC...
MAE, THE ONLY THING I NEED TO SEE IS THE KITCHEN.
AND THAT CAN WAIT UNTIL MORNING.
I DON'T EVEN KNOW IF CECELIA'S STILL HERE, BUT IF SHE IS, WE SHOULD AT LEAST SAY HI.
PLUS, LOOK HOW FANCY!
HUMANITY = CANCER
"We often do, in the right way, something that is wrong."
— Mokhonoana
THE FIRST LINE OF DEFENCE IS PREVENTION
REGULATE THE IGNITED
Ignited = specific immune defense
This is the only way
OMNI
PREVENT Ignited from determining ultimate purpose
Help Ignited find and serve ultimate purpose
Anna Yi, 28
US Army Technical Engineer
WOW, WHAT'S ALL THIS? THAT'S...
...SUPERVILLAIN-Y...

OMNI PRESCRIPTIONS

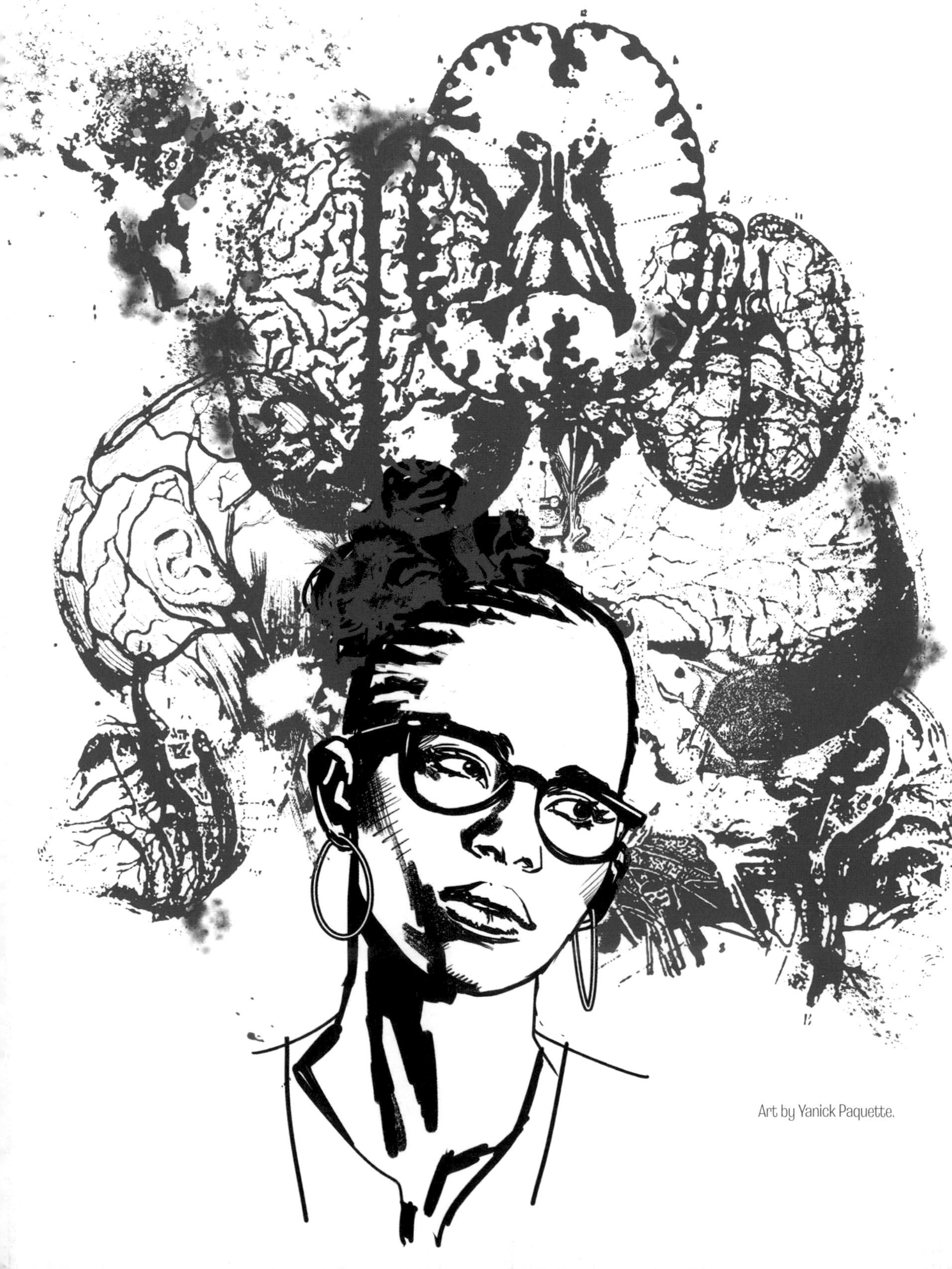

Art by Yanick Paquette.

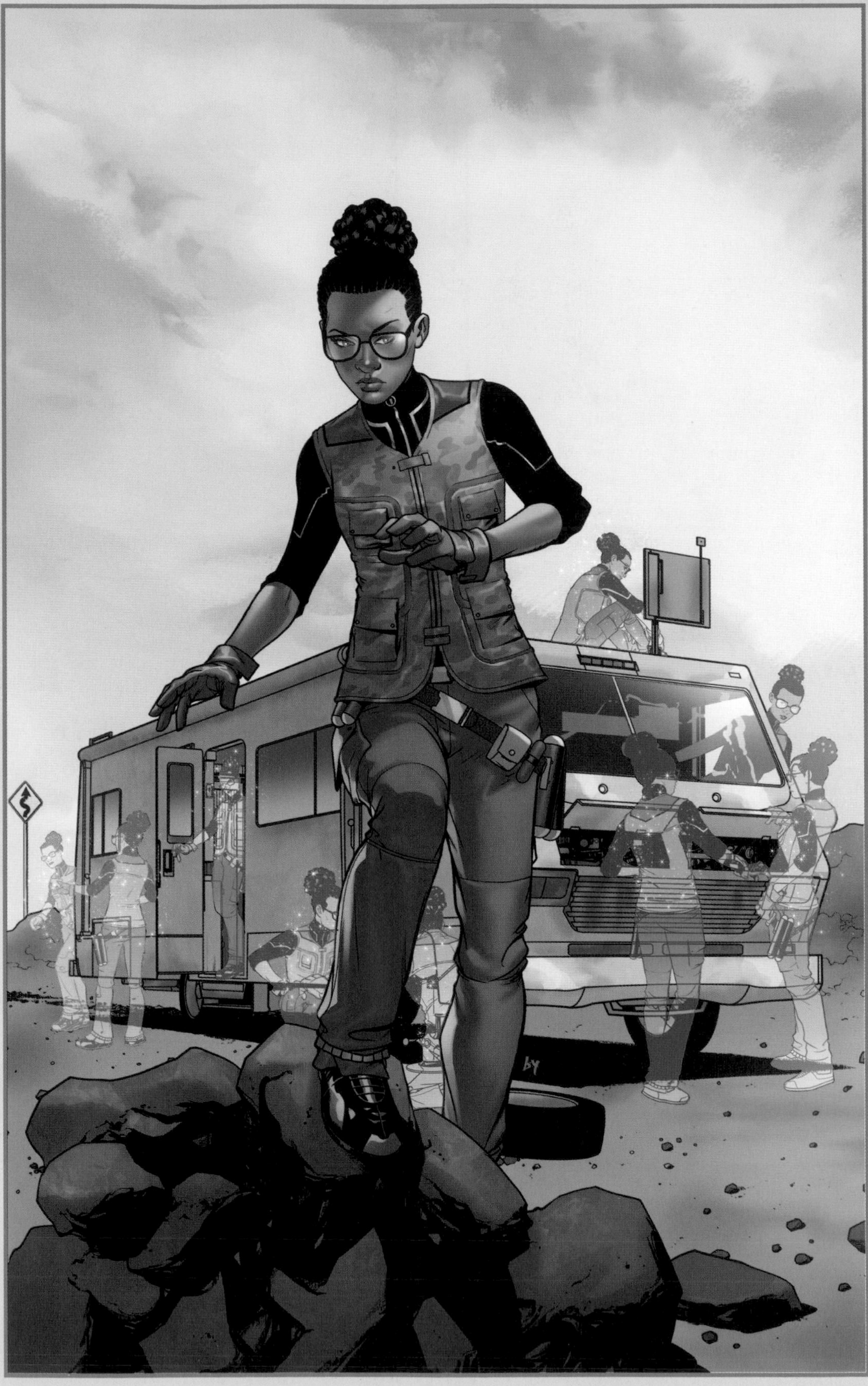

Original cover for **Omni #2** by Mike McKone. Colors by Bryan Valenza.

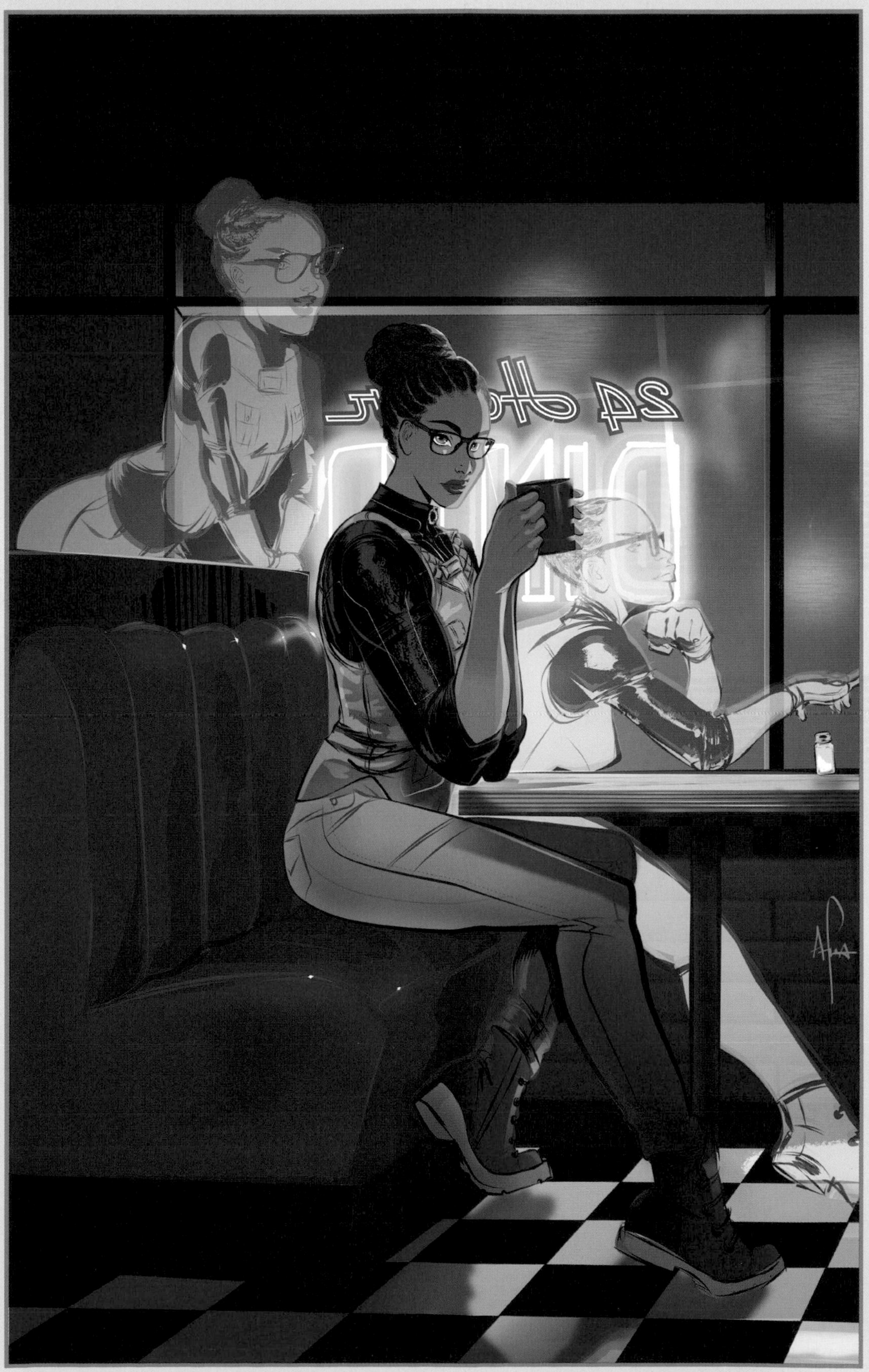

Original variant cover for **Omni #2** by Afua Richardson.

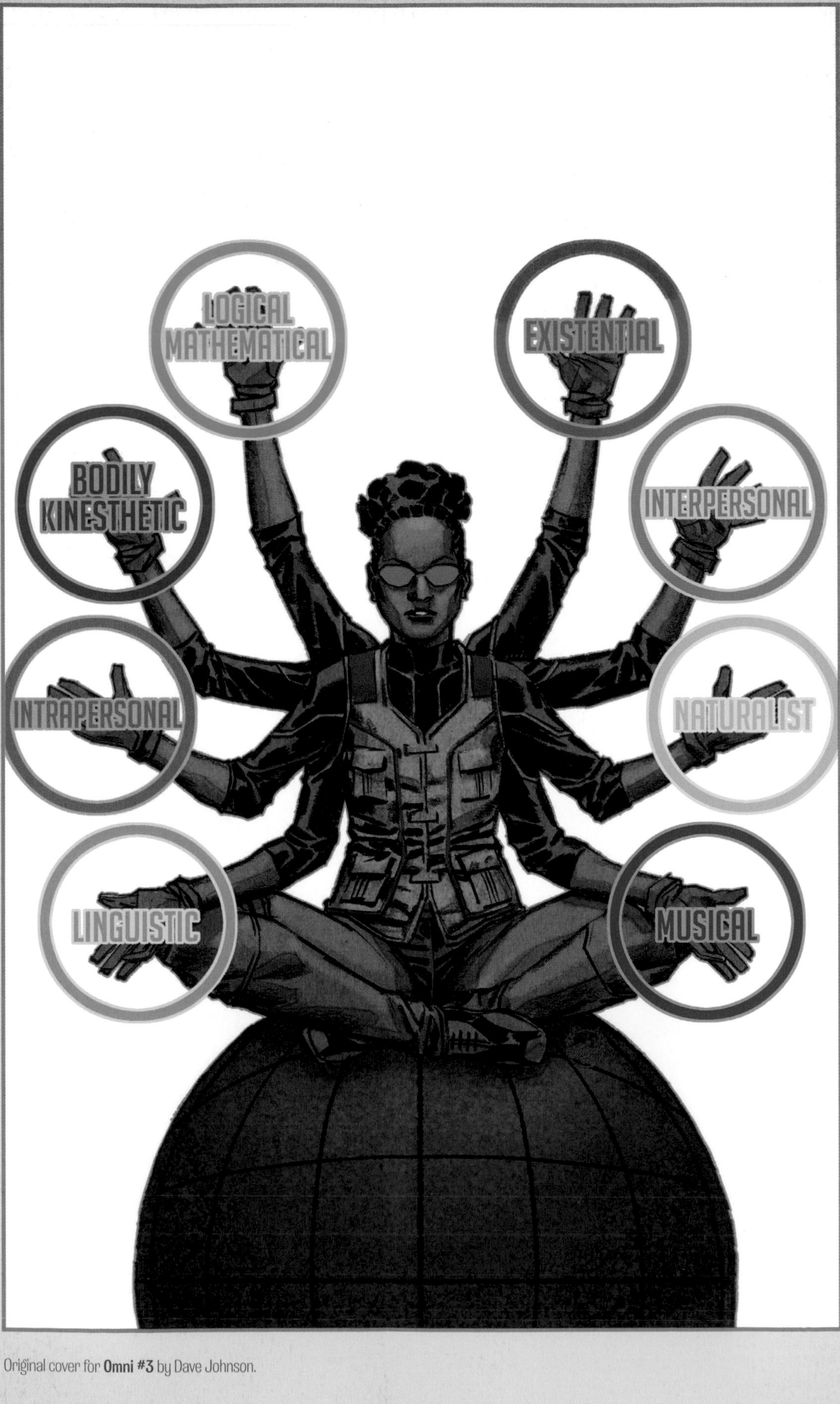
LOGICAL MATHEMATICAL
EXISTENTIAL
BODILY KINESTHETIC
INTERPERSONAL
INTRAPERSONAL
NATURALIST
LINGUISTIC
MUSICAL

Original cover for **Omni #3** by Dave Johnson.